About the Author

Penny Claxton was born and grew up in South-East London. On leaving school, she joined Queen Alexandra's Royal Army Nursing Corps, where she completed her Registered Nurse training prior to emigrating to Australia. Penny has lived and worked in South-Western Sydney for the last twenty years; this is her first novel.

FACING FEARFUL ODDS

Penny Claxton

FACING FEARFUL ODDS

Vanguard Press

To Nan, who believed from the beginning and to Caroline and Karen, without whom this would not have been possible.

Prelude

Next year it was said there would be something permanent, made of stone, and that the wooden memorial currently commemorating the dead would be replaced with something more fitting. It did not seem right that people had died for God, King and Country but were remembered with only a small wooden column in the centre of Whitehall. Designs for a proper stone Cenotaph had been called for and it was anticipated a suitably sombre design would be chosen from hundreds of entries, in what was turning out to be a fiercely competitive event. England and the Empire, although triumphant, were in mourning; for a generation of men who would never know the joy of growing old gracefully in a peaceful world.

Victoria Standish did not care about any of this. For the last hour she had been standing in one spot, trying to ignore the wind which seemed to whistle through Whitehall. She was pleased that the rain which had been forecast had stayed away and that although cold she was at least dry. The tips of her ears and the end of her nose were frozen with cold; she was grateful for the pair of gloves she had been given moments before by a stranger in the crowd as her hands were now slowly beginning to thaw.

The speeches and wreath laying were over. The Glorious Dead had been eulogised by a grateful nation eager to show they would not be forgotten in the years to come. As Big Ben rang out, announcing that it was eleven o'clock, an eerie silence descended on the waiting crowd.

Victoria shifted her weight from her right to her left foot. She had been standing still for so long she was not entirely certain that if she stayed in the same position for much longer, she would be able to march off in a suitably military fashion. She tried hard to concentrate on the moment and not on the extreme discomfort she was starting to feel, as her body objected to the conditions it was being subjected to. Fleetingly, Victoria remembered that it was not too long since she had suffered the deprivation of living through the winter months in a tent in northern France and that she had been lucky enough to survive when others had not.

The war was over, but Victoria could not feel any kind of elation; she had watched far too many of her generation make the ultimate sacrifice, laying down their lives for a cause which seemed impossible to justify and even more difficult to understand.

It was over five years since Victoria had answered her country's cry and left Australia, excited at the prospect of doing her bit in a war which could not fail to see civilised nations triumph. Aware that God was on her side and that good would prevail over evil, Victoria had gone willingly, excited to be doing her bit for the greater good. In the intervening years she had endured the heat, sand and flies on Lemnos and struggled with the cold, wet, frozen fields of France and Flanders; to see the allied nations eventually limp to victory leaving behind the flower of its youth, buried in Turkish and European soil.

The silence and her reverie were broken by a lone bugler playing the haunting notes of the Last Post. To Victoria this, combined with the discomfort she was feeling, made her feel, suddenly, unbelievably weary. As always when the bugle sounded her thoughts turned to home and to people who had come from half a world away, proud to answer England's call, strong in the belief that the fight was just and that linked by the Empire it was their duty; people she had been proud to call friends. It seemed ironic to Victoria that the war which had been brewing for a decade; which the Empire needed to fight, to maintain its values and way of life, had changed the world beyond recognition and that her world would never be the same again.

Chapter One

'The lamps are going out all over Europe;
We shall not see them lit again in our lifetime.'
Sir Edward Grey, Secretary of State for
Foreign Affairs, August, 1914

August 1914 – Camden, New South Wales, Australia

Victoria Standish was on her way to Camden from
Sydney Town. Despite being winter the train had been
warm, crowded and smoky. After disembarking in need
of some fresh air, Victoria decided to walk the rest of
the way home and had left her bags with the station
master, with the instruction that they be sent up to the
house later.

The afternoon was sunny and dry; the smell of
wood burning was strong as houses prepared for the
expected evening chill. Buttoning her coat and adjusting
her scarf Victoria set off for home. The walk would take
her almost an hour but she was glad of the time alone;
she needed to think about her future plans, which for the
moment seemed so uncertain.

Camden was a small township to the south-west of
Sydney, supporting a large farming community. The

land surrounding the town was good grazing land and had been recognised as such by early settlers to New South Wales, well over a hundred years before. Settlers brave enough to live so far from Sydney Town had prospered, cultivating the land and rearing sheep that were durable and bred for the harsh Australian conditions. Their descendants still exerted considerable influence throughout the district, with old families vying for social status in the town; the Standish family had arrived as free settlers early on and were amongst the first brave enough to head westward desperate to find land able to support the fledgling colony. Given a considerable grant of land from Governor Phillip the family had worked hard in the early years, building a sizable concern which they continued to farm.

The community had spread a little in recent years, with the township now extending beyond the church of St John and almost as far as the cottage hospital. From the train station the walk home took in the main street of Camden, which had become a thriving country town and then wound up past the church towards the hospital; Victoria needed to walk beyond this and down into the valley to arrive at her parents' house.

Victoria walked past St John's Church and paused at the top of the rise. Taking advantage of the newly created seating area in Macarthur Park, she sat down and let her thoughts wander for a few moments. Seeing the views from the park to the Blue Mountains always made her realise how much she missed home. For the last four years Victoria had been allowed very little time of her own, the combination of working long hours and studying hard taking its toll.

Settling on the park bench her mind strayed back to the parental resistance she had encountered when she initially broached the idea of embarking on a nurse training course several years previously. Her parents had argued that it was unnecessary and not really acceptable for their daughter to be seeking paid employment. They were concerned their standing amongst friends may be affected by her actions and were worried that the arduous hours may prove too much.

Constance Standish had eventually given in to Victoria's pleading, when she realised her daughter would not give up asking for her blessing and would never be content living the privileged life other young ladies of the district were accustomed to; while they waited for a suitable marriage to take place. Victoria had recently completed her training and her parents' initial doubts had been quelled and replaced with feelings of immense pride, that their daughter had achieved all she had set out to and had shown the more sceptical people of the district what she was capable of.

Over a four-year period, Victoria had learnt everything she could about the modern treatment of disease and how to cope with the back breaking long hours expected of a probationary nurse. It had taken a while to fit into the rigid hierarchical system that made up the hospital environment and, on several occasions, she had come close to giving up and seeking sanctuary back at Oakfield House. Dogged determination and a sneaking fear that her parents would be vindicated if she failed, had kept her from returning home. With her training complete Victoria planned to take a well-earned break, happy to re-join country society, with nothing more taxing than coffee amongst friends to occupy her time.

***

The kitchen at Oakfield House would be nice and warm. The wood-burning stove had been alight since early morning and at the top of the rise smoke could be seen belching from the chimney. Victoria sighed with contentment at the thought, of a day or two exploring the extensive library her parents owned, without needing to pick up a book describing the latest treatment of some obscure disease. She was also looking forward to catching up with her brother Maxwell who she had seen only sporadically over the last few years. She had missed him more than he would ever know.

Victoria began the descent to Oakfield House. The track leading down the hill was lined on either side with Jacaranda trees, bare in winter but beautiful in the late spring when distinctive purple blossom announced the imminent arrival of summer. The house was the largest in the district, a single-story sprawling building made from old sandstone blocks, with a wide veranda encompassing it. The house had several wings added on by various generations as the family became more prosperous and the need to entertain increased. The Standish family were able to boast a distinguished history in the settlement of New South Wales, arriving in the colony in the early days; Hector Standish still farmed the same land his father and grandfather had before him.

Victoria's thoughts were interrupted by the sound of horse's hooves coming at speed over the rise behind her. She turned to see her brother, Maxwell, skidding to a halt on top of a large grey horse, he was as usual riding bareback. Close in age, Victoria had missed her brother a great deal while away gaining her nursing qualifications and was delighted to see him.

'Max! How are you?' she exclaimed. 'I'm so glad you're here and not down in Victoria, as Papa said you might be.' Max climbed down from his horse and hugged his sister before replying.

'I decided not to travel down in the end. I've read in the newspapers about the situation in Europe, it seems to be getting more heated by the day. If it's war, I've heard Australia may be called on to assist and if that happens they'll need some decent horsemen. I can shoot too, which has to be a good thing. I would be perfect for the army. The sheep we were going to buy seem unimportant compared to that!'

Max paused for breath before continuing, 'I thought you were still in town though?'

'There didn't seem much point in staying out at the Coast Hospital once I finished training. Some of the others will be there from now until they retire or get married, or something. I want something different though. So, I've come home until I decide what to do next.'

'Well, now you've done it and proved you can, will you carry on nursing?' Max asked.

'Training was exhausting, at times I never thought I'd finish; now I have it feels a bit of an anti-climax. Midwifery training would keep me in the district and seems the next logical step, but doesn't really appeal. I need to rest for a while, enjoy some home comforts and then look at my options,' Victoria replied.

'You know that there's going to be a war in Europe, don't you, Vic? Everyone's talking about it in town; it's really only a matter of time. The Kaiser has upset most of Europe and now that Archduke Ferdinand has been assassinated it has to happen, even.

'The recruitment boys are heading this way. I've heard they're down in Bowral but will be here in a day or two, they're just waiting for word.' Max came to a halt and opened a gate leading into a large grassed paddock, removing his horse's bridle he closed the gate behind him and carried on walking beside his sister, before continuing to speak.

'There's no way I'll be missing out on this show. The Light Horse should accept me; Pa will be pleased with that. A war will get me away for a bit and out from under his feet. He's never really been happy that I can't see myself as a farmer, but he might just about put up with a son who is a soldier instead.'

'Yes, I've heard all about what's happening, but surely it won't affect us will it? This is all taking place on the other side of the world.' Victoria stopped to take in the first full view of Oakfield House looking warm and inviting in the winter sun and sighed. 'I suppose if there is a war they'll need nurses, won't they? I can see myself looking after the wounded; that has to be more exciting than learning how to be a midwife, but it could be a long way from home.'

August 1914 – London, England

Violet Briggs yawned and got out of bed. She was pleased that it was summer, and that she did not have to contend with the mind-numbing cold and darkness of winter, as well as the early hour. Quickly she washed her face and hands using the stoneware jug and bowl sitting on her dressing table and then put on her morning uniform, which she had carefully laid across the back of a chair the previous evening. Pulling on her boots she looked at the hole in the sole of one of them, hoping that the dry weather would last for a few more weeks before she had to have the boots re-soled. Her mother had come to rely on the little money she sent home each week and she was reluctant to mend her boots until absolutely necessary, even though the hole was irritating the sole of her foot, causing her to limp by the end of each day.

As she ran down the backstairs towards the kitchen the clock began to chime in the hall. Realising she was late, Briggs attempted to make a quiet entrance into the large kitchen in the basement of the house but was unsuccessful. Standing near the entrance to the kitchen Mrs Trent, the housekeeper, was occupied setting trays for breakfast.

Briggs, you're late!' exclaimed Mrs Trent, 'day dreaming again, I shouldn't wonder? You must take more care over your timekeeping.'

'I'm sorry, Mrs Trent, it won't happen again, I was thinking about how much longer this glorious weather will last, I'm hoping to go and listen to the band this afternoon in Hyde Park. I believe the Band of the Grenadier Guards is performing today.'

'Ah yes, it's your afternoon off; which won't be happening unless you get a move on! Now, I want you to start in the drawing room this morning, cleaning out the grate. I know it's August but it looks as though it may be cool later in the day and the Master and Mistress may want the fire lighting this evening. After that report to Edwards in the dining room, where you can help lay for breakfast.'

Briggs left the kitchen and made her way to the drawing room to clean and make up the fire. She had been working for Lord and Lady Hadleigh for eighteen months and still could not believe how lucky she was. Born and raised in south-east London, the eldest daughter of seven children, she had entered into service to help support the family; initially taking a post as housemaid to a doctor with a practice in Dulwich. He had lived on the outskirts of Dulwich Village in a large rambling Victorian house where a portion of the house was set up so he could see patients. A room at the back of the house had been furnished with a long low leather couch; designed for the doctor to easily examine patients attending his surgery. Next door to this was a second room containing shelf after shelf of bottles containing pills and other forms of medication to be dispensed as needed. Briggs was fascinated by this room and made sure she was extra careful if called on to dust the bottles.

When the doctor had eventually made the decision to give up his practice and retire to Eastbourne where his sister lived, his cook, who had heard of the vacancy from a friend, had recommended Briggs apply for her present position. Even after eighteen months she still felt a thrill that she was working in such a prestigious household with such a central address. During this time, she had worked hard to fulfil the exacting standards required and was pleased that recently she had been made responsible for looking after Lady Julia, the eldest daughter of the household.

The household was modest by some standards. The Earl and Countess of Hadleigh had four children. Viscount Gerald Hammond was the eldest, followed by Lady Julia, the Honourable Guy and Roberta. Guy and Roberta were away at school for most of the year, Lady Julia had just returned from an extended period in Switzerland and Viscount Hammond had been commissioned into the Coldstream Guards two years before.

Lord Hadleigh spent most of his time in the City where he was chairman of a large bank; a family concern going back at least five generations. Leaving mid-morning by hansom cab and returning in the early hours of the evening, Lord Hadleigh was occupied most days and was happy to tell anyone who asked, that his family had strong financial connections which still relied on a great deal of work on his part. Heavily involved in decisions made in the House of Lords, Lord Hadleigh took his responsibility as a peer of the realm seriously and never missed divisions when a matter of any consequence was to be debated.

To keep the house running like clockwork the Hadleigh's employed several servants, who made sure their lives were comfortable, well ordered and privileged.

**

Lady Julia Hadleigh sat up and stretched. Looking at the clock she realised if she did not hurry breakfast would have been cleared away and she would go hungry until luncheon. Her parents were adamant that no member of the house should ask the kitchen to provide meals outside of scheduled times as the staff had enough to do. She was surprised Briggs had not yet been in with a cup of tea to gently waken her. Then she remembered instructing she was not to be disturbed, after coming in very late the night before. Lady Julia had been out until the early hours with her brother Gerald.

There was an air of excitement in London, which it was difficult to describe. After years of expectant waiting, war was imminent. Some said this was not before time. Everyone agreed this would be a war for the young who were desperate to show themselves courageous, valiant and loyal to their country and king. Primed and ready music halls rang with patriotic songs urging all young men to take up arms and protect their families from the foe.

The murder of Archduke Franz Ferdinand in some obscure town had excited Lady Julia's brother and his friends; seen as one step closer to war they had spent most of the previous evening discussing how quickly a commission in the army could be obtained, if the right people at the War Office were contacted.

The talk had been exclusively about the situation in Europe and excitement at the thought of going to war at last. The general consensus was that the Hun needed to be pulled into line and that it was up to England to do this. Officers from Viscount Hammond's regiment were all primed for the fight; most having spent their formative years at the hands of a public school cadet system; seeing themselves as there to protect England in any battle necessary for the good of the Empire. Not for one second did any of the young men present think war could be lost, or that they may become a casualty. Most had visions of performing heroic deeds in the heat of battle; but of somehow coming through unscathed, to be feted in glory by an adoring grateful nation. The partying last night had a sense of urgency about it, as though all present knew that they were coming to the end of a frivolous time and that something great was now expected of them all.

Lady Julia reached across and pulled the bell cord to summon Briggs to help her dress for the day. She was lunching with an old school friend, Fiona Moncrieff, and was itching to discuss how best to become a part of 'it'. Somehow this particular conflict seemed bigger than anything that had happened before and closer to home. As a young girl, Lady Julia vaguely remembered the Boer War; an event mentioned in newspapers but very much at the periphery of her life. This she felt would be different and would involve them all. It was with a sense of both excitement and trepidation that she thought of the near future.

Listening to her brother's friends the previous evening had made Lady Julia acutely aware that her world was about to change and that if they were away fighting a war, there would be a lack of young men available to entertain and escort her to the theatre, or the latest club. The thought of sitting at home each night with her parents was simply incomprehensible. She had heard somewhere that if war came it was possible that the government may recruit people to assist nurses in caring for the wounded and rather liked the idea. She had visions of being asked to write letters to loved ones by soldiers too feeble to accomplish the task unaided, or of adjusting pillows to help a soldier rest. Lady Julia was determined to persuade Fiona that volunteering was the only thing to do in the circumstances and that nursing was the most honourable course to pursue.

August 1914 – Kings College Hospital, London

Sister Margaret Brennan adjusted her cuffs and made sure her hat was pinned properly before leaving her room to make the short walk to her ward. As always, she spent the time reflecting on the occupants of each bed and wondered how they may have fared overnight while she had been absent. The evening before she had remained at work until late, as a young man had been bought to hospital after being hit by an omnibus near Camberwell Green. He was unconscious with an obvious fracture of his femur; which, if he did not die first, would require surgical intervention if not amputation. Sister Brennan had received him into her ward, made an initial assessment of his injuries and discussed immediate management with Mr Chardingly, who was the surgeon-on-call for accidental injuries. How well he had survived the night would be crucial in determining further treatment options. As always, Brennan had been reluctant to leave the young man, but had eventually done so; knowing that he was safe in the care of Staff Nurse Blackstone and that if she did not get some much-needed rest she would not be at her best in the morning.

Walking down the ward to her office Sister Brennan observed that the bed where the accident victim had been last night was screened off. Arriving at her office she was surprised to see Mr Chardingly still present, dressed in the dinner suit he had been wearing the previous evening. He looked tired and dishevelled; his dinner jacket was resting on the back of her chair and his bow tie was undone; she could not help noticing how handsome he looked with the morning stubble which was beginning to appear. Mr Chardingly was staring intently into the mouthpiece of the telephone and was speaking to a colleague. His voice was slightly raised, as he tried to make himself heard clearly.

'Yes, yes. We'll give that a go. I don't think I can risk giving the lad any kind of anaesthetic as he hasn't really regained consciousness since the accident; but if we can at least straighten his leg he will be far more comfortable, and we may be able to ease off on the morphia.' Carefully, Mr Chardingly replaced the mouthpiece, gently depositing the telephone on the desk.

'Good morning, sir.' Brennan greeted him as he rose from her desk.

'Ah, Sister; let me explain where we are with the young lad,' Mr Chardingly said. 'I was concerned enough to stay in the hospital last night, as I thought I may have to operate regardless of the poor man's condition. Staff Nurse Blackstone called me at about three o'clock to let me know that he was deteriorating rapidly. He was thrashing about, semi-conscious and moaning, and she was concerned it was too early to give more morphia.' Scratching his chin, he carried on. 'I came straight here to see what could be done, but it is clear now that he would never survive the ether necessary to anaesthetise him. Unfortunately, surgery is what's needed but is not an option at this stage. I have been in contact with a colleague of mine at St Thomas'; he's been doing a lot of work with applying traction to broken bones. Helps straighten the leg, which decreases the pain. I'm hoping if we can rig something up it may help in this case.'

'What can I do to help, sir?'

'His mother is waiting outside; can you give her an update on what's happening and then help Blackstone who is organising the carpenter. We'll need some kind of makeshift pulley system attached to the end of the bed and some sort of splint to immobilise and straighten his leg,' he replied.

As he spoke Sister Brennan started to roll up her sleeves, knowing that as with most of Mr Chardingly's innovations she may be called on to assist in a practical manner.

However, by early evening it was apparent the young lad was not going to survive his injuries; despite a makeshift traction arrangement, which straightened his leg and the subsequent reduction in the amount of morphia given, he remained unconscious. Possibly the omnibus had caused an injury to his head, or maybe the blood loss from the fracture site had been too great, it was impossible to tell. As late afternoon became evening it was clear to all that the young lad was beginning to slip away. Sister Brennan remained with him throughout the day and was present as he drew his last breath. Having closed his eyes and straightened his sheets she opened the nearest window before moving screens into position around the bed. She turned to the probationary nurse who had been present throughout the latter stages of the day.

'I need to let Mr Chardingly know what has happened, and also speak to his mother. Please remain here, Morris, and I'll come back to help you lay him out.' In a rare compassionate voice, she continued, 'I always hate it when they die so young; such a waste of life.'

'Sister, why did you open the window?' Morris asked.

'We need to let his soul go free,' Brennan replied, before walking briskly towards her office.

Later that evening Margaret Brennan was alone in the Sister's sitting room. She had a small glass of whisky on the table beside her and was reading the evening paper. The news was grim with a declaration of war imminent. Soon, in her pledge to support Belgium, England would be at war with Germany. Sighing, Brennan reflected it was only twelve short years since the end of the Boer War, where as a young newly appointed staff nurse she had waved goodbye to her fiancé, who was embarking at Tilbury docks for South Africa. He was a sergeant in the Royal Fusiliers, and although they planned to marry on his return, he was destined to be killed during attempts by the British Army to relieve Mafeking. Brennan, who had never really recovered from his death, had thrown herself into nursing her patients back to health and was rewarded for her efforts with appointment as ward sister at Kings College Hospital in London. Responsible for thirty-six patients she was a passionate advocate, whether helping them to recover, or helping them to die.

Brennan wondered if the nation was truly prepared for the sacrifice that would be needed to emerge victorious in the war to come. Having long ago accepted that she was unlikely to find love for a second time and that she was likely to spend any war assisting in the care of the wounded, Brennan had made the decision to enlist in The Queen Alexandra's Imperial Military Nursing Service for the duration of the impending conflict. The QAIMNS had recently sent Brennan a letter with information on where she should report and to whom once war was declared. She had equipped herself with the uniform requirements listed in the letter and had informed matron of her intention to join up for the duration of war. She had advised Staff Nurse Blackstone of her impending departure and of the need for her to take over the ward. With this in mind she had spent many hours training Blackstone in the additional responsibilities she would have as ward sister.

Margaret Brennan was excited that her life, which had of late taken on a predictable air, was about to take a very different course.

Chapter Two

*'Our duty is clear; to gird up our loins and remember
we are Britons.
We will fight to our last man and shilling.'*
Andrew Fisher, Prime Minister of Australia,
1914

Late August 1914 – Camden, New South Wales, Australia

The Plough and Harrow Inn which stood in the centre of Camden was packed with men enjoying a drink. Young men had come from all over the district on this bright winter's afternoon to socialise and enjoy the monthly country fair. At one end of town there were stalls where local farmers had set up trestle tables to allow their wives to sell home grown produce, in between swapping recipes and discussing local affairs.

Hector Standish had seen that his wife was settled with a group of wives at the showground before setting off with a determined stride in pursuit of a cold beer. Today was one of the rare occasions when he had no business to attend to and he planned to enjoy the time away from his farm, catching up on local news.

At the other end of town, the stockyards were where the serious business of buying and selling cattle and horses took place. Max Standish had ridden into town and had been down to the stockyards to negotiate the sale of his grey horse, in exchange for a slightly more toned-down bay mare. He had heard somewhere that in South Africa, during the Boer War, it was easy for snipers to pick off soldiers riding lighter coloured horses. Not even sure that he would ever leave Australia, Max intended to be fully prepared if he did. As he waited for a call to say he had been accepted by the Light Horse; Max was pleased with the deal he had negotiated for his horse.

A trial ride of his new horse got Max only as far as the Plough and Harrow, where he dismounted, hoping to meet some friends before riding home. Striding into the bar, he was pleased to see Stanley Marshall deep in conversation with the publican, drinking a beer over by the bar. Seeing Standish, Stanley Marshall spoke to the barman before waving him across. Standish gratefully accepted the beer he was offered and took a deep swallow before turning to his best mate.

'I reckon we may be too late you know,' he said. 'The papers are saying it will all be over by Christmas; one big push in France and the Germans will give in. Let's face it the might of the British Army won't be defeated by any number of Hun.'

'I hope you're right, mate. I have no desire to swan off to France to fight a war that has nothing to do with Australia; after all I only agreed to join to keep you out of trouble. I would far rather be chasing that sister of yours; she's grown up into something rather special these days.'

'Definitely a no-go area that is, mate, she's far too good for the likes of you! Not that Vic's around at the moment. She's up in Sydney; she joined the Australian Army Nursing Service a couple of weeks back and has been called up already. Left for town yesterday. A whole group of nurses are getting ready to leave for France. At this rate she'll get to see all the action before we do.' Both men took a long draught from their beer, staring morosely at the bar. 'It's not fair being stuck down here waiting. I have a horse and I'm ready to go,' Max muttered.

A sudden commotion distracted the men from further conversation. Cheering from men in the street could be heard, along with the unmistakable sound of a military band and men attempting to march in step. Joining the crowd of young men thronging about outside the Plough and Harrow Standish craned his neck and watched as behind the band a group of about thirty men progressed along Argyle Street. A couple of men were walking in front, competing with the band attempting a martial tune on mouth organs; following them were two young men holding a banner which stated: "Picton men support the cause, for God, King and Country".

The marching men were of all ages and were dressed in their Sunday best, determined to impress. Their shoes shone with polish, which many of them had spent hours applying and buffing to a mirror-like shine; for some though the effect had been somewhat dampened by the terrain they had negotiated before arriving in Camden.

'Where are you lot off to then?' a man in the crowd shouted.

'Liverpool, they're taking people directly into the First Battalion AIF from there. Quickest way to get involved in the war we reckon; you lot should join us. It's going to be the greatest show on earth.'

Standish looked at Marshall.

'What do you think about that then, could you live without your horse for a while?' he asked excitedly.

After several pints of refreshment and an overnight stay in Camden, the men formed up in the main street early the following morning. Fuzzy headed but determined to continue onward as quickly as possible. Standish and Marshall were amongst them; having taken time out the evening before, to go home and pack a few clothes. They said farewell to their families and were ready to leave; both were nervous in the cold light of dawn, but keen to continue on to Liverpool, convinced they would never again be on the verge of such a life changing adventure.

Hector had watched despondently as his son and his best mate talked with the Picton men and arranged to join them for the journey towards Liverpool. He would have done anything in his power to prevent what was happening, sure in the knowledge a great many of the men would not return; but sensible enough to realise his son was desperate to prove his worth and could not be stopped.

August 1914 – Victoria Barracks, Sydney, Australia

Victoria Standish stood up from the central desk, stretched and prepared to walk around the ward. Lifting a small oil lamp, she moved up and down the ward to check all was well; years before she had become used to walking quietly with a dim lamp and had learnt not to jump at imaginary shadows created by the half-light. She had never quite got used to the silence though and the sense of being alone at three o'clock in the morning, despite being in the presence of dozens of sleeping men.

Standish was tired, because despite working an allocated stint of night shifts, she was still expected to attend embarkation lectures which were held almost daily and covered everything from immediate first aid requirements of injured troops, to care of infectious diseases. Lectures covering first aid techniques were given tongue-in-cheek; although part of the prepared lecture series, it was never really considered a possibility that any of the AANS Sisters would come close enough to the battlefront to need these skills.

Standish had spent very little of the time she had planned at home. Her brother's words proved to be prophetic and within days of his statement Europe was indeed at war. The Australian Prime Minister had immediately pledged support for Great Britain, agreeing to send an initial twenty thousand men. All over the country young men, who until a couple of months before were content to spend their working lives on family properties following in their father's footsteps, were descending on local towns and cities intent on joining up, eager for some martial glory. Standish had made contact with the AANS as soon as war was declared. She felt that, of all people, she was free to go to war. She was qualified, not currently tied down by an important job and had no one dependent on her. The AANS clearly agreed with her, as she rapidly found herself being inducted into military life at Victoria Barracks in Sydney.

Victoria Barracks had been the military hub of Sydney since not long after settlement took place. Construction of the barracks currently occupying the ground between Oxford Street and Moore Park had been completed in 1848. Standish found herself living and working in old colonial sandstone buildings; steeped in the history of those who had gone before. Gradually, over the first few days of her appointment, she became used to military terminology and the vastly different way that things were done. Although Standish had become accustomed to the rigid system encompassing the daily lives of nurses at the Coast Hospital, she was still able to be surprised by some of the seemingly pointless daily orders which were part of military life.

Within days of her arrival she, along with two other nurses, Daisy McMaster and Christina Kelly, were holding the fort on the night shift; other more experienced nursing staff were preparing for immediate deployment overseas. The last couple of weeks had proven busy, with a sudden surge in the number of soldiers presenting with infectious conditions; thought to be brought on by the unprecedented movement of so many people around the State.

Standish was delighted she was to be accompanied overseas by McMaster and Kelly. She had trained with both of them out at the Coast where they had become close friends. Isolated and a considerable distance from the centre of Sydney nursing staff at the Coast had learned to entertain themselves in their off-duty hours, spending time picnicking on the cliffs or paddling in the sea on the beach below.

McMaster came from Kiama down on the South Coast, where her father skippered a fishing trawler. Kelly came from the Blue Mountains where her mother ran a guest house, catering for wealthier Sydneysiders who were keen to escape the relentless Sydney heat in the summer months; her father had died in a mining accident many years before.

For some time, talk in the Sisters Mess had centred entirely on when they could expect to travel overseas and what items were considered necessary to pack in the small portmanteau they were each allowed to carry with them. Each day one of the nurses would return from a trip to the city with news of an essential item they had tracked down; inevitably this would lead to the store concerned running out as everyone present in the mess that night rushed to acquire it. All of the nurses were pre-occupied with the thought of leaving Australian shores for an unknown period of time; but were buoyed up with the knowledge that they would be caring for Australian troops.

When not looking after the troops, Standish spent time rolling and counting bandages before filling large wooden crates with them and other medical equipment destined to go wherever they did.

Late August 1914 – Mons, France

Lieutenant Gerald Hammond was hungry. He and his platoon had been on the move now for forty-eight hours, with almost no rest and very little food. He had been ordered to report to his regiment on August 4th and almost immediately crossed over to France as part of the initial British Expeditionary Force, sent to quell the German advance. The expectation that a swift decisive battle was all that was needed, to send the Hun back to Germany with its tail between its legs, was quickly quashed when it became apparent that the German Army had backbone and were capable of fighting their corner. The British Army had very much been caught on the hop and was now in full retreat heading backwards to the sea; the hastily re-worked plan being to retreat far enough to regroup and attack again. Hammond could not help wondering where the reinforcements were to come from, after witnessing the destruction of large numbers of men at the hands of an enemy who appeared to have a far superior amount of firepower.

Hammond and his men had met the might of the German Army on the canal banks at Mons. German artillery regiments had taken the high ground to the north of the town and once they realised the British had arrived shelled the area continuously. Hammond watched in horror as two thirds of his men and a large proportion of officers were killed in the initial skirmish. Just as the remaining men in his platoon started to gain the upper hand an order had filtered down the line that anyone left was to retreat. General orders were given that in retreating the men were to march south, initially to a small mining town and then on towards Cambrai.

Lieutenant Hammond and his men had become separated from the main attack force when some well-aimed shells had decimated their section of the Coldstream Guards. He had watched helplessly as his colonel and the adjutant had both died as a result of the opening German attack, after a shell landed where he had been discussing battle tactics only seconds before.

Making steady progress away from the fighting, Hammond's priority was to find a place where his troops could rest and regain enough strength to continue. He planned to organise surviving members of the battalion into an ordered force to confront the enemy again; several hours before he had sent Corporal Davis on ahead to look for a suitable area where his men could rest undisturbed. Davis had finally returned after an extensive search of the surrounding countryside, marching up to Lieutenant Hammond he came quickly to attention and saluted: 'Sir, I think I've found cover for a while. There's a farmhouse about half a mile away, with some outbuildings that should give us some protection. The area is deserted; the farmer and his wife appear to have left some days ago.'

'Thanks, Corporal, lead the way so we can get some rest. I have a feeling we will need all our strength in the next few days.'

An hour later Hammond was sat at a table in the farmhouse kitchen, his rifle propped up beside him. A roll call had been taken and he was looking at a hastily compiled list of soldiers from his company and other stragglers, who remained unharmed. Standing at his side was Sergeant Major Jack Lewis, a career soldier who had seen action in South Africa and had been about to retire when war broke out. He had been looking forward to returning to the hop fields of Kent, where his family lived and where he hoped to do nothing more strenuous than tending a smallholding by day and walking to the village pub each evening, to catch up with family and friends. With the promise of early release once the Hun were beaten and a post training recruits at the Guards depot as soon as the preliminary skirmish was over; Lewis had recently been persuaded to defer retirement and sign on for the duration of the war. Dog tired and hungry he was beginning to regret his decision.

'This war is going to see rapid promotion for men I wouldn't normally trust to feed my grandmother's cat, sir.' Lewis observed, as he looked at the list Hammond had in his hand. 'We obviously need to make Corporal Davis up to sergeant, and possibly promote Pearson and Walker to lance-corporal as an interim measure, but we do need some more experienced men.' He sighed. 'Has anyone heard from headquarters recently, sir?'

'No! Runners are only getting through sporadically. I agree Davis should be made acting sergeant and we should trial the other two. Whichever of them does the best I'll recommend their promotion to full corporal in due course,' Hammond replied. 'For the meantime we will have to use what we've got. Can you find all three of them and give them the happy news while I have a few minutes' sleep? Hopefully headquarters will regroup and come through with a plan of attack shortly.'

1914 – France

The opening few days of the war had been exasperating beyond belief. Used to a world where everything was done in an ordered fashion, Brennan had difficulty comprehending that an army which prided itself on an ability to move quickly and efficiently to any theatre of war, seemed to be incapable of moving its medical equipment with any kind of precision. As part of the QAIMNS Reserve she had been called up immediately war was declared and quickly found she was in the thick of a retreat, while attempting to treat men who had been injured in the initial fighting.

Hundreds of walking wounded were treated rapidly and efficiently, with basic first aid being administered before they were sent to join the retreating army; as the retreat progressed the medical teams stayed as close to the fighting as they could, until it became unsafe to remain. Equipment was scarce, often not arriving where it was needed until the hospital had packed up and moved back, closer to the sea.

Brennan was surprised to learn, on reporting for duty, that Mr Chardingly had been gazetted as a major in the Royal Army Medical Corps and was to take charge of her medical detachment in France. Although she knew his loss would be keenly felt by the staff she had left behind; Brennan was happy to be working with a man she knew would do everything he could for the soldiers in his care.

Almost as soon as the first tents had been erected in a semi-permanent place, the wounded started to arrive. Many were carried in by other soldiers retreating from the front, often wounded themselves. Within hours Brennan was looking at a tent with every bed full and with twenty or thirty stretcher cases lying on the ground outside. As the men arrived they were sorted into treatment categories. Those not in imminent danger of dying, were left where they lay. No sooner had a bed been emptied because the occupant had been taken to theatre or had died, then the bed was filled with one of the patients from outside.

Sister Brennan was exhausted, for a number of hours she had been assessing wounds and deciding on treatment options. Removing the bloodied dressing from the leg of a young captain she straightened up. He had been wounded during the retreat from Mons and had lain in a roadside ditch for at least two days before being picked up. Around the site of the injury his leg had swollen and looked almost as though it would explode. Tapping the leg produced a hollow sound, as though there was gas trapped inside.

'Sir, can you look at this next, please?' She asked Major Chardingly, who was staring intently at the wounded arm of a nearby soldier.

'Of course, Sister; can you call an orderly and get this man prepared for surgery? He will lose this arm unless we are quick.'

Major Chardingly crossed to the bedside of the patient Brennan had been removing the dressings from. 'Ah, I've read about such cases, Sister. I think he has advanced gas gangrene. It happens when the wound becomes contaminated with the surrounding earth which is rich and fertile. There's nothing for it but to amputate, we'll proceed with that immediately after the first case. Even then he may not survive; it seems that unless we catch all of the diseased flesh the first time we operate, the gangrene will continue to spread until he no longer has the strength to fight it.' He paused before continuing. 'I do hope the fields of France are not going to make treating the wounded difficult, we have enough to contend with as it is.'

Chapter Three

Silent night, holy night!
All is calm, all is bright.
Round yon Virgin, Mother and Child.
Holy infant so tender and mild,
Sleep in heavenly peace,

German Christmas Carol, 1818

Christmas 1914 – France

Captain Gerald Hammond stopped writing and stood up. Stamping his feet, he started to move around the dugout, at the same time blowing on his hands. For protection against the elements he had taken to wearing woollen gloves knitted by the Red Cross. Chopping the tops of the fingers off gave him the protection needed to keep his hands warm, but also allowed him to write. Hammond felt sure that the Red Cross would understand the necessity of his modification.

What little light there was, pooling at the entrance to the dugout was starting to fade as late afternoon became early evening. Hammond was reluctant to light the lamp he had, as fuel was in such short supply. He had been trying to write to his sister, Lady Julia, in response to a letter he had received from her a few days before. The letter was full of news from home but gloomy about life in the capital city of a country at war. The clubs in Mayfair and Knightsbridge they had frequented so often in peacetime were empty; it was almost as if Londoners felt guilty to be seen enjoying themselves, while so many men were away fighting on the Western Front.

Julia reported nightclubs were springing up in Soho in defiance of some of the new laws drawn up to focus the nation and curb frivolous behaviour. She had accompanied some of their friends to one of the more upmarket clubs when they were either home on leave, or recuperating from injuries sustained during the retreat.

Hammond was overdue for some leave. He had been involved in the war almost from the moment the first shot was fired. After the retreat from Mons he had re-grouped with his men and had been part of the action aimed at halting the German advance. Eventually, with its back to the sea, the British Expeditionary Force had turned and dug in, creating a trench system which spread across Belgium and down through France. Very quickly war on the Western Front had degenerated to a stalemate situation, with neither side able to breach the other's defences. In those hectic early days when the Coldstream Guards had come up against such fierce resistance and lost so many men, Hammond had been promoted in the field to captain and now had responsibility for a company of men, with Lewis as his company sergeant major.

It was so cold in the trench, immediately outside of the dugout, that Hammond was convinced it was about to snow and wondered if he was destined to see a white Christmas from the trenches. The dugout gave some protection from the weather but he felt sorry for his men; the majority of whom were huddled on the fire step trying to keep warm. There was very little activity with no one interested in attempting to engage the enemy; even the snipers had stopped taking pot shots. With only two more days left in the line before being relieved by the Middlesex Regiment everyone thought only of staying alive and the hope that if they did so they would receive news from home the evening they marched out of the line.

***

Christmas Day dawned cold and clear. The area of no man's land separating the British from the German trenches looked peaceful with a frosted covering which could have been mistaken for snow. Shelled stumps of tree trunks were white, with icicles clinging to the remaining branches. It was difficult to believe that only a hundred yards apart two nations were desperately trying to gain the upper hand by killing each other.

The start of the day had been no different from any other. Hammond could hear Sergeant Davis running along the trench calling for the men to 'Stand to' as he went. During the last ten days in the line, the men had learnt that they were living opposite the 55th Regiment of the Prussian Army; a group of men who in peacetime were known as the 6th Westphalia Regiment, soldiers notorious for their battle honours won in various conflicts around the globe. Usually, calls on the part of the British NCOs to 'Stand to' led to a volley of shells being fired from the German lines; a daily morning ritual played out by both sides, to ensure the opposing army knew they were awake and ready for the fight. This Christmas morning was eerily quiet though; following the order to 'Stand to' nothing happened. There was no expectant volley of fire from the Germans.

'What do you make of that then, sir?' Sergeant Davis asked Lewis, who had emerged from the dugout and was standing in the trench beside him.

'I'm not sure; it's very odd that the Hun has not woken us up with the usual barrage. Have you seen Lieutenant Parker? I need him to report to Captain Hammond about activity in the sector overnight.'

'I'll find him and get back to you, sir.'

Ten minutes later Davis returned with Lieutenant Parker who was looking harassed. 'Sorry, Sergeant Major, I was arranging stretcher bearers to take young Gibbs down the line. He was on a night patrol in front of the wire, seems he may have stepped on an unexploded shell, which has taken away most of his right leg. I doubt he'll survive. He's unconscious now from the blood loss.'

'Damn, he was shaping up to be useful sniper; I had recommended him to Captain Hammond for promotion to lance-corporal, sir,' Lewis replied. 'How was the rest of the night, sir?'

'Quiet. I took advantage of the reduced shelling to send out a couple of sorties into no man's land, to check the state of the wire, which is not good. We could do with a couple of men going over tonight to carry out some repairs. The wire directly in front of the trench has taken a battering from the daily bombardment and needs repair, as it could easily be breeched,' Parker replied.

'This lack of activity makes no sense, sir. The Prussians are not known for their reticence. I expected a lively time once we knew they were guarding the sector opposite.'

After half an hour of silence the guards manning the sector began to relax; unsure of what was happening they were a little wary, but happy not to have been subjected to the usual bombardment. Faintly at first but gradually increasing in volume the men became aware of the sound of singing, coming from the trenches opposite. A lone voice could be heard singing the opening words to the Christmas carol, 'Silent Night'. The singing was in German but the tune was unchanged from the English version; as the voice gained in strength other voices joined in reaching a crescendo. By the time the carol reached its conclusion English voices could be heard adding to the sound.

Several other carols then followed, until both sides had exhausted their repertoire. After this, shouted questions could be heard between the troops on either side. The questions were mostly general in nature; it was a little disconcerting as the Germans seemed to know more about the Coldstream Guards than they should have done; at one point a voice was heard asking if Viscount Hammond had enjoyed his breakfast.

Eventually, a German voice, speaking in English, asked if they could safely climb out of the trenches to bury their dead; some of whom had been lying exposed for many weeks. Hearing the request Parker ran down the steps into the dugout and shook Captain Hammond awake to ask his advice. Hammond left the dugout and approached the fire step, where he cautiously lifted first his rifle with a hat perched on it and then, when that wasn't shot at, his head above the parapet. On the opposite side of no man's land close to the German line Prussian soldiers, unwilling to wait for any official orders, could be seen preparing their dead for burial. Hammond welcomed the opportunity to do the same, he was concerned for the increasing number of his men who had died defending their country, but were unable to be buried, as the risk to a burial party had been too great.

'Sergeant Major Lewis, Lieutenant Parker, organise the men into burial parties. Let's see what we can do about clearing up this sector. Ask everyone involved to keep a look out for identity tags, there's nothing worse than a telegram which states only that a chap is missing, presumed dead.'

Unsure of their reception, the men were at first cautious but eventually climbed over the parapet and started work. Closest to the British lines they began to bury the dead and remove identifying tags. The work was distressing, difficult and time-consuming, as the ground was rocky and the earth hard, but there was a feeling of relief that at last their comrades were being given a decent burial.

By lunch time soldiers from both trenches were quite close to each other; inevitably conversations were struck up by the small number of soldiers on each side able to speak a common language. Gifts were exchanged and food was shared; the parcels from home which had begun arriving during the previous week were spread around freely and something of a party atmosphere developed. All over no man's land there were pockets of men enjoying a smoke together and exchanging mementoes. Before long someone produced a football and an impromptu game was organised. Up and down the line a pleasant afternoon was spent by the troops who for a change were happy not to be firing at each other.

As Christmas Day turned into evening soldiers on both sides began to drift back to their own lines; word was spreading that General Sir John French had been informed of the unofficial truce and was determined to make sure it was brought to an end and did not happen again. He and his staff officers were reported to be issuing orders to forbid any further fraternisation. Fortunately, these orders took a while to filter down to the front line; giving Hammond's company the chance to repair and strengthen the wire in front of their sector.

Christmas Eve 1914 – London

Lady Julia mounted the steps leading to the front door of her house, two at a time. She was in a hurry, having spent far too long languishing over tea at Goddard's. She had met Fiona Moncrieff there to finalise details for the evening's entertainment, after some last-minute Christmas shopping; the conversation had inevitably turned to the war and how to become involved in such a way their parents would approve. A significant number of her male friends had joined up and if not in training were, like her brother, already at the front, but Lady Julia and Fiona were having difficulty finding a respectable way to assist the war effort, that their parents would be approve of.

Nursing with the Voluntary Aid Detachment was now high on the list of Hadleigh's options but was not a popular idea with Moncrieff, who was not at all certain she would be able to handle any blood and gore. Lady Julia had been won over by the knowledge that she was more likely to end up in France as a VAD, than by doing anything else for the war effort.

Knowing war was imminent the British Government had recognised a need to consolidate the voluntary medical organisations, which had been springing up all over the country in recent years. By the autumn of 1914 there were nearly two and a half thousand Voluntary Aid Detachments operating; each containing dozens of young volunteers eager to provide support for the men going to war. Once war was declared, the VAD had mobilised and started to convert every available church hall and disused building into a space fit to nurse the wounded; bandages had been rolled and splints made in preparation. Recently the VAD had turned its attention to recruitment and at last Lady Julia had orders to report in the New Year, to the 1st London General Hospital at Denmark Hill. With Moncrieff unwilling to join her she had enlisted the support of Briggs who she was sure would prefer the excitement of nursing the wounded to the drudgery of cleaning. The only flaw with this plan was telling her parents what she intended to do and also persuading them that they may be losing a parlour maid, but it would still be necessary to feed, house and pay her wages for the duration, as a sort of contribution to the war effort.

Lady Julia burst into the drawing room where her mother and father were enjoying a pre-dinner drink.

'Mama! I need to talk to you about something urgently. I've come up with the perfect way for us all to help the war effort. Promise you will listen to me, while I explain,' she panted.

'Julia, please? Your papa and I do not need a whirlwind disturbing a peaceful evening drink. Please take a glass of champagne and sit down before telling us your solution for winning the war.'

In the end it was easier than she thought. Her parents felt that nursing was a genteel, honourable occupation for a young lady in wartime, and were relieved that their son would be looked after by someone from a comparable background, if he needed it. They had read of people, like the Duchess of Westminster, who had taken things into their own hands, loading up ambulances with people and supplies and setting off for France; with the idea of nursing the wounded wherever there was space. Lord and Lady Hadleigh also recognised that Briggs would exert a calming influence on their daughter who had started to develop some wayward tendencies since returning from Switzerland; they were aware that she simply would not be able to nurse unless her wages were maintained, and thought sending her along was well worth the price of a parlour maid's wages.

Christmas 1914 – Camden, New South Wales

The heat was stifling. Summer had arrived with a vengeance a couple of weeks before, and so far there had been no let up from the searing heat. Hector Standish was concerned that if the rain did not come soon his crops would start to die; indeed, he appeared to be fighting a losing battle already in the bottom paddock. The Camden area had been exceptionally dry over winter, and land surrounding the township was brown and parched; not a good sign as generally in December the land was still green and lush, as yet unaffected by the summer heat. Already there was a very real possibility of bush fires, which threatened to take hold most years.

It was nearly a month since Hector had heard from either his son or daughter. He still found it hard to believe his children were on the way to the other side of the world fighting a war. He was concerned they had both gone somewhere that sounded so foreign. Who'd ever heard of Cairo?

The newspapers were full of advertisements from cartographers, selling maps to make it easier to follow the war in France. In an effort to understand the letters he expected they would send, Hector had sent away for a map; he had spent a considerable period of time poring over the various types and had eventually settled on one with place names in both English and French, before hearing his son and daughter were in Egypt. None of his friends at the Plough and Harrow seemed to know what the AIF was doing in Egypt, or where they were likely to attack, so it seemed pointless sending away for anything else. The last letter he had received from his daughter was full of the ancient wonders which she had travelled to with the aid of a local guide. His son sent brief notes complaining of endless drill and other military training thought necessary to produce the perfect Australian soldier.

Hector shook the mud from his boots and stepped into the kitchen. A blast of warm air coming from the word burning stove hit him squarely in the face, which despite the warmth of the day was fully stoked. Inside the oven was a saddle of lamb, slowly being cooked for the Christmas celebrations scheduled to take place later in the day. Constance was standing in the kitchen ruddy faced and perspiring. She had been supervising the cooking of a magnificent feast.

The Standish's planned a festive Christmas and had asked most of the neighbouring farmers to join them over the next two days; determined not to think about what the coming year of war may bring they planned to toast their offspring wherever they were.

Christmas 1914 – Cairo, Egypt

Standish still felt a little strange wearing the tropical uniform of the AANS. The uniform was heavy, hot and uncomfortably designed, but she hardly noticed this while she sat in Forsyth's Hotel waiting for her brother. It was tedious, but she could not arrange to meet him in any of the higher-class hotels because he was not an officer. The British Army had arrived in Cairo with some fanfare and seemed determined to stamp their authority on the city. With their arrival came a set of rules and regulations which the more egalitarian Australian soldiers and nurses thought absurd. Australian soldiers were frequently reported to their superiors for an unacceptable attitude, by British officers unaccustomed to what they saw as an appalling lack of respect.

Coincidently, Victoria and her brother had both arrived in Egypt at around the same time, after sailing in early November on different ships. For Victoria, the journey had taken the best part of a month and was made on a hastily converted troop ship which was carrying mainly men. Unfortunately, the addition of the medical units was made almost as an afterthought; little if any thought had gone into female accommodation, which as a result was cramped and spartan. It had become apparent early on the journey that although the AANS sisters were there out of necessity, their presence was not thought desirable by many of the old school soldiers on board. When the troop ship eventually docked in Alexandria, Victoria was deployed to work with the British, as the AIF had not yet set up any medical units.

Looking across the street Victoria could see her brother hurrying towards the hotel. She noticed he now had the three stripes of a sergeant on his arm and was looking fit and well. Striding into the hotel he noticed her seated next to the window and removed his slouch hat.

'How are you, Sis?' he asked, before sitting down and pouring himself a cup of tea, from the pot sitting on the table.

'Busy,' she replied. 'Unfortunately, there's no shortage of men needing treatment. We've heard that more medical staff are on their way aboard the *Kyarra*; hopefully we'll be setting up our own hospital once they get here and can start looking after Australian soldiers. The British are so much more formal than we're used to and difficult to work with at times.'

'I know what you mean; several men in my company have been in trouble for not saluting officers around town. The British don't seem to understand how much more relaxed things are back home.'

'Have you heard why we're here? Victoria asked. 'It seems such an odd place to be sent to. We should be in France helping to win this war, not stuck here surrounded by desert.'

'I'm no wiser than you are. Stan Marshall has just come back from a machine gun course; I reckon if anyone's heard anything it would be him. Hopefully, he'll join us this afternoon. I told him you were here, and he is rather keen,' Max replied

'Nonsense, I've known him so long it wouldn't feel right; although I'm sure the parents would approve.' Victoria removed her gloves and picked up the menu. 'Congratulations on the promotion. Are you sure you are ready to lead men into battle?' she teased.

'As ready as I'll ever be,' her brother replied. 'None of the AIF have much experience, although the odd man fought in South Africa a few years back. I think we may all end up doing some unfamiliar stuff before too long, but rumour has it we will be doing some intense training in the desert before going anywhere.'

Chapter Four

Blow out, you bugles, over the rich dead!
There's none of these so lonely and poor of old,
But, dying, has made us rarer gifts than gold.
These laid the world away; poured out the red
Sweet wine of youth; gave up the years to be
Of work and joy, and that unhoped serene,
That men call age; and those who would have been,
Their sons, they gave, their immortality.

Rupert Brooke 1914

April 1915 – Gallipoli

It was still dark as the troop ship towing the landing craft began to edge towards the beach. The night was cold and clear, miraculously rain had held off. The Australian Imperial Force, who had been preparing with other nations of the Empire to invade the Gallipoli peninsula, was ready and waiting. In each landing craft there was a sense of expectant nervousness from men who felt as though they had been preparing forever for the task ahead. They had endured months of training to improve their physical fitness in order to survive the rigours of battle at Gallipoli. Soldiers with potential had been weeded out and sent on specialist courses for snipers and machine gunners. Men had been promoted to fill gaps left through illness and injury. The battalions were at full strength, with the prime of Australian youth in their ranks. Men who six months before had been working as farmers, bank clerks and shop keepers had been trained into a cohesive fighting force, ready for action. Each boat contained men bursting with pride, content to know that very shortly they would be called on to make a difference which would hopefully shorten the war.

The previous evening most of Sergeant Standish's company had spent time writing to loved ones; they did this with a sense of urgency, in case they were wounded in the battle to come. Most did not believe they would actually die, as surely the Australian Army was the best fighting force in the world? They were keen only to prove to the Mother Country they were equal to the task and that Australia had come of age.

At last it had been explained why so many months had been spent training and kicking their heels in the desert around Cairo. A plan had been devised in the corridors of power back in London, to capture Constantinople and the Dardanelles. If the Allies could take control of them, Russia would be unimpeded in its efforts to help win the war; leading ultimately to victory on the Western Front. It was estimated that the plan would considerably shorten the war and that the men about to take part would earn the thanks of a grateful Empire, providing, of course, they were victorious.

General Sir Ian Hamilton had addressed them a few days before:

"Before us lies an adventure unprecedented in modern war. Together with our comrades of the fleet we are about to force a landing upon an open beach in face of positions which have been vaunted by our enemies impregnable. The landing will be made good, by the help of God and the Navy; the positions will be stormed and the war bought one step nearer to a glorious close."

Most of the men although uncomfortable and cold were buoyed up with the knowledge that God was on their side, as they contemplated what lay ahead. The night was quiet and the water still. The moon had disappeared over the horizon leaving an enveloping blackness. Apart from the water slapping against the side of the landing craft the only sounds were muffled instructions from NCOs ordering soldiers to put out cigarettes, in case they could be seen. Slowly the troop ships towing the landing craft started to move toward North Beach. Men were tense, listening for any sign that the Turks hiding in the hills may be aware of their approach. As the landing craft neared the beach head it looked as though they may be able to take the enemy by surprise.

The first wave of men had been thoroughly briefed about the terrain and assured that there would be only small pockets of resistance from the Turkish. Once on the beach they should be able to take the high ground with ease; providing covering fire for the second and third waves landing after them.

As the landing craft crept towards the shore a sudden burst of machine-gun fire disturbed the silence of the night; two men in Standish's boat fell back, hit from the gun. Wave after wave of machine-gun fire began raking the boats, from the cliffs surrounding the beach head. Men cried out as they fell, only to have their sounds muffled by the stutter of machine-gun fire. The midshipman in charge of the landing craft started shouting orders to disembark, but his voice was lost in the general commotion and confusion, as men tried to take cover from the hail of bullets passing too close for comfort.

Making a quick assessment of the situation Standish realised that if his men stayed where they were there would soon be no one left alive to fight on the beach. Quickly, he ordered his men to climb over the side into the shallow water surrounding the boat. Jumping in after them Standish struck out for shore. With full kit on his back it was not an easy task but eventually he was able to make his way up the beach to some sand dunes in the lea of a cliff face; running in fear of every minute he was exposed to the ceaseless machine-gun fire from the Turkish guns overhead. Looking back towards the beach he could see the bodies of men lying at the water's edge where they had fallen. Some men had drowned after jumping over the side; weighed down by the equipment they were carrying; no one had time to stop and help.

After several minutes Corporal Marshall arrived and lay panting beside him. He was followed almost immediately by their company commander, Captain Crowley, and several other men. Crowley ordered them all to take off their packs and leave them.

'I'm not sure where we are, Sergeant, but this cliff is not meant to be here. The ground should be flat. Bloody typical the Pom's have cocked things up again; I think we may have drifted north,' he said. 'We will need to take only essential ammunition, to scale upward and secure the ground; hopefully if we can do this, we can pick up what's left behind later.'

'I agree, sir, but I think we've got a bigger problem that needs to be sorted out immediately. The men on the beach are being hammered by machine-gun fire coming from the right. Unless we deal with the machine gun they won't be able to establish any kind of base on the beach head below. I think if we can follow the shadow of that rock face we may have an element of surprise,' Standish replied. 'Corporal Marshall, can you cover me with a bit of fire? I'll see if I can get close enough to take the position out.'

Without waiting for a response, Standish ran to the base of the rock face; taking advantage of the gloom and dawn shadow he edged quickly towards the Turkish gun emplacement, which had been causing such devastation for the troops landing on the beach below. The closer he got the more nerve-wracking the journey became.

A steep path ran up the cliff face to where three men were manning a gun positioned in a sheltered natural hollow. One man was firing rapidly in a sweeping motion, picking out Australians on the beach below, while another fed belts of ammunition through the gun. The third man was protecting the other two with a rifle which he was firing sporadically into the area just below the gun emplacement. It was obvious that he could not see the area directly, but was firing in a random manner hoping to catch anyone approaching. Standish somehow managed to dodge the fire as he cautiously approached.

Extracting a Mills bomb from his ammunition pouch Standish pulled the pin and threw it into the middle of the enemy gun site. Ducking quickly, he waited for the resulting explosion, which was loud enough to make him cover his ears; he then stood up and looked at the damage he had caused. There was nothing left of either the machine gun or the men who had been manning it, where the gun emplacement had been a large crater was left in the side of the hill.

The relief for the men down on the beach head was instant, with no further gunfire. It was possible to hear a second machine gun firing from further up the cliff face, but the majority of soldiers were out of range.

Quickly headquarters were established and plans made to attack the high ground in a more ordered fashion.

Once the day became lighter it was easier to see where the troops had landed and evaluate the situation they found themselves in. The Australians had landed directly in front of a sheer yellow sandstone cliff, which did not have any easy access routes to the top. The plan for domination of the peninsula depended on swift movement of the landing troops, with an element of surprise to gain a substantial foothold. As the day wore on it was obvious this would not be possible; some troops began to dig in close to the beach, to provide support for those scaling the cliffs above.

Standish and his men continued to fight on through the day, eventually attaining the high ground on 400 Plateau. Two of his men were killed instantly when a shell landed in the middle of them, as the platoon rested for ten minutes. A third man was badly wounded, but was carried to where the wounded were being laid in rows on the beach before being evacuated to hospital ships anchored in the bay. Many died waiting to be transported as they had wounds which were too extensive to survive a day with the medical teams in disarray, desperately trying to organise themselves in the chaos on the beach.

April 25th 1915 – ANZAC Cover

Sister Standish pulled her cloak around her shoulders in an effort to feel warmer. It was not quite light yet and although the night was still, a chill drifted up from the surface of the sea below. Victoria shivered, not quite sure if she was shivering from the cold or at the thought of what the day would bring. Somewhere out there on the Aegean Sea her brother was waiting for daylight and orders to wade ashore. Alongside him were men she had known all her life, going to school and church with them and more recently to bush dances. She was particularly fond of Stanley Marshall; a larrikin who had grown up with her brother and had spent almost as much time at Oakfield House as he did his own home. She desperately hoped they would both come through the next few hours unscathed, but knew the chances were poor.

The sound of gunfire strengthened with the break of dawn. Standing on the ship's deck with her Kelly looked toward land and sighed.

'Do you think we'll see many wounded?' she asked.

'I hope not, but I have a bad feeling about this. From what I've read the land is barren and inhospitable. I hope the landing points have been chosen with care, or they'll have trouble getting to the top of the cliffs. I'm sure, despite what everyone is saying, the Turks will be waiting,' she replied.

After the frustration of working in Cairo, Standish and Kelly had been given orders to serve on the *Ariadne*; a hospital ship, which had been sent to the peninsula, equipped to transport the wounded after the battle began. Military planners had not expected too many wounded, as they expected minimal resistance, but had set up hospitals in Cairo and Malta to deal with any overflow, just in case. Knowing that the landing was imminent, these hospitals had been emptied to cope with the expected influx once the battle began. Hospital staff had prepared for months to receive casualties, sending requests for bandages and dressings and stocking up on morphine supplies. Military red tape meant medical supplies were not always given priority and often requests had to be made on several occasions before they arrived.

The *Ariadne* had been hastily converted from a luxury liner at the start of the war. The state rooms had all been cleared of pre-war fixtures and fittings and had been replaced with basic hospital equipment. Row upon row of hospital beds now filled every available space on board. A couple of state rooms had been set up as operating theatres to treat soldiers needing urgent surgery.

Once dawn broke it was possible to see action on the beachhead in the distance. The noise of machine-gun fire and shells exploding could be heard quite clearly, although the ship spent the early part of the day constantly manoeuvring out of range of the Turkish guns. After several hours of waiting, troop ships began to arrive with soldiers injured during the initial landing. Most had crudely applied field dressings over shrapnel and bullet wounds. Standish and Kelly set about tending to the wounded, who were lifted from the troop ships and taken to the makeshift wards. Once the wards were full they were lifted on to the open deck and left lying under awnings; erected as soon as the ship's captain realised the numbers of wounded arriving greatly exceeded expectations. The work was relentless, with some men dying before they could receive any treatment at all.

After several hours of back breaking work on deck Standish stood up to find Matron Veronica Gillespie standing beside her. Gillespie was a seasoned campaigner who had served in South Africa several years before; returning to Australia she had been employed as matron of a large Melbourne hospital. She was looking dishevelled, for once her immaculate turnout was awry. Her sleeves were rolled up, her dress bloodstained and her cap was crumpled.

'Standish, I want you to finish what you are doing here, take a ten-minute break to have a cup of tea and then go and assist Captain Francis in the operating theatre.'

'Of course, Matron. Who will take over here?'

'I'm sending Kelly up, she's been assisting in theatres and needs fresh air for a while. It's quite claustrophobic inside so I'm trying to share out the work down there. I'll try and make sure you are relieved before too long.'

In the end, Standish continued to work until she could hardly move from exhaustion. The day passed by with wounded after wounded being lifted on board, taking the place of the newly dead. The AANS sisters working alongside the medical staff stripped and dressed wounds, identified who required surgery and how urgently. Throughout the day the ship remained vulnerable from shell fire, despite the large red crosses painted on each side. Turkish batteries high on the hillside sent a constant barrage of fire until the inevitable happened and the ship suffered a direct hit.

Kelly was working on the foredeck when the shell hit, she was carrying out an initial assessment on a sergeant who had been winched on board minutes before with abdominal injuries sustained in the fighting on Plugge's Plateau. The shell landed just behind her, throwing her sideways and killing her and the sergeant instantly. Two other men in the immediate vicinity sustained further injuries to add to their original ones, dying before anyone was able to attend to them.

Hearing the explosion, Standish left the theatre to see what had happened; running quickly up on to the foredeck she was greeted by the sight of wounded and dying men and women. Looking across the deck she was shocked to see Christina Kelly lying where the force of the blast had thrown her. Running over she bent down and felt for her pulse but quickly realised there was nothing she could do; she stood up and looked around, her eyes resting on a wounded officer who needed urgent attention. Automatically, years of ingrained training took over as she began to help the survivors.

Initially Standish blamed herself for Kelly's death, having swapped to the comparative safety of the operating theatres. As darkness began to fall on what had been a momentous day, Veronica Gillespie found her on deck standing at the bow of the ship looking toward land.

'Are you all right?' Gillespie asked. 'I know that Kelly was a close friend of yours.'

'Yes, Matron, I'm fine, it's been a very tiring day. We trained together you know? Out at the Coast.' Victoria paused before continuing. 'It all seems such a long time ago now. She was so excited about all of this; saw it as a huge adventure and a way of escaping the parochial restraints of home. Her mother will be devastated by her death,' she added. 'It would have been me you know, if only a few minutes earlier.'

'You mustn't blame yourself for this, Standish. It was my order which caused you to swap duties. You had no choice in the matter. I have spoken to the padre and the ship's captain and the plan is to bury her at sea tomorrow morning, along with the other soldiers killed at the same time.' Gillespie continued, 'The captain has indicated that we are almost fully loaded and will leave soon for Alexandria, so we can offload and then return for another batch of wounded. Can you work for a little longer?'

'Of course, ma'am; I'll just go and freshen up before reporting to Captain Francis. He still has several badly wounded men to operate on.'

The following morning the ship slowed its engines almost to a standstill and in the cold light of dawn the padre conducted a short ceremony committing Christina Kelly and seven men to the deep. The ceremony was necessarily brief, submarine activity in the area had been reported as high, with a supply ship sunk by torpedo action the night before. After the ceremony, the *Ariadne* wasted no time in increasing to full speed wishing to offload it's wounded in Alexandria as quickly as possible. From there the wounded would be transported on to hospitals in Cairo.

May 1915 – London, England

Lady Julia Hadleigh was tired and her feet ached. She had been at work since seven o'clock after being woken much earlier by Briggs with a cup of tea. They had changed quickly into newly starched VAD uniforms and had been driven to work by Bates the coachman. Up until a few years before, Bates had taken care of the horses in the mews behind the house, but the advent of the motor car had changed his life considerably; now he had sole charge of two gleaming family cars, which when he was not driving he spent the day polishing and tinkering with their engines. Despite being May the weather at such an early hour was still cool and Bates made sure they were both warmly wrapped, before setting off to cross over Vauxhall Bridge, on the way to the 1st London General Hospital at Camberwell.

Hadleigh was taking a moments respite from the exacting demands of Sister Blackstone, who seemed to have taken an instant dislike to her when she started work on the ward several months before. She was sitting next to the sink in the sluice; a small room located to the side of the ward, where bed pans were kept and cleaned and where she was fairly hopeful Sister Blackstone would not venture.

After joining the VAD with a certain amount of self-satisfaction at the thought of helping in such a positive way, Hadleigh had not been over impressed with the welcome they both received on reporting for training. She had, as instructed, been kitted out with a uniform at Salmon's a small retail shop specialising in such outfitting, located in a side street not far from Regent Street.

On the evening the uniforms arrived, she and Briggs had been persuaded to model their attire in front of a group of Red Cross volunteers, invited by her mother to help knit socks for the soldiers at the Western Front; she had felt proud that they were both going to do their bit shortly and would soon be making some sacrifices, thereby showing loyalty and empathy for the men in France.

Hadleigh's first day had been exhausting. In no uncertain terms Sister Blackstone had made it clear that VAD nurses were a rather quaint social experiment, aimed at placating a few old dowagers with influence in Whitehall; ladies who were convinced that aristocratic nurses may cheer up the wounded officers from the front, as surely they would have more in common than anyone nursing professionally? Blackstone was not in favour of the arrangement and resented the intrusion of a group of VADs on her ward. From the outset she had made life as difficult as she possibly could, in the misguided belief that the VADs would soon tire of such exhausting work and return to the drawing rooms of Kensington and Belgravia to find less arduous tasks to assist the war effort. She had not bargained on the reputation she would soon earn in those very drawing rooms, where VADs returning from a period on duty would discuss in detail her unique foibles; where indeed it had become a badge of honour to be able to say you had survived a stint on her ward. After several months of being in the firing line, Hadleigh was slightly dispirited but had not succumbed to pressure and when not carrying out the more mundane tasks nursing entailed was even beginning to enjoy herself.

Hadleigh wriggled her toes inside the unflattering lace-up boots she was wearing and briefly contemplated removing them to give her feet some relief. As she reached forward to undo her bootlaces she could hear voices coming her way.

'I'm sure I last saw Hadleigh preparing for the back round, Sister,' she could hear Briggs explaining. 'She was going to look for some methylated spirit in the sluice,' she continued.

'Well, find her and then report to my office immediately,' Blackstone replied.

Briggs banged open the door of the sluice. 'Come on, Lady Julia, look sharp. Sister wants us in her office.'

Hurriedly straightening their caps and smoothing imaginary creases in their immaculate aprons, Hadleigh and Briggs knocked nervously on Sister Blackstone's door and waited for the command to enter. Both were mentally going over possible transgressions they may have made, from the myriad of rules which encompassed their working lives. Hadleigh had until this moment believed she was having the best week yet, having thrown out no more than two bandages accidentally and not breaking anything at all.

Sister Blackstone was seated at her desk writing when they entered. She continued for several minutes before signing a letter with a flourish and blotting it carefully; only then did she look up and come straight to the point.

'Firstly, I would like you to know, that despite my misgivings, you are shaping up to be reasonable nurses. Given time, you may even become good nurses. Are you both prepared to put in the effort required to achieve this?' she asked.

'Yes, Sister,' they both replied in unison. Not knowing what else they could possibly say, or indeed what else could be expected.

'Good,' Sister Blackstone continued, 'I have a proposition for you. I have taken a commission in the QAIMNS and have been asked to set up a ward dedicated to nursing men from the Gallipoli Peninsula. The war there is not going as planned and although there are several hospitals in Cairo, Alexandria and Malta, current planning indicates a need for a hospital closer to the battlefield; so, we will be setting up a field hospital on an island called Lemnos. Trained nursing staff will be assigned from various places; I believe some may even be Australian. I'm committed to taking some VAD staff out with me, as the War Office continues to believe you are useful and has indicated service overseas for the VAD has become a necessity. This will allow a wider spread of appropriately trained staff.' Hadleigh and

Briggs stood waiting for Sister Blackstone to continue. 'I would prefer to take VADs I have had a hand in training and have worked with. The work will be difficult and distressing but no harder physically than you are used to. You have a day or two to think things over, but I will need an answer by the end of the week.'

With a nod of her head Blackstone indicated the audience was over and picked up her pen to start writing. Hadleigh and Briggs left her office rapidly and only just managed to get out of earshot before eagerly discussing the conversation they'd just had.

'What do you think, Briggs?' Hadleigh asked excitedly.

'Well, I'm sure I don't know what to think, Lady Julia, fancy being asked to go to somewhere foreign. I've never even been to Margate before!' Briggs paused. 'I suppose you'll need someone to look after you.'

'If we go you'll be flat out looking after yourself,' Hadleigh answered. 'I don't know that it'll be that comfortable, I shall have to learn to put up with the conditions. We must go home and persuade Mama to let us go. Then I think another trip to Salmon's will be in order for some summer uniforms.'

Chapter Five

I have a rendezvous with Death
At some disputed barricade,
When spring comes back with rustling shade
And apple-blossoms fill the air-
I have a rendezvous with Death
When Spring brings back blue days and fair.
It may be he shall take my hand
And lead me into his dark land
And close my eyes and quench my breath-
It may be I shall pass him still.
I have a rendezvous with Death
On some scarred slope of battered hill,
When Spring comes round again this year
And the first meadow-flowers appear.

Alan Seeger

May 1915 – London

Captain Gerald Hammond had spent a relaxing leave at home. It had taken several days to get used to the mundane sounds of London in comparison to the sound of shelling in the trenches. The sound of a car backfiring had him instinctively flinching but remembering just in time not to dive for cover. For the first twenty-four hours Hammond slept, much to his sister's disgust, as she had managed to take some time off and was keen to introduce him to friends she had made since she last saw him. She was also longing to find out what France was really like, not believing for a second the rubbish the newspapers were reporting.

Viscount Hammond walked into the drawing room on the second day of his leave looking spruced-up and rested. His uniform had been carefully cleaned while he was asleep and looked worn but presentable. As he sat drinking coffee he and his sister discussed plans for the next few days.

'I need to go to Bingley and Throckmorton to order a few things to take back with me, after that I'm all yours, old thing,' Hammond stated.

'That's good; I need to check out some of the overseas kit they've got, as I can't imagine Egypt will be too comfortable. Perhaps you can give me a bit of advice on things I need to take with me,' his sister replied. 'I still can't believe we've been asked to go, you know. Such a strange thing for Sister Blackstone to do, after making our lives hell for months; mind you saying yes to going hasn't improved things, if anything she's worse.' She continued, 'She seems to think we need to be capable of working like a professional nurse before we leave England. I do so want to remind her I'm a volunteer but am keeping as quiet as possible in case she changes her mind about taking us with her.'

'Learn all you can, while you can, Julia,' Hammond replied. 'If it's like France it will be hell out there and any extra training you are exposed to before you get there can only be good news.'

With the task of shopping for essentials out of the way, Hammond's leave passed by rapidly in a whirl of social activity. Most of his friends and associates had taken a commission in the older more established regiments of the British Army and although several had already departed for the Western Front or for Gallipoli, enough remained to help him enjoy his leave. He managed to catch all of the latest shows, but found the sudden rush of patriotic fervour a little hard to warm to. Almost every performance ended with a stunningly beautiful young lady belting out the words to 'Your King and Country want you', accompanied by a chorus of women wearing military clothing. Following this; children would descend into the audience handing white feathers to any man of an appropriate age not in uniform.

After months spent dodging bullets and shrapnel on a daily basis, Hammond felt unable to appreciate this kind of military jingoism. The steady stream of recruits, joining as a result of patriotic fervour, filled the gaps left by those who had been wounded or killed, but did not address the problem of why the war was being fought in the first place. Although happy to serve King and Country as a professional soldier, Hammond saw no reason why anyone else should be daft enough to join him.

At six o'clock in the morning on the day his leave ended, Hammond was woken by Edwards in preparation for his return to the Front. After breakfasting on scrambled eggs and kippers, Bates drove him the short distance to Victoria Station; where his mother was waiting, having already been at work in the canteen for several hours. He had deliberately left very little time for farewells and after a quick hug and kiss with promises to write, he boarded the first-class compartment of the train.

***

Victoria Station was an emotional place as it was the gateway to the Western Front from early on in the war. Troops arriving from France on the leave train would disembark at Victoria before crossing London to catch trains to destinations around the country. Troops embarking for France also departed from Victoria, in the early morning chill every day; often accompanied by relatives unable to hold back tears, terrified this was the last time they would say goodbye.

After seeing her son off to France in August of 1914 and observing Victoria Station was a functional but austere place, Lady Hadleigh began encouraging her friends to support the idea of setting up a canteen at the entrance to platform nine. She planned to give out tea and cigarettes to returning troops knowing that the journey from the Western Front was an arduous one, sometimes taking days. Once she had gained support and some capital for the idea she set about encouraging her friends to give practical help.

A committee had been formed to provide comfort for the men who were away fighting, by knitting socks and having fundraising drives. Its members were a little surprised that Lady Hadleigh appeared to think they would be willing to wait on the troops; but acknowledged it may be good for men who arrived covered in mud, straight from France, to encounter ladies in their best evening dress serving tea as they alighted from the train. Most vowed to recruit their daughters to the cause, knowing their presence would be an additional morale boost; so that within weeks of the canteen opening it had become a popular place for soldiers passing through the station.

War Office staff quickly realised that trains carrying the wounded had a terrible effect on troops preparing to leave for France; some hasty arrangements were called for to ensure hospital trains arrived long after the morning leave trains had steamed out of the station. Lady Hadleigh on hearing of these arrangements called an extraordinary committee meeting to canvass the ladies of Belgravia.

'I believe, of all people, the wounded need us most. I've noticed that often some of our brave boys, although horribly wounded, are left on the platform for considerable periods of time before being taken away in an ambulance,' she announced. 'I've approached Teddy Moncrieff at the War Office and he's happy for us to go right onto the platforms when the trains come in, to see what we can do. Can we get together a roster of people willing to give up an hour or so in the early evenings, do you think?' she asked.

A spirited debate followed, with some of the ladies present arguing that although this was an admirable suggestion, would it really be necessary to meet every train? After all, Lady Monksford argued, some of the soldiers would not be from the kind of background to appreciate such a gesture. Perhaps a roster could be made up of servants from some of their households to work at the station?

Lady Julia Hadleigh, who had a rare day off was sitting quietly in the corner listening to the debate, but found she was unable to remain silent. She stood up and moved to the centre of the room, where she interrupted Lady Monksford and addressed the ladies present.

'Most of you would know that for several months now I have been doing my bit at the 1st London General Hospital. The work is hard and some of it very distressing. I have looked after both officers and men during this time and have come to realise that if we are to win this war, it will only be with the help of the men some of you seem keen to abandon on the station platform,' she said. 'Mostly, they are pathetically grateful for anything I do for them and certainly appreciate that I am not from the type of background that would be found nursing in peacetime; I believe this war will break down a lot of social barriers and people of my generation will be able to lead lives away from London's drawing rooms,' she continued. 'I think everyone returning from the Western Front should be received and thanked for their contribution which is all that is keeping the German Army from marching through the streets of London.'

The sheer impossibility of predicting which trains should be met, led to a vote to meet them all. Once the decision was made the ladies did this smiling and as tradition demanded wearing full evening dress, despite the trains arriving during the late afternoon.

Often soldiers returning to France would arrive in the early hours of the morning, anxious not to miss the leave train which left at eight o'clock. Some came with relatives, wives and girlfriends desperate to spend the very last moments of time together.

Many said goodbye at the station entrance rather than go through the acute pain of a platform separation; where they could see their loved one's distress until the train had left the station and rounded the first bend in the track. It was far easier to deliver a quick peck on the cheek underneath the station clock and then disappear at speed into the enveloping crowd on the station concourse.

May 1915 – France

Intense fighting around Ypres had begun a couple of weeks earlier and the staff at the hospital had become accustomed to being called at all hours of the day and night, to deal with casualties as they were moved down the line. Sister Brennan existed on minimal amounts of sleep, in a constant state of near exhaustion. She found herself living life entirely dependent on when the next convoy of wounded arrived. Often she would be woken from a deep sleep to be told another convoy was on the way and it was necessary to prepare theatre for any number of life threatening injuries. She and Major Chardingly developed a routine; as each convoy of ambulances drew up, they briefly assessed and prioritised the wounded and then started to operate, stopping only when there was no one left requiring surgery. Assisting them in theatre was a padre, who initially called to minister to the dying was asked to deliver anaesthetics whenever he was free, releasing medical staff to attend to other gravely injured men.

Gradually the days and nights merged into one with only short breaks possible to eat and sleep.

The start of the day was unremarkable; a convoy of ambulances had arrived in the early hours of the morning and the wounded were gradually being attended to by available medical staff. Sister Brennan had again been called from her bed to assist Major Chardingly in theatre, as several patients required urgent surgical attention for wounds which were days old. They had been working steadily for a number of hours, pausing only for a quick cup of tea between cases, when an orderly came searching for Chardingly.

'Sir, a runner has been sent down from a casualty clearing station closer to the front line,' he stated. 'Apparently, some kind of poison gas has been released by the Hun and is knocking the Guards down like flies. I've been asked to let you know that a lot of the men are having difficulty breathing and are turning blue. The worst are being evacuated now and are on their way down here. Word from the Front is men are dying, gasping for breath in their hundreds.'

The hospital staff was well used to the arrival of ambulance convoys and had developed procedures to ensure a swift calm offload of the wounded, but nothing could have prepared them for these ambulances. Standing at the entrance to the hospital, drinking in the early dawn air during a short break, Brennan observed the start of an endless procession of ambulances crawling slowly down the hill towards her. Long before the first one arrived she could hear the sound of coughing, spluttering men, gasping for breath.

As the first men were lifted from the back of each ambulance she noticed that some were unable to see, making the situation they were in all the more terrifying. Men cried out as they were jolted by stretcher bearers, who had become careless because they were exhausted from the long night's work. The initial response from many of the nurses was consternation and distress. There was nothing tangible to treat; once the men were propped up with as many pillows and makeshift bolsters as could be found, little else could be done. The nurses had never expected to have to cope with a situation like this; in essence nursing was a practical skill and until now men either died or survived dependant on the nursing and medical treatment available. Having to watch helplessly as men died, without being able to intervene, was harder to accept than the exhausting backbreaking hard work of looking after the physically wounded they were used to.

Several of the men died very quickly, as the acute bronchitis bought on by the gas caused them to drown in fluid which accumulated rapidly on their lungs. These men could be heard trying to gulp in air from some distance away; a smaller number died slowly over a few days, gasping for breath until eventually slipping into unconsciousness and dying shortly after. However, the majority of men survived, recovering slowly and returning to the Front after a few weeks spent convalescing. The enemy achieved much by launching a gas attack, momentarily rendering troops in the line useless; isolated breakthroughs occurred, briefly penetrating the allied line, ultimately though these attacks were rebuffed, and the Allies managed to fight back and hold on leaving the line intact.

On the second morning after the gas attack Sister Brennan returned to the ward after a brief period off-duty; she had been able to sleep for a few hours and was feeling ready to face the inevitable onslaught of fresh wounded. Crossing the road separating the tented nurses' accommodation from the hospital she became aware of a captain pacing up and down before the entrance to the hospital. He had obviously been in the front line recently, as his clothes and boots were muddy and he looked tired.

'Are you all right, sir?' Brennan asked as she drew level with him.

'Yes, fine thank you, Sister,' he replied, before continuing. 'I'm trying to find out how one of my platoon sergeants is. He was gassed fairly badly yesterday near Ypres. An orderly went in to find out for me a while back, but hasn't returned.'

'If you come with me, sir, I'll take you to the wards where the gassed men are being cared for. The orderly's probably been caught up; it's fairly busy in there,'

Brennan responded, walking quickly towards the building.

Hammond, who was glad to have found someone able to help, followed after her.

June 1915 – Gallipoli

The war to claim the Gallipoli Peninsula was not going as planned. The objective to take the high ground and witness the withdrawal of all Turkish troops had not been achieved. At North Beach Australian and New Zealand troops were starting to dig in; preparing for a war of attrition. Trenches had been dug anywhere that the ground supported them and much like France quickly became home for the troops involved in the initial assault. Sergeant Standish and his men were occupying an area close to the Nek, where fighting seemed to have come to a temporary halt. The area was exposed and vulnerable, with the Turks sending up a shower of gunfire every time they saw movement. The track leading down to the beachhead had several points that were in clear view of Turkish snipers; making it hazardous for messengers sent from HQ to forward parts of the line.

Sergeant Standish was on his way to HQ for up to date orders and had taken the opportunity to have a swim; although still within range of gunfire many men took the chance of a cleansing dip in the sea when they could. A few men with the same idea were already in the water throwing a ball around. The sea was cold but inviting; after joining in the ball game for a few minutes he emerged feeling invigorated and clean. Rapidly rubbing himself dry Standish dressed and walked towards the southern end of the beach.

North beach was a hive of activity. At one end of the beach a makeshift casualty clearing station had been set up under temporary canvass shelter. Wounded men bought down from the trenches were left there on stretchers, waiting for darkness to fall; after dark it was safe for landing craft to leave the hospital ships, which were anchored further out to sea, to load the wounded and transport them.

Supplies and ammunition were stockpiled on the beach waiting to be taken up the cliff side under cover of darkness. Several donkeys were tethered close by to assist moving supplies.

The general staff had set up headquarters at the southern end of the beach, where a natural cave provided some relief from the occasional shells exploding around them. Sergeant Standish made his way to HQ. Sitting behind a desk made up of wooden boxes which had originally contained tins of bully beef, a corporal looked up on his approach.

'Sergeant Standish?' he enquired. 'The colonel is waiting to speak to you, go right in.'

Separated by a curtain Colonel Hathaway had a small private area, with a desk and camp bed. Sergeant Standish stepped into the inner sanctum and saluted the colonel who was sat at his desk signing dispatches. At his side stood his adjutant, Major Brown, who looked up when Standish entered.

'Ah, Sergeant Standish, good news I think,' Major Brown commented. 'After your action on the day of the landings, Captain Crowley recommended you for a bravery medal. It seems they agree in London as you have been awarded the Victoria Cross.'

Nodding, Colonel Hathaway picked up a piece of paper. 'Stand at ease, Sergeant. You can take a copy of this with you, but I'd like to read the citation which accompanies the award.'

"For conspicuous bravery and devotion to duty. On April 25th 1915, Sergeant Maxwell Standish identified an enemy machine gun emplacement, which was raking the beach with sustained fire, wounding and killing large numbers of men as they attempted to leave their landing craft during the initial assault on North Beach. With total disregard for his own safety and requesting only covering fire, Sergeant Standish stormed the gun emplacement, killing the occupants and disabling the gun. It is estimated that this single act of bravery saved the lives of countless men and assisted them to land without further incident on North Beach."

Standish was stunned. The Victoria Cross was such an unobtainable honour. During his youth he had occasionally seen a man who was reputed to have lost his leg and won the Victoria Cross during the Zulu War at the end of the eighteen-seventies. He apparently had wanted a little more adventure than rural Camden was able to provide and as a young man left the township to see the world. After jumping a ship bound for South Africa he had worked his passage before disembarking in Durban; here he had joined the Natal Native Contingent, as a non-commissioned officer, and had gone on to defend the hospital at Rorke's Drift. Standish and his friends were a little scared and a little in awe of the man, who used to sit in the local park on Sunday afternoons listening to the band playing.

'The King will want to present the Victoria Cross to you,' Colonel Hathaway continued. 'When we get word, we'll arrange leave and get you to London, but I doubt it will be any time soon as there's too much fighting to be done, and the King will recognise that we need every available man at this time.'

June 1915 – Alexandria

The *Ariadne* had docked several hours before in the early morning half-light, after a rough voyage across the Aegean Sea. Ambulances were lined up along the quayside waiting to take the wounded to one of several hospitals set up to cope with the influx, for some, this meant a short journey to a hospital train and further travel to Cairo. It had been a time-consuming, painstaking operation to offload the wounded without causing them any further pain. As the last ambulance disappeared into the distance Sister Standish turned her attention to cleaning and re-stocking the operating theatre. She had arranged to meet McMaster later in the day at the Palace Hotel, where she planned a soak in the bath, a long sleep and then a decent meal, before boarding the *Ariadne* for the return trip to the peninsula.

Since the first day of the Gallipoli landings the *Ariadne* had spent as little time as possible in port. Endless numbers of wounded needed evacuation from the battle zone; some of whom had been lying all day exposed on the beach, with little or nothing to drink. Wounds needed to be carefully soaked to remove bandages and clothing which had dried in the heat of the day and become stuck to the wounds they covered. The first time a covering was eased off was always an anxious moment; sometimes the dressing was all that prevented a man from haemorrhaging and bleeding to death.

Standish had become used to the movement of the ship as it steamed towards port with a full complement of injured men. She was able to move swiftly amongst the wounded in tune with the rocking of the boat. Often it took several hours after arriving in port before her legs would acknowledge she was back on land.

Inevitably, during the journey several men died; too many to be able to wait until the ship reached Alexandria before burying them. Each morning the padre would conduct a brief ceremony to bury the dead at sea; Sister Standish always took time, when she could, to attend the service, reluctant to allow them to go without paying her respects. It did not feel right that men who not long ago had been full of life and hope should be consigned to the deep without a suitable send off and without anyone present who would truly mourn.

Standish arrived at the Palace Hotel to find a letter waiting from her brother and another from her parents. She was surprised to learn about the Victoria Cross, not because her brother had been so brave, but because it had been awarded so swiftly. The general staff were not renowned for quick thinking, or for their love of Australian soldiers; rumours abounded that a number of quick awards had been made to convince the Australian public that they had a worthwhile part to play, in what was turning out to be a prolonged war of attrition. It was said by the more cynical that reports of heroic behaviour on the part of individual men would divert attention away from the appalling number of dead and wounded, which probably occurred as a result of poor military planning and a lack of accurate maps of the peninsula.

Her parents' letter made her feel homesick. At home the days would have started to draw in and would be cooler. At night, when Victoria was home, her parents would sometimes light a fire and sit around discussing farm business; sharing gossip picked up in Camden at the weekend fair. If her brother was home, he would be full of news from the latest town dance and Victoria was always happy to thrill the family with tales of her latest hospital exploits.

Standish could not help wondering how she would describe what was happening now. She, along with the rest of the Australian nursing contingent, had been horrified to learn that the Australian Imperial Force had landed in the wrong place and were struggling even now to gain a foothold on the peninsula. The casualties from the initial landing were far higher than anyone expected and almost every spare space in Alexandra and Cairo had been requisitioned and turned into a makeshift hospital. Daisy McMaster was currently engaged setting up a temporary hospital in an abandoned warehouse close to the port. Alexandria, which had only a few weeks before been full of soldiers keen to live life to the full, was now a place where the laughter had gone; replaced by the wounded and dying. It was impossible not to be affected by the atmosphere in town; Standish was relieved when later that evening feeling rested and clean, she found her way back to the port and re-boarded the *Ariadne*.

Chapter Six

August 1915 – Lemnos

Lady Julia Hadleigh and Violet Briggs had at last arrived in Mudros Harbour, along with Sister Blackstone and a party of nurses from the 1st London General Hospital. The voyage out from England had been fraught with danger, with enemy submarines a constant threat. The German Navy had recently proved they had an effective torpedo system, when to an appalled outcry from members of the public, they sank the Lusitania; this act alone was enough to cause a degree of nervousness amongst the passengers on board the ship bound for Lemnos, a Greek island in the Aegean Sea. The days at sea were punctuated with emergency drills triggered by a siren, designed to prepare the passengers for U-boat attack and alert them to the procedure for abandoning ship. In the event nothing happened, but everyone on board was very relieved to finally see land.

When the ship dropped anchor, the weather was hot and dry despite being six o'clock in the morning. Ahead, Lemnos appeared barren with hills gently rising from the Mudros quayside. A hastily constructed hospital had been made from large white canvas tents; which stretched row upon row as far as the eye could see. Alongside the tented hospital a road had been constructed, lined with painted white boulders; as if to let anyone passing know that the area was a military one. In front of the tents were small areas of scrub suitable for the wounded to sit out when the weather was clement.

Each tent contained a number of beds arranged along both sides with minimal space between them. In the middle of the tented area was a small amount of space where a desk was positioned to enable the nursing staff to sit and keep notes on each patient's condition. Next to the desk was a central wood-burning stove with a flue, which extended upwards through the centre of the tent.

Away from the hospital further up the hill were more tents. These were smaller and somehow looked rougher; as though erected with less care; the neat rows of painted boulders did not stretch this far. Each of the tents was set out to accommodate up to four nurses and at best could be described as functional.

Sister Blackstone gathered up her nursing staff and set off up the incline at a rapid pace, anxious to settle in and then see what needed to be done. As yet the hospital was empty; waiting for the wounded to arrive from a major summer offensive planned to take place shortly on the Gallipoli Peninsula.

Hadleigh and Briggs were assigned to a tent together with two other VADs, Joan Bishop and Veronica Thorpe, who had worked at the 1st London but were unknown to them. Hadleigh soon discovered she had been to school with the sister of one and had friends in common with the other. After rapidly unpacking the few items she had been allowed to bring with her, Hadleigh sat down on the flimsy looking camp bed and sighed.

'I have a feeling this tent is going to be hot and uncomfortable in a few hours,' she observed, 'and God help us if we are still here when winter arrives. It could get very cold, if you ask my opinion,' she continued.

'But no one is asking your opinion Hadleigh,' came the voice of Sister Blackstone, who had appeared at the opening of the tent. 'If you have finished unpacking, come with me. The dust and sand are thick in some of the tents that we intend to use to nurse the wounded. I think an afternoon of brushing and cleaning is necessary. These tents may be spartan but are adequate for you all for the time being. If we are still here when the weather gets colder, I will discuss the situation with the hospital superintendent.'

Without waiting for a response, Sister Blackstone set off down the hill, secure in the knowledge that the occupants of the tent would follow her without question.

Arriving at the first long narrow tent intended to be used as a hospital ward, she opened the front flap and peered into the gloom. Walking inside she began to open some of the flaps running along each side of the tent to let in some natural light. Before long she had the VAD's cleaning and sweeping, until each tent was ready to receive the predicted influx of wounded.

August 1915 – Lone Pine

Second Lieutenant Maxwell Standish stepped from the boat onto the improvised jetty that had appeared at the beachhead. The jetty did not stretch far enough out to sea to accommodate the larger boats engaged in supplying the troops dug in on the peninsula, but was useful for troops returning in smaller launches; they no longer had to wade through the surf to shore and at least started the climb to the trenches, dry.

After news of his Victoria Cross, Lieutenant Standish had returned to the trenches in front of the Nek and had continued to fight for a further month; before being advised he had been commissioned in the field and was to attend an officer training course in Cairo. The course had been tough, but a welcome break from the war; he had been able to catch up with his sister on the odd occasion that she was in port and he could get away from Cairo.

Alighting, Standish felt a little self-conscious, he had become used to wearing an officer's uniform in Cairo and had enjoyed the additional privileges it afforded; but was not sure if he could return to the trenches and command a group of men he had known since they were all children.

Leaving his valise on the beach, with instructions to a supply sergeant about where it was to be delivered, he reported to headquarters. Colonel Hathaway was still in command but his adjutant, Major Brown, had been replaced by a younger man leaning heavily on a stick. Standish was informed that Major Brown had unfortunately been killed in action a week before; following a routine inspection of the line he had been shot traversing an open area of gully where a sniper was known to have his sights trained. Although he had cautiously attempted the crossing, the sniper had been waiting and with deadly accuracy had shot him before he managed to travel ten yards.

Major Albert Smith-Barton looked young to be a major, but the stick and Military Cross ribbon demonstrated this was not his first experience of war; he had in fact been out in France at the start of it all. On loan from the Sussex Regiment, Smith-Barton had seen action during the retreat from Mons in September of 1914. He had been wounded in the thigh while attempting to repulse a small number of German soldiers who had broken through the British defences and were playing havoc with the retreating army. For destroying the attacking force, with minimal men available to assist him, he had earned the Military Cross; but had also spent some months convalescing in a military hospital in Kent. As a reward for his heroic behaviour at Mons, Smith-Barton had been sent first as an instructor to the training battalion and then to Gallipoli; where Churchill was still predicting a swift decisive victory.

Colonel Hathaway motioned Standish to join him at a map, which was laid out on a trestle table, in the centre of the room. The map was an assessment of trenches surrounding a place called Lone Pine; named by Australian troops who thought it odd that the Turks had felled all of the trees in the vicinity, but left a single pine standing.

'Good to see you, Lieutenant Standish. You've arrived back just in time for the battle which will see us break through and march onward to Constantinople. The British are planning to launch an attack to the North at Suvla Bay; we've been asked to support them and take out some of the Turkish trenches close by. It's hoped if we can do this the landing will go smoothly with little loss of life, and we will be assisting to achieve the final objective.' Hathaway pointed to an area of trenches marked on the map. 'I'm sending you back to C Company, as a replacement after a few of the company were injured last month. Captain Crowley is still there and will be in command.' He continued, 'Very best of luck, I am sure we will meet again after the battle.'

Lieutenant Standish saluted and left headquarters. Following a well-worn path, he made his way up onto 400 Plateau. The going was tough as the road up was narrow and with a major offensive imminent traffic was heavy. Ammunition and other supplies were being carried up to the plateau by any means possible. Some men were leading donkeys; laden down with last-minute equipment which had suddenly become essential. The path up was surrounded by debris from earlier fighting. The dead had been buried where they had fallen and a number of cemeteries had sprung up clinging to the hillsides, with simple crosses marking each grave. Most were carved in haste with minimal details; but some had epitaphs added by the men they had fought alongside.

Eventually, Standish arrived at a holding area just before the entrance to the trenches. Rounding a corner, he came across his old platoon, who were sitting on the fire step filling old jam tins with nails and bits of shrapnel. With a detonator added, the tins were instantly converted to a hand held bomb and were every bit as effective as the bombs sent up the line from the arsenal below. After greeting his old platoon and exchanging news from home, picked up in Cairo from Australians who were fresh off the boats arriving each week;

Standish asked Marshall to show him where Captain Crowley was and brief him on what had been happening while he was away.

'Victoria's been asking after you, mate,' Standish commented as they disappeared out of earshot from the rest of the platoon. 'She's asked me to see if you will write to her? I said I'd ask,' he continued.

Marshall stopped and pulled a cigarette packet from his pocket; he offered one to Standish. Lighting up he drew smoke deeply into his lungs before exhaling slowly. 'I'm not sure it would be a good thing,' he replied. 'We've been told it's the big one coming up and if we don't gain the ground they want we'll die trying. I'm not so sure it's a good idea to get too involved at this stage.'

'She thought you'd say that, but wants you to know she'll be thinking of you from now until she hears you are safe.' Standish stubbed out the remains of his cigarette and with a wave walked off towards the officers' dugout.

August 1915 – Gallipoli and Lemnos

Watching from the deck of the *Ariadne* Victoria Standish felt as though she was witnessing history in the making; ships anchored close to ANZAC Cove were carrying out a sustained bombardment of the area around Lone Pine. The noise was deafening and it was obvious that some sort of attack was planned to start soon. The *Ariadne* was prepared for an onslaught of wounded, but the medical staff had not been advised to expect any more casualties than usual. Instruments were sterile and the operating theatre had been scrubbed on the journey out, as part of the routine maintenance carried out each time the ship returned to the peninsula.

When the ship had sailed from Alexandria, Sister Standish assumed they were going to evacuate the wounded from the sporadic trench fighting which had been going on since the initial landings; it became clear this was not the case only when the ship arrived in ANZAC Cove. Immediately apparent was the frenetic activity at the beachhead. The cove was alive with small boats; transporting supplies and ammunition from larger ships waiting further out to sea. From where the *Ariadne* was positioned it was possible to see hundreds of men climbing the steep paths up to the plateau. Periodically, the Turkish troops, safe on the high ground, let out a volley of shrapnel fire which cascaded down onto the beachhead and the boats in the bay. During the day, a trickle of wounded were ferried out to the *Ariadne* and Standish was kept busy attending to their needs.

At almost five o'clock in the afternoon, the guns on the ships in the bay fell silent and an eerie silence spread throughout the peninsula, announcing to both sides the fight was about to begin.

***

The shrill short blast of a whistle let everyone in the trench know that it was time to go over the top. In the end the men were relieved to go, having spent several uncomfortable hours in cramped conditions sitting or standing wherever they could; every front-line and every communication trench was filled with the additional troops needed for the battle to come. The constant barrage from ships in the bay, which saw shells bursting overhead, was unnerving, at one point a misdirected shell exploded in a communication trench killing several men and wounding more. The cry for stretcher bearers could be heard echoing down the line, serving to unnerve the men further.

Each man was weighed down with personal supplies, a water bottle, ammunition and a rifle, making it cumbersome to climb the trench ladders which had been propped at intervals in front of the fire step.

Captain Crowley climbed quickly out of the trench and started to run towards the Turkish line. He was followed by the men of C Company. They immediately attracted sustained gun fire from the trench they were charging towards. Smedley and Ferguson were hit on exiting the trench, dying where they fell. Large numbers of men were wounded as they exited the trench system; causing problems for the men following afterwards who had to climb over them before starting the run across no man's land. On arrival at the enemy lines no one expected the lengths to which the Turks had gone in an effort to protect themselves. The pine trees which had originally lined the ridge had been cut down and logs now topped the trenches, protecting the men from attack. Although the run across open ground, in full view of the enemy, had been dangerous and several men had been wounded or killed, the real fighting didn't start until the Australians attempted to break into the trenches.

Standish quickly realised that men were dying attempting to dislodge the pine logs, as the Turks were able to fire through the gaps but were protected themselves. Jumping over the forward trench, Standish was able to take over a part of a communication trench, which had a substantial dugout attached and afforded some relief from the constant firing. Captain Crowley and three other men who had survived the initial dash soon joined him. Standish and Crowley set about securing the trench, posting men at intervals to make sure they were not attacked from behind.

The first task was to eliminate any Turkish soldiers in the immediate area. Standish and his men did this using a combination of rapid fire and by throwing some of the bombs each of them carried. As the party advanced around each corner some hand to hand bayonet fighting was necessary, to rid the area of all enemy action. Dead soldiers were lifted up onto the parapet to clear the trench for other soldiers crowding in. Bloody fighting continued until nightfall, when there was a lull in activity and the guns fell silent for a while.

Corporal Marshall was injured very early in the attack. Climbing out of the forward trench, he was unable to move quickly as there was a number of wounded blocking his path. Skirting round them he began to run toward the Turkish trenches, but was wounded by a stray bullet which hit him in the left thigh; causing him to fall heavily into a shell hole, created by the intense bombardment earlier.

Momentarily stunned with intense pain Marshall did not immediately take in his surroundings; when he did it was to see two other wounded men sharing the hole with him. Both were from D Company and had been alongside him in the trenches only hours before, discussing the best way to survive the push, desperate not to become part of the peninsula's mounting dead. One had a bad head wound and was unconscious but moaning, while the other had been shot in the chest and although conscious a rattling sound was coming from his lungs.

Marshall looked around for help; aware that if he did not act quickly both men would die. Lance-Corporal Roberts looked the more seriously wounded of the two, but was at least responsive. Propped upright, his lips were blue as he sucked in air, gasping with every laboured breath.

'Look, mate, we're going to have to see about getting out of here and back into the trenches, so we can both get seen to.' Marshall started to drag himself across the crater towards Roberts. The pain in his thigh was excruciating, but grunting with the effort and with sweat pouring down his face he eventually made it. Pulling himself into a sitting position he began to assess Roberts' chest wound, before extracting a large field dressing from his tunic pocket to cover the bullet hole.

The peninsula was getting dark now and men could be seen stumbling around in the half-light looking for the old front line. Marshall called out softly to a man who was passing, asking for help to get Roberts in; which between them they managed. Much later, Marshall learned that the other occupant of the shell hole died before he was able to be moved and was found by a burial party working under cover of darkness.

The noise of daytime shelling gave way to night-time cries from the wounded, lying in no man's land with little prospect of being stretchered to safety; as the night wore on the cries grew steadily fainter as men succumbed to their wounds.

August 1915 – London

Lord and Lady Hadleigh had decided to remain in London for August rather than attend the Cowes Regatta as they traditionally did at this time of year. The decision to do this was never really discussed but happened as a process of omission; Lady Hadleigh simply failed to inform the servants of the usual travel plans and Lord Hadleigh continued to attend the bank several times a week, happy to go away only if his wife wanted to.

A couple of weeks earlier the youngest Hadleigh children had come home from school for the long summer holidays; Guy had been home for only a couple of days before taking off to join his Cadet Corps for exercises on Salisbury Plain. He had celebrated his eighteenth birthday on July 20th and was keen to hone his military skills, as he intended to take a commission as soon as it could be arranged. His brother was something of a hero amongst his school friends, remembered by the older boys from his time as head prefect of School House.

Guy was thankful each day at school prayers that his brother was not listed as missing or killed-in-action by the headmaster; who insisted on reading out the latest news on old boys who had sacrificed themselves for King and Country. He appeared oblivious to the grief he sometimes caused younger siblings, who were not always aware of their relatives passing until it was announced to the school in morning assembly. On at least one occasion his eulogies to the fallen had caused an anguished cry; followed by swift removal of a grief-stricken boy, as other masters attempted to repair the damage done.

Roberta, the youngest of the Hadleigh children, was almost sixteen and spent most of the year at a remote Suffolk boarding school not far from the seaside town of Southwold. The Prudence Bradford School for the Daughters of Gentlemen had been set up some twenty years previously; initially catering for the daughters of officers serving the East India Company out in Calcutta. More recently its reputation had spread and the gentry had started to educate their daughters there. The school was far removed from the war; the official policy seemed to be that any news was too distressing for young girls who wouldn't understand anyway. As a result, anyone visiting the school who was remotely connected to world events was instantly surrounded by a host of girls asking questions. Roberta's brother had been a sensation when he arrived unannounced several months earlier and had whisked her and a friend away for tea.

Lady Hadleigh and her daughter spent the day in London shopping and had just taken tea at Goddard's when the Zeppelin appeared overhead. As they waited for the doorman to summon a hansom cab to take them home it was possible to hear the sound of an engine, high above the London traffic; a huge shadow fell across the street causing them both to look up as the engine noise became louder. Directly above, they were confronted by a large cigar-shaped silver balloon gliding slowly towards Belgravia.

The balloon was large enough to support an enclosed flight deck hanging below and still remain airborne. People could be seen operating controls and steering the balloon through a large tailfin. As the people in the street gazed skyward in silent awe, two large cylindrical tubes fell from the Zeppelin; the resulting explosions shook the ground around them causing shocked cries from the onlookers, who immediately ran for cover.

Lady Hadleigh appeared unfazed by the attack. She had read about the Zeppelin bombing of Kings Lynn earlier in the year and half expected that once the Zeppelins managed to get through inadequate English coastal defences, London would also be targeted. It was a nuisance though, that the Germans had chosen late on a Friday afternoon when she was expecting twenty for dinner and needed to get home to change and supervise the preparations. Five minutes after the Zeppelin had passed over normality returned to the street and Lady Hadleigh and Roberta managed to persuade a hansom driver to take them to Belgravia.

As the hansom rounded the corner into Essex Square the true nature of the devastation caused by the Zeppelin became apparent. The house inhabited by the Hadleigh family for over a century was a pile of rubble. The houses on either side had also been hit but were in part still standing; the rest of the Square was unscathed sustaining minimal damage. With a sigh Lady Hadleigh surveyed the devastation before marching determinedly in the direction of a harassed looking fireman who was dealing with the public. 137 Essex Square had taken a direct hit with two bombs landing directly on top of the roof. The resulting explosion had caused the internal walls to collapse, killing everyone who was inside the house at the time. Firemen were beginning to scrabble around on the bomb site; hoping they may find someone still alive.

Lord Hadleigh was found some hours later having spent an agreeable afternoon at his club; he often retired to Wyndham's secure in the knowledge the club only allowed men through its hallowed portals and he was unlikely to be disturbed by the general trivia of life. Lord Hadleigh had in fact spent the afternoon entering into a lively debate with Rear-Admiral Peters about the situation in the Dardanelles; arguing that perhaps it would be reasonable to consider withdrawing from the peninsula, as too many lives were being lost. Peters had only recently dined with his good friend Winston Churchill and was of the opinion that the sacrifice being made on Gallipoli was worth it; as the taking of Constantinople would shorten the war. The spirited discussion that took place between the two men would later be attributed with saving Lord Hadleigh's life, as he remained at his club for far longer than intended and was absent when the bomb hit.

Mrs Trent was also spared the bombing as she had taken a rare afternoon off, catching an omnibus to Charing Cross Station before boarding a train to New Cross; the area of London where her family lived and where her brother was on leave from France. She had spent a pleasant afternoon, taking tea with her elderly parents and listening to her brother's stories of life on the Western Front, before arriving back in Essex Square shocked to see the what had happened in her absence.

No one else stood a chance, having sat down to tea only five minutes before the bombs hit and the house collapsed. It was to be a number of days before their remains were removed from the rubble.

Chapter Seven

*Those heroes that shed their blood and lost their
lives... You are now living in the soil of a friendly
country. Therefore rest in peace. There is no difference
between the Johnnies and the Mehmets to us where
they lie side by side here in this country of ours... You,
the mothers, who sent their sons from faraway
countries, wipe away your tears; your sons are now
lying in our bosom and are in peace, after having lost
their lives on this land they have become our sons as
well.*

Atatürk, 1934

August 1915 – Camden

The congregation of St John's Church, which stood
proud on the hillside overlooking Camden, were
listening to the Reverend James Sharpe as he began to
read the latest dispatches and casualty lists from the war.
Although most of the district's fighting men were over
in Gallipoli a few had somehow found their way to
France.

Listening to the dispatches had become a regular
Sunday event following matins; the Reverend Sharpe

was kept abreast of events by his colleagues in the centre of Sydney and felt the news he received should be shared. The solemn reading of names from the casualty lists was usually preceded by a short address describing where the fighting was taking place and which division was fighting there; prayers were offered for individual men known to be fighting in a dangerous area.

'The men of Camden and its surrounding district have acquitted themselves with honour in the recent fighting,' Sharpe started his address. 'The latest news from Gallipoli is full of Australian heroics during the battle of Lone Pine. In the early evening of August 8th your sons, brothers and fathers left the trenches at Lone Pine, crossed no man's land and engaged in heavy fighting with the enemy. The subsequent glorious victory was achieved with a large loss of Australian life, but I defy anyone to argue that these men did not lay down their lives willingly, knowing that they have sacrificed themselves for a worthy cause, which will ultimately secure the freedom of all civilised nations. I grieve with each and every one of you who has borne a loss and pray that in the fullness of time the pain you are feeling now, may become bearable. Let us pray now for the wounded, missing and dead of the last battle, that they may be at peace.'

Following several prayers, the service ended with Sharpe reading a list of casualties from the local area.

Constance Standish gasped when she heard Stanley Marshall's name on the list of seriously wounded and prayed fervently he would recover. As soon as the service was over and she could get away without offending any of the parishioners who relied on the weekly service to hear her news; she took the trap and drove toward the hospital, further along Menangle road. She knew Marshall's mother would be preparing luncheon for the patients admitted there; as she did every third Sunday, before going down to an afternoon meeting of the Camden War Society, an organisation set up by the local farmers' wives to assist the men and their families caught up in the struggle.

When Constance arrived at the hospital she found Mrs Marshall stirring a large bowl of beef broth; the smell of freshly made bread baking in the oven gave the kitchen an inviting air and she soon began to warm up after the morning spent in a cold church. Mrs Marshall made a pot of tea and the women sat down to discuss news from the fighting.

'Have you heard how badly he's been wounded?' Constance asked, after extending her initial sympathy at hearing the news.

'Yes. I was sent a telegram to say he's being looked after somewhere in Greece. He's been hurt in the leg. I think they needed to operate to take out some shrapnel. They're worried because it was a while before he got medical attention and his leg may be infected,' Mrs Marshall answered.

Moving over to the oven she checked the bread before continuing. 'I have spoken to Matron here and she tells me he could be out of action for months, depending on the size of his wound. Maybe he'll get sent to England to convalesce. I wish they would just send him home. I think he's done his bit now and would be better off here with me to look after him. There are plenty of other men around here who have yet to sign up.'

September 1915 – Lemnos

Lady Julia Hadleigh could hardly stand from exhaustion, but with a supreme effort stood up and walked over to the small table which had been turned into a washstand. Hurriedly, she splashed water from the ceramic bowl onto her face in an effort to wake up, slowly she then dressed in her uniform. On the opposite side of the tent Briggs was yawning while lacing up her boots. Neither woman spoke as the effort to get ready took all of their concentration.

The battle for Lone Pine had started over a month earlier and fighting still continued, without respite. Hadleigh and the other VADs had been called on to help with the admission of casualties whenever a hospital ship steamed into Mudros harbour. The arrival of ships was erratic, but often occurred in the hours just before dawn. She had lost count of the number of times she was shaken awake with a cup of tepid tea and advised a ship had docked. Once a ship arrived, every available person from the hospital was needed to assist and settle the wounded.

Thousands had been injured and evacuated from ANZAC Cove. In the early days of fighting the beachhead had been overwhelmed with wounded; moving them to the troop transporters tied up at the end of the pier had been fraught with problems and had been a painstaking, time-consuming operation. Delays cost lives and several of the wounded died where they were, without receiving anything more than basic medical attention. For the stretcher cases lying on the beach, the heat and the flies caused almost as much damage as the wound itself; the longer the wounded remained waiting evacuation, the more dehydrated and sicker they became.

Hospital ships, once loaded, set off for the nearest port containing a field hospital not listed as being at capacity. As the weeks wore on it became impossible to determine which hospitals could cope with more wounded and which were at breaking point. Ships captains made the decision of where to sail to solely on where the previous ship had gone; this crude method at least helped ensure the casualty load was spread out across the region and hospitals did not receive several ships all at the same time.

Mudros harbour was a hive of activity. Ships were at anchor everywhere, engaged in replenishing supplies and making minor repairs before sailing once again for the peninsula. Tied up by the quay were two hospital ships that had arrived as dawn broke and were busy off-loading stretchers. A number of ambulances and horse drawn traps were queuing to accept the wounded being offloaded from the *Ariadne*.

Victoria Standish had been hard at work since the ship docked; she finished the cleaning and replenishment of supplies in the operating theatre and then went to look for Matron Gillespie, who was supervising the disembarkation of the wounded.

'Theatre is clean and ready, ma'am,' she reported.

In response Gillespie looked at her watch. 'You may go then, Sister. I shall expect you back by eighteen hundred hours, ready to sail within half an hour.'

Standish left the ship via the portside gangway, descending rapidly onto the quay. Scanning the ambulances ready and waiting to transport the wounded, she recognised a driver she had often spoken to in the past. After a brief discussion he agreed to take her up to the hospital on the hill above Mudros. They arrived at the top of the dirt track, where the sprawling tented hospital had increased markedly in size since the last time the *Ariadne* was in port.

At the start of the battle of Lone Pine two hundred patients were being treated, mainly for medical conditions like dysentery bought on by the appalling insanitary conditions the troops were forced to put up with. Four days after the start of the battle eight hundred wounded were being treated; the medical patients having been evacuated to hospitals further away from the fighting.

Hadleigh and Briggs stepped out of their tent just as the first ambulance drew to a halt outside of their ward. In the distance they could both see Sister Blackstone, sleeves rolled up, directing operations. She had obviously been up for some time, causing Hadleigh to wonder if she ever slept. It had been apparent since arriving on Lemnos that Sister Blackstone was never likely to ask anything of her staff she was not prepared to do herself.

'Hadleigh, Briggs, come over here,' Blackstone called, as soon as she saw them. 'We've got two abdominals, a head and a leg in the back of this ambulance. I need you both to help get them into beds; then look at their wounds and get back to me. You may need to burn their clothing, which is filthy and lice encrusted. Some of these men have been lying in no man's land for a number of days before being brought in.' Without waiting for a response, she disappeared to look at the wounded in the ambulance behind.

With the help of an orderly, the difficult task of undressing the four men was eventually accomplished, accompanied by groans as each man was moved. Hadleigh made a brief assessment of where each new admission was wounded, logging the results in a large admissions book. She was careful not to dislodge any of the field dressings the men had arrived with, knowing that the wounds underneath may require instant attention once disturbed. Assessing the patients took a considerable period of time as the men could only be moved slowly, to cause the least amount of pain. With a final look at all four of them Hadleigh went to find Sister Blackstone.

As she left the tent, Hadleigh almost collided with a lady dressed in the uniform of an officer in the Australian Army Nursing Service. The hospital had taken Australian wounded from Lone Pine as well as British troops from Suvla Bay and she had become used to hearing the strange Australian accent over the last few weeks, so was not surprised when Victoria Standish spoke.

'I wonder if you can help, Nurse. I'm trying to find an Australian soldier, Corporal Stanley Marshall. He was wounded several weeks ago and was transported here. Is he likely to still be here or will he have been moved to Cairo?' she asked.

'I remember him, Sister,' Hadleigh replied. 'I think he was moved a couple of days ago to the convalescent tents further up the hillside. The men there are waiting to be taken to Cairo or England for further treatment.'

'Thank you very much; I shall look for him there,' Standish replied before striding in the direction Hadleigh pointed to.

Hadleigh paused for a moment as she watched the Australian heading toward the convalescent tents. She remembered Corporal Marshall well, he had arrived not long after the start of the battle at Lone Pine and had been seriously ill. The shrapnel had damaged a considerable part of his thigh muscle, creating a large gaping wound; surgery had been necessary to remove debris and tidy up the area. It had been necessary to leave a long thin silver drain, poking out from underneath the bandaged area.

Rumour circulating amongst some of the other men, described how he had managed to drag Roberts back to the allied lines although badly wounded himself. This act, combined with the length of time he was exposed in the extreme August heat, left him with a deeper dirtier wound, which was going to take several months more of painful dressings. In the last month Hadleigh had become used to looking after him; initially nursing him through a period where morphia was required before it was even possible to remove his dressings and clean his wounds. She was happy he appeared to be recovering and would soon be moved off the island to recuperate; knowing that this would be a welcome break for him from the fighting.

September 1915 – Brighton

The weather was still hot, with an absence of the usual autumn winds. Friends of Lord and Lady Hadleigh, who had come down to Brighton to escape the London summer heat, had long since returned to the city. With nowhere to return to, the Hadleigh's remained in their suite of rooms at the Pavilion Hotel on the seafront, while negotiations were underway to buy a house in Bedford Square.

The aftermath of the Zeppelin raid had been a traumatic time for the family. They had lost a total of five household members in the bombing. The servants who died were dug out from their basement quarters, where they had been having tea prior to starting on dinner preparations. Lord and Lady Hadleigh experienced the harrowing task of letting relatives know what had happened and then helping make arrangements for their funerals. Once this had been done and the rubble was cleared they had retired to Brighton for some rest.

Guy Hadleigh had come home from Salisbury Plain and immediately started lobbying his father to allow him to join the fight. Determined, at first, to follow his elder brother and take a commission in the Coldstream

Guards, he settled in the end with the London Rifle Brigade who were scheduled to run an officer training course much sooner. A week before, he had disappeared into the Kent countryside for an initial officer training course; full of enthusiasm and keen to get through the initial training period so he could be posted to France.

Brighton was a seaside town on the south coast of England. Popular since Georgian times with an exotic Pavilion constructed at the request of George IV, the sprawling building was a symbol of the pursuit of pleasure. Used for more than a hundred years, the town was popular as a means of escape for London aristocracy once The Season had wound down.

Brighton had become popular for soldiers on leave, wanting to escape the bustle and noise of London. Hotels located on the front were full of newly wed couples attempting to extract every precious moment together, knowing that this time was all too brief. The town came alive in the evening with the Palace Pier Theatre running a raucous nightly show, successful because it helped the audience forget they were at war.

Although temporarily in exile, Lord and Lady Hadleigh continued to lead active lives. Lady Hadleigh had become a member of the local Red Cross, which met in a church hall behind the Brighton Pavilion and was intent on making life easier for those at the Front by sending socks and other useful items. She also volunteered for several hours a week at the Pavilion itself, which had been turned into a hospital for Indian soldiers wounded in France; she found it comforting assisting in any way she could, knowing that if either of her sons were wounded far from home, she would hope someone was doing the same.

Lord Hadleigh entered the foyer of the Pavilion Hotel and enquired if his wife was home. He had taken the early train down from London after a week spent arguing against conscription at various sub-committee meetings. In town he stayed at the Wyndham, where the chef was fully committed to the war effort, churning out various inedible recipes designed to show the club knew how to economise; he was desperate to take his wife out for a decent lunch. On hearing Lady Hadleigh was in their suite Lord Hadleigh hurried upstairs.

'Darling,' he called as he entered. 'Have you time for luncheon? I saw Teddy Moncrieff at the War Office yesterday and mentioned your idea to him. He wants you to meet him in London next week to discuss it.'

September 1915 – France

For some of the wounded the rocking of the hospital train was soporific and they managed to get their first real rest for days; relaxed in the knowledge that they had acquired a 'Blighty Wound' and that for them the war was at the very least delayed, if not over. For others, every nerve shattering jolt of the train was felt, causing cries of pain and requests for morphine.

Sister Brennan had been posted to the hospital train a couple of months before, initially to give her a rest from the relentless work at the Casualty Clearing Station. In theory the work was more predictable, as once the train was loaded, there were no more unexpected convoys arriving in the middle of the night and the workload was constant. Reality had proven a little different; the journey she was currently undertaking had begun two days before when the train had offloaded several hundred wounded in Calais. Here several hospital ships were waiting to transport the wounded on to England. The train staff had to cope not only with interminable delays but also with an unpredictable workload where the very rattling which was so soporific for some, was the death knell for others; the rattling over the tracks capable of easily dislodging blood clots which had formed tenuously over fragile wounds and were all that prevented a catastrophic haemorrhage.

Glad to have handed over responsibility for her latest wounded, Sister Brennan set about making the train as clean as possible for the journey to whichever railhead they were directed to.

After waiting around while two important looking staff officers consulted lists, the train was eventually sent towards Arras, with instruction to pick up wounded

126

in the area and then proceed to Boulogne. The arrangements were haphazard, if Boulogne had no ships waiting the train was likely to be moved back to Calais or on to another Channel Port, where it was hoped a hospital ship would be ready to load; the influx of trains from all over the Front being so unpredictable that it wasn't possible to allow arriving trains simply to wait, without a knock-on effect.

Brennan had supervised the loading of nearly four hundred wounded, a slow painstaking procedure that took most of the day. She was nursing on the train with three other QAIMNS sisters and a dozen orderlies, along with two medical officers, who were kept busy operating on the patients who haemorrhaged in transit and as a result required urgent surgery. Moving up and down the train without stumbling into the bunks of the wounded was a skill which all of them learnt rapidly. In the half-light of the carriage, Brennan also developed an uncanny ability to know exactly when to pay attention to someone before their wounds got the better of them, saving many a man from certain death had she not shone her lamp their way.

Fortunately, on this occasion apart from being shunted into sidings with monotonous regularity and being made to wait there for no apparent reason, the trip was uneventful, arriving in Boulogne only a few hours behind schedule. Despite being exhausted from the fragmented sleep and long hours on her feet Brennan was mildly excited and looking forward to the end of this particular trip.

Several months before, Brennan had come across a captain of the Coldstream Guards looking a little bewildered as he tried to locate one of his men. She was able to direct him to where he needed to go on that occasion, but subsequently could not help noticing he made a lot of visits to the hospital and seemed to bump into her frequently. Gradually she began to enjoy these occasions and began to look forward to them; finding the brief snatched conversations a welcome relief from discussing wounds and hospital business.

Eventually the captain plucked up enough courage and approached her, asking if she would dine with him the next time they were both free. With this he disappeared and was absent for several months. After a while Brennan gave up all thought of dinner; not sure if he had been wounded, killed or had simply changed his mind. She was pleasantly surprised one morning when she collected her mail, to find he had written suggesting they meet. He was attending a staff officer's course near Boulogne and was sure the train would eventually stop there. Touched that he had somehow tracked her down she agreed.

Later that evening having brushed mud and debris from her uniform Brennan walked to the Café Angleterre, located in a back street behind the station; she arrived early, half hoping to have time for a glass of wine before Captain Hammond arrived, to build up some courage. This was not to be though, as he was already sat by the window with an unopened bottle of champagne in a bucket beside the table.

Hammond stood as she approached, 'I'm so pleased you could make it, Sister, can I pour you some champagne?'

Chapter Eight

The consideration which did go straight to every man's heart was the tragedy of confessing failure after so many and well-loved comrades had given their lives to the effort. The men hated to leave their dead mates to the mercy of the Turks. For days after the breaking of the news there were never absent from the cemeteries men by themselves, or in twos and threes, erecting new crosses or tenderly 'tidying-up' the grave of a friend. This was by far the deepest regret of the troops. 'I hope', said one of them to Birdwood on the final day, pointing to a little cemetery, 'I hope they don't hear us marching down the deres (gullies)'.

Charles Edwin Woodrow Bean 1924

November 1915 – France

The Casualty Clearing Station was experiencing a lull in activity. Troops in the trenches were digging in for winter and were more interested in making their lives bearable than attacking the enemy. The weather was so cold the ground was frozen, making it impossible to increase the size of dugouts in the trenches and so provide the men with better protection from the elements.

Major Chardingly finally had some free time but was not a happy man; he had watched from afar as Captain Hammond courted Sister Brennan. He was unhappy because he had become increasingly fond of her over the years they had worked together and was kicking himself for not asking her out first.

Up until recently Brennan had been away for days at a time, as the hospital train crawled around France and Belgium picking up the wounded and delivering them to hospital ships waiting to take them to England. After a spell of leave she had returned to work at the Casualty Clearing Station, which made her trips out with Captain Hammond all the more difficult to ignore. Major Chardingly was pacing up and down in the small room he called his office wondering what to do about the situation when there was a knock on the door.

'Sir, I need you to look at Sergeant Price. His leg wound is looking badly infected; I don't think it can be saved,' Brennan said, as she hurriedly entered the room. 'If you are happy to have a look I'll go and prepare theatre, at the very least I think we need to cut away the dead tissue surrounding the bullet wound, but it may be too late.'

Major Chardingly sighed, his thoughts returning abruptly to the present. 'I will take a look at him shortly, Sister. Set up for an amputation, although hopefully it will not come to that. When I last saw the wound this morning it looked worse than previously but I'm not convinced amputation is the only option left. Can you arrange for another nurse to assist me? I will need you to give the anaesthetic, as Captain Strachan has taken the leave train to Paris for a few days' rest.'

'Of course, sir,' Brennan nodded. She had become used to delivering anaesthetics on board the hospital train, where the scarcity of qualified medical officers meant she had no choice. The train had been equipped with a very cramped operating theatre; used in the event of an emergency to patch up soldiers suffering from life threatening complications, which could not wait until the train reached its destination. Brennan had become adept at administering ether as the train rocked from side to side.

Within half an hour Sergeant Price had been stretchered into the operating theatre and was lifted onto the table. Brennan had prepared her anaesthetic mask, which she intended to place over Price's face before dripping ether onto it to induce unconsciousness. Once Price was anaesthetised, Chardingly quickly removed the dressings covering his thigh and scrutinised the wound.

'This looks bad, Sister,' he commented. 'The wound is far deeper than I first thought and needs exploration. Its full of dirt and, I think, some shrapnel. We'll be lucky to save his leg.'

Painstakingly, Major Chardingly began the process of exploring the wound and bit by bit repairing the damage. Finished, he carefully inspected his handiwork before pouring Eusol over the wound which he then wrapped with clean bandages. Sister Brennan made sure Price was deeply anaesthetised throughout the operation, adding ether to the mask as she felt necessary. Once surgery was over she stayed with him for the immediate post-operative phase, where vomiting caused by the anaesthetic was expected; Sergeant Price did not disappoint. It was late in the evening before she finally told Major Chardingly that she thought Price would pull through.

'He should be fine now, sir,' Brennan reported. 'He has stopped vomiting and is asleep. Hopefully the wound is now clean enough and will have a chance to heal.'

'Let's hope so, Sister.' He paused before continuing, 'It's late and we both need to eat, will you join me at the local café?' he asked.

Half an hour later Major Chardingly guided Sister Brennan to an alcove in a café which stayed open late.

'Sister, I am so pleased you were able to spend time dining with me. I have often wanted to tell you how much I admire the professional way in which you conduct yourself. If we had both remained at Kings College Hospital and the war had not intervened, I believe we may eventually have come to a mutual arrangement, which could have ended in marriage. War has changed everything though. I notice that a young captain in the Guards has been paying you some attention. Are you walking out with him, or is there still a chance for me?' Chardingly asked.

'I'm very sorry to disappoint you, sir. I am fond of no one else as much as I am you, but I have fallen in love with Captain Hammond. If we both survive the war I hope we may spend our lives together,' Brennan replied.

'Then we must celebrate your good fortune with some champagne,' Chardingly responded. 'I hope that we will be able to remain friends whatever happens.'

November 1915 – Lemnos

The weather had finally turned, with the dust and flies replaced by rain and mud. The VAD contingent continued to be accommodated in tents, despite the vociferous complaints levelled at the hospital commandant by Sister Blackstone. His response to her requests for an improvement in living quarters was to post a notice informing all voluntary staff that, if they were unhappy, they could break their agreement and return to England. The commandant was a man who could not be persuaded to change his long-held opinion that war was a man's game and that a woman's place was at home waiting; despite witnessing first-hand the effect a woman's touch had on the wounded every day.

The commandant had in fact made life as difficult as he could for the hospital staff from the day he was appointed in overall charge. He was a crusty old surgeon dug out of retirement at the start of the war; having been something of an authority on care of the wounded during the Boer War several years before. He was not up to date enough to give a reasonable medical opinion on any of the types of wound soldiers presented with from Gallipoli; accepted medical treatment having advanced well beyond his scope of practice. Nursing and medical staff constantly had to justify the supply requests they submitted, as he appeared to be ignorant of modern medical treatment.

Sodium hypochlorite solution or Eusol as it was commonly known, had been around for a while and was used primarily to flush out dirty looking wounds; initially the hospital was in very short supply and until the commandant was persuaded of its necessity, had to borrow what they could from neighbouring hospitals. Bandage rolling had become a nightly task for the VADs not engaged in looking after the patients; due to the commandant's economies all but the dirtiest of bandages were salvaged, boiled and washed to remove any bloodstains and were then used again.

Late autumn had created its own set of problems for the nurses on Lemnos. After Lone Pine there had been no further major battles; both sides settling into a stalemate situation. Injuries continued as a result of minor skirmishes, but the hospital did not receive anywhere near the number of wounded it had in August. The wounded were replaced by men who arrived in their hundreds with dysentery and other illnesses caused by the unsanitary conditions on the peninsula. More recently an increasing number of casualties arrived with frostbite, as the weather had become unexpectedly cold within a very short space of time and most of the men did not have the warm clothing necessary to survive the sudden drop in temperature. Socks were in short supply, despite hundreds of women knitting them back home. They were thought to be needed more in France, so had been sent there.

Hadleigh had been down collecting her mail at the orderly office when she heard the rumour. Running back up the hill to the Mess Tent she burst in just as Briggs was pouring tea for herself and Veronica Thorpe.

'I say, Briggs, have you heard the latest?' she asked excitedly. 'Corporal Smith has just told me we're going to pack it all in and leave Gallipoli, because the army needs more men in France. Recruits are not being trained fast enough, so they need experienced men. The word is we will never be able to get through to Constantinople. Do you think we will get to go too? I fancy somewhere a bit more civilised than this windswept muddy place.'

Before Briggs could answer, Sister Blackstone arrived, noisily drawing back the tent flap and letting in a blast of cold air, she stepped inside. She was accompanied by the tall Australian sister that Hadleigh remembered meeting a couple of months earlier.

'Please, don't get up,' Blackstone said as the three VADs struggled to their feet. 'I'd like you to meet Sister Standish. She has been posted here from the *Ariadne*, where until now she's been transporting the wounded. I've been ordered to Cairo to take charge at one of our hospitals, while the supervisor there takes some much-needed leave. It's not permanent, only for a week or two. In the mean time I would expect you all to show Sister Standish the same amount of respect and devotion to duty that you do me.'

Seeing an opportunity, Hadleigh spoke out. 'Sister, is it true that the troops on Gallipoli are going to be withdrawn?'

Pulling up a chair Blackstone sat down and accepted the cup of tea she was offered, before replying. 'Nothing has been decided yet, if I hear anything in Cairo I'll let you know. The winter is going to make things very difficult for our men. Frostbite is already a major problem and can only get worse the longer they stay in such awful conditions. Serious consideration needs to be given to leaving though; although it may be prudent to withdraw without sacrificing more lives, people at home will ask why such a loss of life was necessary and if we achieved anything fighting this campaign?'

Briggs, who had been listening quietly, looked up. 'If we can't achieve what we set out to, would it not be better to leave now rather than sacrifice more men to a campaign we can't win, Sister?'

Standish spoke for the first time, addressing the group. 'A number of my countrymen have lost their lives fighting on the peninsula and many more have been wounded. I would hate to think it has happened in vain, the idea that taking Constantinople would shorten the war was a good one, it just hasn't been possible to achieve. It feels as though we are breaking faith with the dead if we do not continue the struggle, but I think we will pull out in the end and accept defeat.'

December 1915 – Gallipoli

Lieutenant Max Standish stepped out of the dugout and started to walk along the trench. He had been to a meeting at headquarters and was a little surprised at the instructions he had received. He was about to deliver the news to the rest of the company that there was a plan afoot to evacuate the peninsula. Stunned by the information, his immediate thoughts were of the difficulty he would have persuading his men that Gallipoli had been a worthwhile battle and that their friends had not died in vain.

Australians and New Zealanders had lost an enormous number of wounded and dead in a campaign which established both fledgling nations as countries in their own right, with histories to be proud of. They would never again be known as colonies of the British. The fact that so many men had answered the call and gone to the defence of Great Britain, was in itself a heroic act. In addition, the tenacious grit shown clinging to a foothold of hostile peninsula, until ordered to leave meant that Gallipoli would remain at the forefront of services commemorating the dead in years to come.

Standish was looking for Sergeant Marshall to explain details of the evacuation plan. Marshall had been back on the peninsula for less than a week. After a prolonged convalescence in Cairo he had been sent on a sergeant's course before returning to Gallipoli in early December. Although passed fit by a medical board he found it difficult to remain on his feet for hours at a time and was hoping he would be fit enough for any imminent fighting. Standish found Marshall sitting alone on a fire step cleaning his rifle.

'Well, its official, Stan,' Standish said, as he sat down beside him. 'We're going to leave Gallipoli to the Turks. Plans are being made now for the withdrawal. It's to be hoped we can get out with minimal loss of life.'

'What? You mean we're going to run away?' Marshall asked. 'The men won't like that, Max. They will only be happy now, if they end up drinking beer in Constantinople.'

'We're going to have to persuade them that it's for the best,' Standish replied. 'A successful evacuation will depend on that. We have come up with a plan so Johnny Turk has no idea what we're up to. Can you round up the men for a briefing in half an hour's time?' Standish stood up and walked off down the trench.

Half an hour later Captain Crowley left the officers dug out and surveyed the men in front of him. 'Gentlemen, I appreciate this will be hard but it has been decided we are to evacuate and must prepare to leave this all behind. The majority of you will be leaving friends and colleagues buried in these sandy hills. I have no doubt you will leave with a sense of regret, that we were not able to achieve the primary objective and take Constantinople. I share this regret with you, but feel the decision to withdraw now is the right decision; to stay would involve far greater loss of life. We are needed in France, to strengthen the line and assist our Allies in defeating the Hun. The fate of the civilised world depends upon us.' Crowley paused for a moment before continuing.

'We have devised a timetable of distractions aimed at convincing the Turks nothing is different and we are here for the duration. Lieutenant Standish and I will give you details of these plans shortly. Good luck with the evacuation. It has been a privilege to serve here with you.' Crowley then saluted his men, turned and left the trench.

***

For the next two weeks the Australians at Gallipoli waged a war of deception on the unsuspecting Turks. The aim of getting the Turks to accept that nothing was wrong was achieved using several different strategies. On command, the Australians would randomly cease all communication and normal trench activity. After an hour or so of complete silence the Turkish troops began to suspect something was wrong and would climb into no man's land to check. A couple of well-placed machine guns were all that was necessary to convince the Turks that the Australians were still there.

Further deception involved activity down at the beachhead. Supply deliveries continued with boxes being offloaded at the pier head. The Turks would never know that the boxes were empty and that some excess supplies were in fact being taken off the peninsula. Every night, once darkness fell, a host of small ships sailed over the horizon, intent on collecting supplies and equipment no one wanted the Turks to inherit. Troops were removed from the peninsula each day, until by December 18[th,] less than half remained. If the Turks had chosen to attack they would have been virtually unimpeded in their run to the sea.

Sergeant Marshall was nervous. Over the last few nights he had watched as the trenches gradually emptied of human life. C Company remained alone; defending what seemed like an impossibly long stretch of trench. Hundreds of rifles and spare billycans had been sent up from the beach and had been converted into timed firing devices. With a little water and a few holes punctured in one of the cans it was possible to make the rifles fire shots randomly; convincing the Turks that the trenches were still full of men.

At last it was time to leave. The night was cold and cloudy. Men were warned not to smoke, as a naked flame seen by the Turks, would bring down a hail of bullets. They trod softly on the floor of the trench; blankets and canvas sacking had been laid earlier to deaden the noise as they crept out. The journey down to the beach took only twenty minutes but felt like a lifetime, with every strange sound magnified and echoing in the dark. Once the men were clear of the trenches and walking down through the gully, they paused every few yards, to pull out barbed wire they had buried in the bushes earlier; cutting off the track behind them.

The beach head was full of activity with officers marshalling the men onto small boats as soon as they arrived on the beach. The evacuation ran smoothly with thousands of men loaded and transferred to larger ships anchored further out in the bay, beyond the reach of the

Turkish guns. The midshipmen manning the small boats returned again and again to pick troops up off the beach; apparently oblivious to the danger they were in. Eventually, in the early hours of the morning the last man left the beach and the ships made ready to leave the peninsula.

Lieutenant Standish and Sergeant Marshall stood at the stern of the troop ship watching as Gallipoli receded behind them. Neither spoke as the ships moved off, each man lost in his own thoughts; marshalling together memories of the last few months. So many men had died, if not of wounds, of disease bought about by the appalling living conditions endured on a daily basis. Men who had arrived in the peak of physical fitness were leaving wracked with chronic disease, which some would never recover from.

For the last time, Standish looked across the bay at the moonlit hills surrounding ANZAC Cove, putting into words what many were thinking. 'Do you think the sacrifice was worth it?' he asked no one in particular.

Chapter Nine

Eternal Father, strong to save,
Whose arm hath bound the restless wave,
Who bidd'st the mighty ocean deep
Its own appointed limits keep;
Oh, hear us when we cry to Thee,
For those in peril on the sea!
O Christ! Whose voice the waters heard
And hushed their raging at thy word,
Who walked'st on the foaming deep,
And calm amidst its rage didst sleep;
Oh, hear us when we cry to Thee,
For those in peril on the sea!

Traditional Hymn

January 1916 – Mudros Harbour

The *Ariadne* was alongside the quay at Mudros waiting
to take on several hundred wounded. Following the
evacuation of the Gallipoli Peninsula just before
Christmas the stream of wounded had dried up
completely, although some cases of dysentery were still
being admitted in a sporadic fashion. The news, when it

came, started in the orderly room as a barely contained rumour gleaned from the rapidly arriving ships.

Breathless, Hadleigh arrived in their tent. 'I say, Briggs! Have you heard? We're going!' she exclaimed before throwing herself onto her bed. Briggs looked up from the painstaking act of darning some old socks.

'Going where?' she responded.

'I don't know! Just out of here and away from the flies.'

***

The commandant, clearly excited at the idea of leaving such a godforsaken place, immediately recalled Sister Blackstone from Cairo to supervise the embarkation. He was determined to be seen as a model of efficiency by the War Office, as he already had his eyes on a posting to India; wishing to live out his days in a colonial backwater, sipping gin and tonic at the local polo club.

The staff spent a fevered week packing supplies into crates, leaving out a bare minimum of necessities for the patients and staff staying behind. Sister Blackstone directly supervised preparation of the wounded for embarkation, reporting to the commandant when she felt all was prepared.

'The hospital is ready to be decommissioned and the wounded transferred to the *Ariadne*, sir. The care of men too sick to be transported has been handed over to one of the hospitals remaining behind. If you would care to join me for a tour of inspection, I will advise you on how we should proceed from here,' Blackstone reported.

'That won't be necessary, Sister. Carry on as you have planned and inform me once embarkation is complete. You will find me in the Officers Mess.'

The ships company of the *Ariadne* had all been engaged in loading supplies from the moment the ship had docked several hours before. A dozen ambulances could now be seen making their way down the hill with the first of the wounded. The sickest patients were loaded first, to give them time to settle before the ship sailed.

The *Ariadne* had been converted into a hospital ship at the start of the war, but still retained some of its majestic charm. Men who only moments before had been looked after in freezing canvas tents, suddenly found themselves lying on beds in the Grand Salon; looking at ornate ceilings, plush carpets and gilded fixtures which were still in evidence throughout. Internally nothing much had changed on the *Ariadne,* apart from the obvious erection of beds wherever space could be found; externally the ship had been painted white with large red crosses painted in several places along each side. Secretly, Sister Blackstone was of the opinion that the stark white paint was not a good idea and may in fact attract the enemy.

None of the nurses noticed the *Ariadne* pulling away from the quay, as some of the wounded had not fared well travelling even a short distance from the tented hospital. The jolting of the ambulance over stony ground, caused one patient to haemorrhage as he was lifted on board; Sister Standish was called to go and assist in theatre immediately she arrived at the quayside. The rest of the nursing staff was busy administering morphia to settle the patients in case there were rough seas ahead.

It was a little after ten in the evening before any of the nurses had time to themselves. After a final round of her makeshift wards Sister Blackstone chose to take a turn around the deck, even though it was a cold evening. As she neared the stern of the ship she came across Hadleigh standing by the rail looking at the stars.

'Do you think this war will ever end, Sister?' Hadleigh asked, as she saw Blackstone approach. 'So many men I know have died and we don't seem to be getting anywhere. Gallipoli doesn't seem to have achieved anything really.'

'I think we have a long way to go and many more will die first. We have to hope that in the end what is good and right will triumph. I could not bear it if what we have seen has been in vain,' Blackstone replied, before visibly pulling herself together and speaking more briskly. 'Why don't you come inside, I've made friends with one of the crew and he assured me earlier that he would be able to find some brandy if the occasion demanded. I think now is just such an occasion.'

***

The torpedo hit at a little after noon. The gong had sounded minutes before summoning the staff and walking wounded to the dining room. Of the nursing staff on board half of them were eating luncheon. The rest remained with the more seriously wounded and were scheduled to eat at a second sitting. At first, apart from a dull thud, it was difficult to tell anything was wrong and the chatter in the dining room, which had ceased when the torpedo hit, gradually resumed; however, within minutes the ship began to list to one side and plates began to slide across the tables.

Afterwards, Hadleigh was to remember the feeling of calm which seemed to spread quickly through nurses and patients alike. She moved out onto the deck and started to help the ship's crew loading the lifeboats. In the distance she could see Sister Blackstone and Sister Standish marshalling men into the boats, but was a little concerned she could not see Briggs, Thorpe or Bishop, all of whom were at the first sitting for luncheon. Concentrating on the task at hand, Hadleigh began assisting the wounded into boats, only obeying the instruction to climb into a lifeboat once every other available space was occupied. Initially she protested, reluctant to leave the ship, but it soon became apparent she would be needed to take care of the wounded in the boat.

Almost as soon as Hadleigh was seated the lifeboat was swung clear of its davits and lowered with a jerking motion to the sea below. The sea was choppy and grey, reflecting the cloudy sky above, a chill rose from the water lapping the side of the boat. Men, who could, began to row and within a few minutes the lifeboat was clear of the *Ariadne*, which was listing heavily to one side. Hadleigh watched as several other lifeboats were lowered, pulling quickly away from the ships side. As the boat started to list and roll with the sea a lifeboat was seen being lowered as theirs had been. Halfway down, the line securing the stern to the davit came adrift; screams could be heard as the wounded and everyone else in the boat were jettisoned into the sea.

Occupants seated in the lifeboats watched in horror as the ship sank; the stern rising higher and higher, until a man in the lifeboat commented in wonder, that she was about to go. Almost on cue the ship started to slip rapidly beneath the waves and in a few short seconds was gone. A collective sigh could be heard from the lifeboat occupants as the stern disappeared from view.

It was bitterly cold in the lifeboats, but far colder in the sea itself. As the *Ariadne* finally sank, men jumped over its sides directly into the sea. Some were able to swim to the lifeboats, which remained close by; boats with space hauled them in, wrapping blankets around their shoulders. Others were not so lucky, clinging on to pieces of wreckage until the mind-numbing cold of the water caused them to fall asleep, lose consciousness and ultimately their lives. Men who had survived for months on the arid land of Gallipoli with shrapnel exploding around them, were to die quickly in the Mediterranean as the winter sea claimed them.

After several hours a ship loomed out of the dark, searching for survivors. The HMS Cornwall was delivering supplies to Malta when the distress call came. Altering course, the ship arrived in the area and began to pluck survivors from the lifeboats. While waiting to be rescued Hadleigh's boat lost two men, both dying from a combination of their wounds and exposure.

It was to be a number of days before Hadleigh learnt the fate of her colleagues and friends. Joan Bishop and Veronica Thorpe lost their lives going down with the ship; no one reported seeing them in the water after the attack and they had both been known to be working down in the Third-Class Salon. A number of the more seriously wounded were being nursed there on makeshift beds.

Initially, Briggs also stayed with a some of the wounded men who were too badly injured to move, giving as much comfort as she could. Waiting until the ship was about to sink she jumped directly into the sea where, unable to swim, she clung to a piece of debris until picked up by a lifeboat. Hadleigh heard she was alive but gravely ill, the cold water having taken its toll.

The commandant also died; unable to persuade any of the men manning the lifeboats he was a priority for embarkation, he retreated to the bar, where in the time he had left he managed to empty a bottle of malt whisky. He then took out his service revolver and shot himself in the head, as the *Ariadne* began its final descent beneath the waves.

February 1916 – Camden, New South Wales

The Reverend James Sharpe came to a halt on the gravelled circular driveway of Oakfield House, leant his bicycle up against a wall and removed his bicycle clips; smoothing out his trousers, he shook each leg before marching round to the back of the house where the kitchen was situated. He was not expected, but for once was visiting with good news. Over the last year he had become used to delivering the worst type of news, as telegrams arrived at the post office in Argyle Street and he was then called on to comfort people after they had read the contents.

Rapping loudly on the kitchen door, Sharpe stepped inside. It was already a hot summer's day, although the church clock had struck nine only ten minutes previously. He was glad to step into the coolness of the sandstone building.

'It's good news,' the Reverend Sharpe hastily said, as he saw the look on Constance Standish's face. 'I have news of Victoria,' he continued. 'She was picked up from the sea and taken to England on the HMS Cornwall, which was in the area at the time and responded to the distress call. She is unharmed and is currently recuperating in London. Someone she worked with on Lemnos has been kind enough to allow her to stay until she is fit to decide on what to do next; I've got the details here.'

Constance Standish sank down into a chair, at the large kitchen table and burst into tears. Sharpe, who was used to an emotional response whenever he delivered news, crossed to the range and started to boil a kettle. Opening a cupboard, he removed a bottle of brandy and poured a liberal amount into a teacup; adding some freshly brewed tea, he handed it to Constance.

Constance gulped down some of the tea before speaking. 'Sorry, you must think my reaction odd at such happy news; but I had convinced myself she was dead. I've read of hospital ships being torpedoed with all lives lost and thought, somehow, she couldn't have survived. It's winter over there so it must be easy to die of cold; you must excuse me, Vicar, I have to go and find Hector, he will be delighted.' Pausing only to hang up the apron she had been wearing and throw on a hat, Mrs Standish bustled out of the kitchen.

Later in the afternoon Hector prepared the trap and they both travelled into Camden. Hector had decided a celebration was called for. On hearing his daughter was alive and well he had taken himself off to the gardener's shed, where he was able to sit undisturbed for a while; a man of few words and even fewer emotions, Hector needed time to understand the range of feelings he had experienced in the last few days. Much later he entered the dining room for luncheon and announced he intended to drive into Camden.

'I have decided to buy every man in Camden a drink, to celebrate my daughter's rescue. After we eat I would like to take the trap and drive to the Plough and Harrow,' he stated. 'The ladies lounge will be serving tea and as its Thursday I'm sure you will have plenty of people to talk to if you wish to accompany me,' he continued.

The war had brought about many changes for rural communities throughout Australia. By late 1914 war fever had affected every town and village in the country, sweeping through and claiming its youth; turning them overnight into military men, before shipping them across to countries no one had ever heard of. For the townsfolk left behind it was necessary to adapt; so that the men enjoying a quiet beer in the Plough and Harrow were only mildly surprised when Hector walked into the bar that afternoon followed by his wife; who on the way into town had declared if any celebrating was to be done she would be there too.

March 1916 – France

Lady Hadleigh was worried. High above her, cradled in a sling, the family motorcar was being lifted from the deck of a supply ship by crane and gently lowered to the dock. Crates, full of everything they could possibly need, had already been removed from the ship and were piled up on the quayside; the crates were waiting to be transported a few hundred yards, to a small brick building she had been allocated just inside the dock gates.

It had been almost six months since the Zeppelin raid had caused such devastation to the house in Belgravia; during this time the Hadleigh's had been busy. They had bought and furnished a new house in Bedford Square, moving back to London just before Christmas. Mrs Trent had returned to their service as housekeeper and had been instrumental in getting the new house habitable. In Belgravia the rubble had been sifted through to see if anything could be salvaged. A few family portraits and a number of items from a silver tea service remained undamaged and were recovered. A few more family possessions were found damaged but repairable; Trent took a personal interest in making sure these items were repaired and returned to the new house.

New servants were engaged to take the place of those who had died. This was achieved with a certain degree of difficulty as all men of fighting age were expected to have taken the King's shilling. Those who hadn't were not the sort of people that Lord Hadleigh wished to employ; they were also likely to be called up soon, as a bill for conscription had recently passed through parliament after some vigorous debate. In the end the Hadleigh family engaged a butler who had been invalided out of the Royal Navy after twice being on board ships which had sunk; originally Chief Petty Officer Buxton had survived the sinking of HMS *Audacious* in October of 1914 and more recently the sinking of HMS *Triumph* in May. After the second sinking, despite the improving weather, Buxton had been left with residual lung problems; which deemed him unfit for further military service. At the time of his appointment Lord and Lady Hadleigh had no idea how fortuitous that appointment would be; within a matter of months Buxton would be providing support for their daughter and the Australian nurse she returned with, after the sinking of the *Ariadne*.

Trent breathed a sigh of relief as the motorcar was lowered to the dockside without incident. She had fully expected the motorcar to break free of its restraints and come crashing down at any moment. Lady Hadleigh climbed up into the driver's seat, calling on Trent to join her. Lady Hadleigh had learnt to drive after Bates was killed in the bombing and was proud of her skills, although most people travelling anywhere with her, would at best describe her driving skills as erratic. With Trent cranking the engine from the front the motorcar was soon purring contentedly, apparently unaffected by the trip across the Channel on the deck of a supply ship.

The dockside was teeming with soldiers, standing around near the transport office. Going on leave to England, while exciting, was fraught with problems. After travelling to the closest railway station and boarding a train to one of the ports where a leave boat was expected, it could be several hours before the boat arrived and was ready for boarding. During this time there was very little shelter if it rained and nowhere for the men to relax and wait; crowds of men got in the way of dock workers, who were trying to make ready leave boats for the trip across the Channel.

After he was forced to spend a prolonged period waiting on a rain swept quayside, Hammond had complained to his mother. Lady Hadleigh sprang into action, the germ of an idea beginning to form as she listened to her son. Speaking with Teddy Moncrieff at the War Office, Lady Hadleigh managed to acquire a large red brick shed, previously used as a dockyard canteen, standing near the entrance to the docks. She and Trent had arrived as the advance party of a group of ladies who intended to transform the shed into a café and rest area for the troops. Fundraising for the venture had been taking place in London drawing rooms for many months.

For the next few days Lady Hadleigh and Mrs Trent worked hard, scrubbing and stocking the area. The ovens caused the most trouble, as they did not appear to have been cleaned since they were installed, but after a session of elbow grease they were fit for use. On the second day a furniture van drew up in front of the shed; several tables and dozens of chairs were offloaded. On enquiring, Lady Hadleigh was informed the delivery was at the instigation of Teddy Moncrieff, who felt he should be allowed to help out and felt sure the tables and chairs would be needed. Teddy Moncrieff also sent his daughter who would train as café manager to enable Lady Hadleigh to return to England.

A couple of days later, Lady Hadleigh left her hotel and made her way to the café. In complete contrast to the dockyard the streets were deserted; the dockyard was full of soldiers standing around waiting for the ships to come in. Looking out into the harbour two transport ships could be seen in the distance, bringing supplies badly needed at the Front. A couple of hospital ships were already tied up ready to take on the wounded once trains, which had travelled through the night, arrived from all over France.

For Lady Hadleigh, today was the culmination of several weeks' work, with the Grand Opening scheduled for later on in the morning. The café had recently been named the Union Flag Café and last evening the sign writer had worked late, creating shop front signs to let everyone know the café was there. Outside on the pavement a queue of soldiers had started to form, keen to know if at last there was somewhere they could get a fresh brew and a sandwich.

March 1916 – London

Lady Julia was excited at the prospect of her first real night out in London since joining the VAD. After the *Ariadne* sank, the HMS *Cornwall* had plucked her and her colleagues from the sea and had taken them to Gibraltar. Initially stunned by what had happened, the nursing staff stuck together; scarcely able to believe that they had survived in the face of such an appalling loss of life.

Most of the wounded who perished when the ship sunk were unable to get to the lifeboats; dying in their beds as the ship slipped rapidly beneath the waves. Two hundred and fifty-four men and women were listed as missing, presumed drowned, when the final tally was published.

After several weeks in Gibraltar a transport ship arrived to pick up the survivors and take them to

England. After an uneventful journey, it was with a huge amount of relief that the nurses finally disembarked at Southampton and took the train to London. Briggs, along with other wounded, was taken directly to a military hospital in Southampton; where she was nursed until considered well enough to move to a convalescent home in London.

Victoria Standish looked in the mirror and sighed, she could see that she had aged after her ordeal in the Mediterranean and felt this was reflected in the mirror. Everything she owned had been lost when the ship sunk, apart from the clothes she had been wearing. Frantic telegrams to her family generated much-needed funds, allowing her to visit Salmons to replace her uniform. Another much-needed shopping trip was made to Howards, one of the largest fashion houses in London, to buy civilian clothing and a couple of gowns suitable for evening wear.

After a final look in the mirror, Standish left her room and ran down the stairs to the drawing room, where Lady Julia was drinking sherry with her father. Lord Hadleigh had returned from the city half an hour previously and had not yet dressed for dinner. With his wife away in France and his daughter and her friend planning an evening out, Lord Hadleigh planned to dine late at his club. After dining he hoped to catch up with some of the more reasonable characters who frequented the smoking room, before meeting Teddy Moncrieff for a nightcap.

Approaching the drawing room, Standish could hear raised voices. She entered to see Lord Hadleigh standing with his back to the fireplace, waving a cigar he was holding at his daughter.

'No, my dear, you are wrong! Success in the Dardanelles, would have shortened the war. I voted with Winston on that one. Anything to stop the senseless carnage in France was worth a try!' Looking over at Victoria he spoke again. 'Come in, my dear, you look lovely. Would you like a sherry?' he asked.

***

London was full of soldiers and officers on leave. After an initial lull in activity at the start of the war, London had come alive with people intent on having a good time. Soldiers on leave were determined to spend every last penny of their pay before returning to France; all over London private clubs and bars had sprung up, full of forced gaiety and laughter, its patrons very aware that time was so short.

Lady Julia had decided she was going to show Victoria the town. She had arranged dinner at the Metropolitan with several friends who were on leave and then planned to join more friends at Club 23 for some late-night dancing. When they arrived at the

Metropolitan, the hotel was bustling with activity. The dining room was full, with every table occupied. Most of the men present were in uniform. After eighteen months of war, public opinion still favoured the idea that all men of the right age should be fighting and that those who weren't were somehow letting everyone down, although no one was saying that all the Germans required was 'a bloody nose' to have them running, any more.

During the daytime, groups of young ladies could still be seen on street corners handing out white feathers to any man who looked to be of military age but was not in uniform. For men not allowed to join up, because they were already serving the country in a vital capacity, it had been necessary for the Government to produce a badge for them to wear, declaring their service to "God, King and Country". Even so, the pressure on young men to leave government service and enlist was immense, with many unwilling to run the gauntlet of ladies handing out feathers every day.

After a relatively sedate dinner the party moved on to Club 23; an exclusive Knightsbridge venue catering almost exclusively to the sons and daughters of the English aristocracy. Present in the party that night were several offspring of the country's leading families. Standish was more bemused than overawed that she found herself in the company of men who would become the next generation of England's power brokers, if they survived the war. She could not help thinking how beautifully uncomplicated life in Australia had been before the war and how much she longed to be back there.

***

Two days later, Victoria Standish found herself again mixing with the cream of London society. Max Standish had arrived in England at the end of February and with the rest of his battalion had begun training for trench warfare in France. Standish had been promoted to captain and was immediately dispatched to a staff officer training course; although he vowed never to leave his men for the safety of headquarters. His best friend Stanley Marshall had been commissioned after Gallipoli and had completed basic officer training not far from Aldershot; returning to lead the same men he had fought with on the peninsula.

Several days earlier Standish had been summoned to see the colonel. Waiting in the outer office at headquarters he attempted to find out what was happening from Major Smith-Barton who sat at a desk signing letters; he was keen to know that he was not about to be posted away from his men, as seemed to happen so often to men completing courses.

'Do you have any idea why the colonel wants to see me, sir?' Standish asked, after Smith-Barton had finished writing and capped his pen.

'No idea, old chap,' was the response he got. Fortunately, Standish did not have to wait too long, as an orderly emerged from Colonel Hathaway's office and asked him to enter.

'Ah, Captain Standish, how was the course?' Colonel Hathaway asked.

'Not too bad, sir; although the tactics we were taught seemed outdated. They may have worked in South Africa, but would not have worked at Gallipoli,' Standish replied. 'The book on tactical warfare was written in nineteen hundred and three, so I'm not at all sure it was relevant.'

'I agree, but as every officer with recent military experience is needed in France it's difficult to find people who are up to date to teach these courses,' Hathaway responded. 'Anyway, that's not why you are here. This has arrived.' Colonel Hathaway handed Standish an envelope.

The envelope was made of heavy velum and was embossed with the royal crest. Pulling out the piece of stiff card contained in the envelope, Standish astonished to read a request that he attend Buckingham Palace, to receive his Victoria Cross from King George V, in person. The date of the ceremony was only a few days away.

'You may want to see a London tailor before the investiture,' Hathaway commented. 'I've arranged for you to take some leave, effective from now. Congratulations! It's good to see the Australian Imperial Force is receiving some of the recognition it deserves.'

Standish saluted and left the office. Outside Major Smith-Barton stopped what he was doing and looked up with a smile on his face.

'Well done, Standish, have fun in London!'

The investiture took place at Buckingham Palace a few days later. Standish had sent word to his sister that he would be arriving in London and intended to stay at Wyndhams, a club his father had been a member of since studying at Oxford University decades before.

The invitation requested that Captain Standish and his guests arrive at the West Gate of Buckingham Palace no later than eleven o'clock, as the ceremony was scheduled to start at midday. Standish had managed to visit Bingley and Throckmorton and was kitted out in a new uniform for the occasion, which felt stiff, new and uncomfortable. The purple ribbon of the Victoria Cross already stitched above his left breast pocket was all that showed he was not new to life as a soldier.

Standish had been waiting at the gates to Buckingham Palace for almost half an hour when a hansom cab drew up and his sister jumped out followed quickly by Lady Julia who had accompanied her.

'So sorry we are late, it was impossible to get a cab. Mama has taken the automobile to France,' Lady Julia announced, eager to explain their tardiness. 'After this is over and done with we must pop to the Metropolitan for a well-earned drink. My younger brother Guy is in town and is looking forward to meeting someone who fought at Gallipoli,' she continued.

The ceremony was simple but moving. Arriving in an anteroom Captain Standish was separated from his guests and marshalled into a line of men, who were to be presented to the King. Lady Julia grabbed his sister by the hand and led her through to a large room where the presentations were to be made; choosing seats which were close to the front of the room, to give them the best possible view of the ceremony.

Slowly the line of men being presented to the King snaked forward. All of the men present were receiving an award for bravery in the field. As each man arrived and was introduced to the King, the original citation was read out; leaving no one in any doubt that they were in the presence of some very brave men.

Chapter Ten

"Our pilots come from all sections of the British Empire; from our public schools and universities; from the counting house and office desk in London, Manchester and Glasgow; from the wheat farm in the Canadian North-West; the sheep station in Australia and New Zealand; from the gold mines on the Rand— in fact, from every section of His Majesty's Dominions these boys have come to 'strafe the Hun'."

Lord Rothermere 1918

April 1916 – Army Central Flying School, Upavon, Wiltshire, England

Lieutenant Guy Hadleigh stood up and walked across to the window of the hut for the third time in half an hour. Peering up at the sky he was unhappy to see the cloud which had so far prevented him from flying was, if anything, denser than the last time he looked and that the possibility of doing a few circuits was becoming less likely every minute.

Several months earlier, in the wake of a Zeppelin raid on his parents' house, Guy Hadleigh had joined the London Rifles. Initially, he was happy simply to be a part of everything and flung himself into training with vigour; he was keen to complete officer training and be posted to France, where he planned to avenge the deaths of everyone who had died when the family home in Belgravia had been bombed. However, in the middle of his training Hadleigh had bumped into George Sprockmorton, a contemporary at school, who had finished basic training with the Royal Artillery and then immediately transferred to the Royal Flying Corps. Sprockmorton was full of excitement at the prospect of fighting the war from the air. The idea had instantly appealed to Hadleigh, who could vividly remember the excitement when Bleriot crossed the Channel only a few years before and could see a kind of poetic justice in the idea, that he would be the person dropping bombs in future. After some determined lobbying, his father eventually agreed to use his contacts at the War Office to help him transfer and learn to fly.

Hadleigh had also persuaded his father that it would be much easier for him to come home and visit if he had the means of transportation at his fingertips and was now the proud owner of an AJS Model D motorcycle. His father had enquired about what was around and had decided that this particular make was value for money. He was not happy his son would be roaring around the countryside in such a newfangled mode of transport, but conceded it couldn't be more dangerous than learning how to fly a wooden box.

Lieutenant Hadleigh started his flying career out at Brooklands where he learnt the basics before being commissioned into the Royal Flying Corps. Although a civilian course it was expected that he would learn how to fly before reporting to the Central Flying School at Upavon for further instruction; he managed to complete the required hours by flying at weekends and other times when there was a break in his officer training.

Hadleigh was obsessed with weather conditions which impacted on his flying hours. At Upavon there were hours of flight theory to master, as well as the practical aspects of taking off and landing. He was also instructed in mechanical theory, which included stripping down an aircraft engine; at some point it was expected that he may have to crash land and make running repairs to his aircraft. Suddenly the hours spent in the mews at the back of the Belgravia house pestering the chauffeur seemed to have been well spent as Guy mastered the mechanical lessons with ease.

Later in the afternoon the sky started to clear and after a final check it was judged safe to fly. Hadleigh pulled on his thick flying boots and leather jacket. Carrying his flying helmet and goggles he walked out to the aircraft. His instructor was already standing by the plane and watched as he performed the pre-flight checks necessary before every take off. At one side of the plane a mechanic stood ready to help start the plane by spinning the propeller when the order was given.

Hadleigh climbed onto the wing and then into the pilot's seat of the BEc2; strapping himself in he made sure he was comfortable before carrying out standard cockpit checks. His instructor Captain John Rochford climbed into the forward seat of the plane and turned to him.

'Taxi down to the start of the runway; after take-off, I want you to take her up to a couple of thousand feet, so we can do a little altitude flying,' Rochford ordered. 'Then we'll practice some more take off and landings. I'm hoping that with another hour or so this afternoon you'll be able to go solo tomorrow.'

'OK, sir,' Hadleigh replied, excited at the prospect that at last he may be allowed up on his own.

Steering carefully, to avoid some of the bumps in the grassed area in front of the hanger, Hadleigh taxied to the end of the runway. Given the all clear, by Rochford, he pulled back on the joy stick; the aeroplane began to rapidly increase speed. As always, the sound of the wind and the accompanying roar of the engine, had an immediate effect; his heart started to beat so quickly and strongly, that he could feel it pounding in his neck and echoing in his ears. His mouth dried up and he began to feel slightly nauseated, with a strange feeling in the pit of his stomach. Pulling back on the stick still further, the aeroplane began to rise above the ground. Hadleigh quietly breathed a sigh of relief, as he had managed to take off without stalling. Looking down at the runway there was a large patch of scorched earth, where a pilot had stalled on take-off; the resulting explosion and fireball had been seen several miles away and served as a reminder to all pilots, that learning to fly was a dangerous game.

Flying high above the clouds was exhilarating, Hadleigh had never quite got used to how far away everything looked, a study in miniature; spread out below him was a patchwork of fields and tiny houses that looked as small as his sister's dolls house. Country lanes looked like thin pieces of string winding through the fields; occasional farm wagons could be seen transporting equipment and people.

After some altitude flying and an hour practicing turns and other manoeuvres, Rochford indicated that Hadleigh should land the plane. The landing was smooth and went without a hitch; as Hadleigh slowed almost to a standstill Rochford climbed out onto the wing. Tapping Hadleigh on the shoulder he spoke.

'Take her up and circuit the aerodrome. See how you go without me,' he then jumped off the wing and started to run towards the dispersal hut. With a final look at Rochford's retreating back Hadleigh turned the plane around to face the runway and began taxiing towards it.

April 1916 – Camden, New South Wales

The organising committee for the Camden Show were happy they had left nothing to chance and had made every available contingency plan should there be inclement weather. The preceding weeks had been cool, with several days of driving rain giving the committee a few sleepless nights, concerned that the showground may be too wet for the Show to go ahead.

The town had been humming with activity for the best part of a week, with people arriving from all over the State to take part in a country show with a reputation for being the best, outside of the Easter Show itself. Although most families were affected by the war in Europe, life for the community of Camden continued in much the same way as it had for decades. The Camden Show was an agricultural event which had been held annually since 1882; it was not about to be cancelled because some of the districts young men were away fighting. This year, bringing in the harvest had been a drawn-out affair, with most farms taking longer; it was with a sense of achievement that the crops were finally gathered.

The show committee with Hector Standish as chairman had been meeting for several months to ensure the show was a success. A program had been produced, with competition classes for local farmers to enter livestock; recognition for the quality of their cattle would lead to increased prices at the next sale. Ribbons were awarded for the best crops and the biggest and best quality fruits. All of the ladies had devoted considerable amounts of time baking cakes and making jams; the best of which would be entered for judging at the Royal Easter Show, in the weeks ahead.

A corner of the showground had been designated a family area, with travelling carousel and shooting gallery operators allowed to set up for the two-day show. Sideshow alley also had smaller stalls selling herbal remedies and household gadgets of dubious quality; the stall owners knew that by the time the ineffectiveness of their particular product was discovered they would be long gone.

A fortune teller had erected an exotic looking tent, covered in large cut out pictures of the sun, moon and stars, with placards exhorting people to come inside, so that they may find out what the future would hold. Business was brisk with a queue of people hoping she would confirm the safety of relatives serving with the Australian Imperial Force and be able to provide reassurance that all would be well in the future.

Constance Standish was pouring cups of tea for the wives of men who were next door in the beer tent, discussing the finer aspects of surviving in a country at war. Talk in the men's tent was exclusively about the effect war was having on the local community and included the difficulty of milking without help and problems encountered breeding quality stock. In general, it was agreed that although this year's Show had been good, stock quality was poorer; most farmers had to work harder with less assistance, to produce the feed needed to keep their cattle in the best condition.

In the ladies' tea tent, Constance was asked to recount, over and over again, how Victoria had survived the sinking of the *Ariadne* several months before. The Show attracted people from all over the district. Some people came into town only once a year; things that had happened several months before were often still newsworthy. Conspicuous by their absence were two of the more prominent local families who had lost sons at Gallipoli and were still mourning their loss.

The Camden Show organisers had decided that a proportion of money earned from the show would be used to support men fighting overseas. It looked like the war was not going to end in the near future; plans needed to be made for on-going relief. Several stalls were dedicated to sending the men who were overseas, comforts from home. Money was also raised for the support of families, who were finding it difficult to cope with the head of the house away. Collection points were established for people to deliver clothing and other items to be sent to France. Constance was able to arrange for more regular meetings of the Camden War Society, in the year ahead.

On the final evening of the show most of the district's families gathered in the Plough and Harrow for a farewell drink to toast a successful show, before returning to their land with a renewed commitment to support the nation's fighting men.

May 1916 – France

The Union Flag Café was full to bursting; the café had broken all records since opening and was bustling with activity. Fiona Moncrieff had quickly settled into the role of café manager, she had become adept at accurately predicting the provision levels needed to feed everyone arriving, without running out and without any waste.

Each day there was a steady stream of soldiers, all in need of refreshment. Journeying from the Front was a lengthy frustrating business; leave trains pulled in sporadically, often hours late because of problems with the track. Regular heavy shelling caused enough disruption to make the track impassable for several hours, while a mobile team of labourers repaired the damage. Men often spent the first few precious hours of leave in railway sidings, waiting for other more urgently needed trains to use the tracks ahead. Although spring, the nights were still cold and with no heating on the trains it was difficult to sleep; men arrived at the café cold, tired and hungry but excited at the prospect of leave and the thought that in a few short hours they would be with their loved ones.

The café specialised in hot, quick, basic food, which for men who had endured months of trench food was paradise. A team of volunteers baked pies and made soup which was sold with crusty French bread; the men could also buy packets of decent cigarettes, after months of going short.

Lady Hadleigh was excited because her son Gerald was due for leave. He had been caught up in fighting around Ypres for a number of months without respite; the sector had been relatively quiet with no major offensives over the winter period, but men still died caught by snipers.

Quite suddenly more men than usual had been given leave, causing speculation that a spring offensive was planned; large numbers of Kitchener's Army had finally arrived in France and had set off marching, to camps outside of Calais and Boulogne, where they endured weeks of further training.

Kitchener's Army had been recruited at the start of the war. Lord Kitchener had sold the idea to the War Office that men were more likely to enlist if they were allowed to join alongside their friends. Dozens of battalions had been formed comprised entirely of local recruits; men who worked together in civilian life were now trained to fight together. This short-sighted strategy was to have repercussions for decades to come, with whole towns decimated, losing all of their men within a few short hours.

Each new battalion was desperately short of officers; initially old soldiers who had fought in previous wars were recruited. As the recruits became trained, it was possible to promote from within and dispense with their services; many remained though, keen to see out the battle.

Lady Hadleigh finished setting the table and stepped back. With every inch of available space taken, and wanting privacy, she had spent some time turning an old store room at the back of the building into an acceptable temporary dining room. Her son had sent word that he would be on the leave train arriving that day and that he would not be alone. Lady Hadleigh was a little intrigued as it sounded as though he would be bringing a lady with him and she could not imagine where he would have met anyone, while fighting in the Belgium trenches. If his train was reasonably on time, she expected he would have several hours before boarding the boat to England and intended to have a hot appetizing meal waiting.

Lady Hadleigh had learnt to cook many years before, as a child on the family estate. Fascinated by the whole process of preparing a meal, she had spent many hours hounding the cook, until she was allowed to sit at the large kitchen table and watch what was happening; as long as she promised not to disturb any of the other servants going about their daily routine. Somehow, she had retained knowledge of the basics, an invaluable skill over the last few weeks.

Walking back into the kitchen, Lady Hadleigh quickly checked the oven; looking at the rolled mutton she had stuffed with capers and anchovies earlier, she then moved into the café. She was surprised at how busy the café was despite the relatively early hour. Two trains had arrived half an hour earlier, disgorging hundreds of men anxious to board one of the two boats tied up next to the dock. After reporting to the transport office some were lucky enough to be allowed to embark immediately, others though, were given movement orders for boats arriving later in the day and immediately sought out the Union flag, intent on a refreshing cup of tea and something to eat.

Lady Hadleigh was standing at the till when she saw him. Standing in the doorway he looked exhausted. His uniform boots were covered in mud and his greatcoat looked worn and old. He was carrying a rifle, which many of the officers defending his part of the front line had started to do; a captured German sniper had recently confessed that it was easy to pick out the officers and shoot them, as they did not carry rifles. Leaving his rifle at the door and shrugging of a small back pack, Captain Hammond walked quickly over to his mother; grabbing her he gave her a hug and kiss, to applause from some of the men sitting around the tables, who were watching proceedings with interest.

'Mama!' he exclaimed, 'What in Heaven's name are you doing over here? I could not believe it when I received your letter, this café is a very welcome relief for soldiers waiting hours for a boat; such a splendid idea, it looks as though you have been kept busy.'

'We have been providing a service, darling,' Lady Hadleigh replied. 'It has to be better than knitting endless pairs of socks and packing Red Cross boxes,' she added.

In the excitement Lady Hadleigh did not immediately notice the young lady standing just inside of the doorway. Suddenly remembering he had not arrived alone, Hammond turned and grabbed Sister Brennan by the hand pulling her into the centre of the room.

'Mama, let me introduce Margaret Brennan. She has kept me sane for the last few months.'

Lady Hadleigh turned and looked sideways at the young lady now holding her son's hand. She was immediately struck by how astonishingly beautiful she was, despite the general air of exhaustion and the worn look of the uniform she was wearing. Having spent a considerable period of time involved with the café, Lady Hadleigh instantly recognised Brennan's uniform as belonging to the QAIMNS reserve, rather than the regulars. The thought that a possible daughter-in-law was serving only for the duration of the war was somewhat heartening; only a few short months ago such a liaison would have been impossible to contemplate and although happy for her son, Lady Hadleigh looked forward to the future with a degree of trepidation. Looking at Brennan she spoke.

'It is such a pleasure to meet you, my dear. You must come and warm yourself by the stove and take some refreshment. I am very pleased to see Gerald has finally met someone suitable.'

For Margaret Brennan a few short hours were enough to make her feel she had known Lady Hadleigh for years. Any doubts she may have had about Gerald's background were immediately dispelled, giving her hope for the future

Early June 1916 – The Somme

If anyone had asked, Captain Max Standish would not have been able to describe what it was like to be in northern France during the spring of 1916. The men who were in France had all volunteered to serve the colours and believed in the cause they were fighting for. There was a sense of purpose, with all men certain they were moving toward a common goal; almost overnight men with differences appeared reconciled, as though the trivia of daily life was nothing in the scheme of things. It was well known that some kind of big offensive was planned for the weeks ahead, but no one was quite sure what, or where and rumour was rife.

A few miles back from the Front, row upon row of tents had been set up in the fields. The weather was fine and warm, with an atmosphere far more reminiscent of a scout camp, than of a group of men preparing to go into the biggest planned battle of the war so far. Training was intense, with hours spent walking in an unwavering line towards a distant goal. The men could not see the point of this exercise but recognised it must be important as they were timed over and over again, until eventually the staff officers present nodded in agreement writing results in their notebooks.

The camps were filled with soldiers from every country of the Empire. Men from India trained alongside Canadians, ANZACS and South Africans; but by far the most men present were part of Kitchener's Army. These men had answered England's call and had joined up at the start of the war; full of pride and wanting to fight with their pals for God, King and Country. They had endured training which lasted for nearly two years; making them fitter than they had been in their lives. Finally, they were ready for whatever battle they were called on to fight and for most of them it was not a moment too soon. Some had friends who had joined regular regiments at the same time as they had joined and had been in the thick of fighting for months now.

Kitchener's Army was desperate to swagger home on leave, with tales of taming the Hun. Excited beyond belief at the prospect of finally fighting for what was right, they put up with the endless shouting from drill sergeants and the repetitive nature of their training; knowing that soon they would be called on to prove they were the best and would not be found wanting.

After Gallipoli, the Australians were given some local leave in Egypt, before being sent to England for trench warfare training in preparation for moving to France. They had finally marched into camp a month before and had been kept busy training for the spring offensive that no one was willing to admit was going to happen.

Captain Standish looked in the mirror and fiddled with the knot in his tie; then picking up a clothes brush, he brushed his uniform jacket once again. His jacket was in fact as clean as it could be in the circumstances. He had been in France now since late March and the jacket, although only worn behind the lines, had not been properly cleaned since he bought it on leave in London. On the opposite side of the tent Second Lieutenant Stanley Marshall was making the final adjustments of his own dress, ready for the evening ahead.

To his delight, Standish had received news from his sister the day before; after months of waiting she had been posted to France. The AANS had blocked her posting for weeks; Matron Gillespie who was now in charge of postings was convinced that she had done enough and after the sinking of the *Ariadne* had wanted to send her home. It took some determined lobbying on Victoria's part to be sent to France instead. She had written to tell her brother that she had spent the best part of a fortnight settling in, but was able to get the evening off and planned a quiet evening meal at a restaurant in the local town. Standish had called in every favour he could, to borrow a motorbike from the transport pool, so that he and Marshall could join her.

Although Standish was excited at the thought of seeing his sister, he was far more excited at the prospect of renewing his acquaintance with Lady Julia, having met her when he received the Victoria Cross. The luncheon at the Metropolitan had been a pleasant affair which led to several other meetings; Standish had accompanied Lady Julia to several concerts and had become her constant companion before reluctantly reporting to his battalion in preparation for France.

The Café Bleu was located just off the town's main street, but was well signposted, with chalk signs pointing the way. Shell damage from earlier in the war had destroyed a lot of street signage and left shops boarded up; many inhabitants of the town chose to relocate further from the fighting until the war was over. The café's owners had decided to stay and take their chances and, so far, this decision was paying off.

Located in the basement of a building which had suffered some shell damage, but appeared safe enough, the café had become a welcome retreat for troops training in the area; Standish and Marshall could hear raucous singing coming from the café as they negotiated the stairs down into the basement.

Standish pulled back the heavy blue curtain covering the entrance to the café. Stepping inside he was surprised to see he had entered a large cavernous space which was full of soldiers eating and drinking. The air was thick with cigarette smoke. In one corner a piano stood by the wall and was being hammered by a lieutenant from the Lifeguards who was singing "It's a long way to Tipperary" at the top of his voice. Although fairly early in the evening it was apparent that everyone present intended to enjoy themselves before returning to the reality and uncertainties of daily life. Looking across the room Standish was able to see both his sister and to his intense pleasure Lady Julia Hadleigh, deep in conversation drinking a glass of wine each.

'Come along, Stanley, I think we have earned a little wine and good company to fortify us,' Standish remarked before striding across the room.

Chapter Eleven

Now God be thanked who has matched us with His
hour,
And caught our youth, and wakened us from sleeping,
With handmade sure, clear eye, and sharpened power,
To turn, as swimmers into cleanness leaping,
Glad from a world grown old and cold and weary,
Leave the sick hearts that honour could not move,
And half-men, and their dirty songs and dreary,
And all the little emptiness of love!
Oh! We, who have known shame, we have found
release there,
Where there's no ill, no grief, but sleep has mending,
Naught broken save this body, lost but breath;
Nothing to shake the laughing heart's long peace there
But only agony and that has ending;
And the worse friend and enemy is but Death.

Rupert Brooke 1914

June 1916 – Brooklands

Guy Hadleigh was happy that at last he was about to
enter the war. After several weeks of flight training he
had been passed fit to fly solo and had been sent on

leave for a short period, before being asked to report to the Sopwith Aviation Company at Brooklands. His orders were to collect a Sopwith 1 ½ Strutter, which he was to fly across to France; where he would join his squadron.

Arriving at the aerodrome, Hadleigh parked his motorcycle and walked into a hut next to the hangar belonging to Sopwith Aviation. Sat behind a reception desk a young man in overalls was attempting to clean his hands with an oily rag, which looked only marginally cleaner than he was. Peering at Hadleigh through a pair of round, steel-rimmed spectacles he spoke.

'You must be one of the three pilots I'm expecting,' he observed. 'I've just been testing the kites you three are taking across. All of them sound sweet and should get there without any problem. You may want to touch down close to Calais to refuel and stretch your legs,' he continued.

'Have you any tips for flying this plane?' Hadleigh asked. 'I've only ever flown the kites used for training at Upavon and have no idea how different this will be.'

'It's much lighter on the controls, so go easy. On the whole though you'll find easier to manoeuvre, once you are airborne.'

Hadleigh followed the mechanic out of the hut and across a grassed area, to where three identical Sopwith's were parked. The aeroplanes were new and smelt of the glue used to attach the canvas sections to the fuselage. For the first time a British plane had been designed with a forward firing machine gun capable of firing in synchronisation with the propeller. Aerial combat had suddenly become safer for all concerned; the observer no longer had to hang over the side to fire a gun and there was less risk of shooting the propeller off. Happily, Hadleigh saw that the planes also had a seat for an observer; which he hoped he could use as a storage area for the trip across.

Within half an hour the other pilots making the trip had arrived and introduced themselves as Lieutenants Julian Horton and Andrew Fitzgibbon, Hadleigh knew them both slightly, as they had been at the Central Flying School when he arrived for training. After some hurried introductions the three men set about examining their aircraft, to personally make sure each plane was airworthy. Just before they were scheduled to take off two RFC observers appeared, with orders to join the same squadron. Hadleigh agreed to fly solo carrying the other pilots' baggage in the place of an observer.

The day was cloudless with a sense of early morning summer heat. As Hadleigh taxied to the start of the runway he could feel the day promised to be a very hot one with little breeze. Although hot on the ground Hadleigh was well aware that up above the clouds the temperature would be very cold indeed, so was suitably dressed in a flying helmet which covered his ears, as well as a leather greatcoat, which covered his uniform completely. Hadleigh pulled back on the stick of the unfamiliar plane to take off; the plane handled well and as he had been told was sensitive once airborne, turning with the slightest application of pressure on the rudder.

All three planes flew in formation towards Dover and then started to cross the English Channel. Looking down it was possible to see a number of troop ships waiting to take on soldiers travelling to the front. The port looked busy, as though in anticipation of the battle to come. Supply ships were everywhere, jockeying for position, their captains wanting to load supplies and return to France.

Once England started to disappear behind him, Hadleigh experienced a slight feeling of nervousness as he thought about the future. It was well known that for pilots fighting on the Western Front, life expectancy could be measured in weeks rather than months. Aeroplanes were becoming more sophisticated but remained death traps for the inexperienced; the sensitive nature of the plane he was flying made Hadleigh keenly aware that any loss of concentration may have disastrous consequences and caused him to wonder how he would concentrate and fight the Hun at the same time.

In the end the crossing was uneventful and the three Sopwith's touched down in St Omer in good time. After sending a telegraph to the airfield just outside of Amiens the pilots and observers entered the Officers Mess, keen to warm up with some vintage French cognac and learn about France from some more experienced pilots.

The following morning, Hadleigh and the other pilots took off and flew directly to Amiens. The cloud cover was low, making it difficult to land. Hadleigh was happy that he landed with only one small bounce, acutely aware that he was probably being watched by every member of the squadron not flying. As he came to a halt, he was further relieved when he noticed out of the corner of his eye that Captain John Rochford was striding purposefully towards his plane.

'Welcome to France, Lieutenant Hadleigh. How did you find the kite?' Rochford asked.

'After lumbering around in a BEc2 at Upavon, it was a joy to fly, sir,' Hadleigh replied. 'It took a bit of getting used to though, I thought I was going to stall on take-off, but somehow managed to get airborne. Have you been posted here as well, sir?'

'Yes, it would seem I am needed here, in charge of the squadron you are joining,' Rochford replied.

June 1916 – The Somme

Sister Standish sank into a chair in the Sisters Mess and accepted the cup of tea passed to her by Sister Blackstone. Standish had arrived at the Casualty Clearing Station as soon as she could arrange passage;

after being informed that her application to return to a field hospital had been approved. She had travelled with Hadleigh, who had taken time off after the sinking of the *Ariadne*, vowing never to put herself in danger again; only to find she missed the work and the friends she had made, making a return inevitable.

Soon after joining the Casualty Clearing Station, Standish realised the pressure was on to stabilise and transfer as many wounded as possible, by hospital train to Calais and then to England. Although the spring offensive was a hushed affair, it was obvious that the fighting would be concentrated around the Somme area and casualties may be heavy. For several days transfer of the wounded had been a priority in an attempt to free up as many beds as possible. Additional supplies had been arriving by the crate load, with bandages and dressings stockpiled in tents behind the main hospital.

Standish had recently dined with her brother and knew that wherever the fighting took place he would be involved. She was frightened for him, but acknowledged he had trained well and could not be better prepared. Following the last evening out she had spent a considerable period of time writing to her parents, describing France and letting them know about the dinner party. She had also written to Mrs Marshall, keen to let her know how well thought of Stanley was, by his mates.

Several days before, sitting in the basement café, Standish and Hadleigh had waited with nervous anticipation for the two men to arrive. Hadleigh recently came to the realisation that Maxwell Standish was a decent man who she wanted to get to know better.

Hadleigh had the time of her life when Captain Standish was in London. He had wined and dined her, as though each occasion was their last, and following his transfer to France he had written almost every day. His letters were full of daily trivia and didn't really say much, but Hadleigh was pleased to receive them as they confirmed he was thinking of her.

The evening had been hugely enjoyable everyone dining in the café encouraged to join in the popular songs, sung by a couple of officers from the Lifeguards. In the end they had parted from each other not knowing when or if they would meet again and the evening had taken on a slightly sombre air. Captain Standish had given his sister a letter to be posted to their parents if he did not survive and Marshall had done the same, asking that if necessary she seek out his mother and let her know how much he thought of her every day.

***

With a start, Standish realised that Blackstone had been talking to her while she had been day dreaming about Stanley Marshall.

'Is there anyone left you feel could be moved safely?' Sister Blackstone asked. 'I can't help feeling we are unprepared for the number of wounded we will see in the coming days. Everyone we can get out, we must,' she added.

'Yes, I've got two,' Standish replied. 'Sutton, in bed fourteen, has superficial shrapnel wounds to the scalp. He has recovered from the injury but is still getting a lot of headaches; normally we would keep him and send him back to his regiment, but he will not be able to take things easy, with the spring offensive expected so soon. Clarke has been shot in the shoulder. Again, not a case I would normally send to England.'

'All right, let's arrange for them both to go on tonight's hospital train. I'll let Major Chardingly know how many wounded we are left with.' Blackstone quickly drained the rest of her tea, stood up and left the mess. Standish did not linger for long, keen to let Sutton and Clarke know it was their lucky day.

***

Hadleigh folded the letter she had been reading earlier and returned it to her dress pocket. The letter was from Briggs who was slowly recuperating in London.

Eighteen months into the war, it was becoming difficult for those left on the Home Front. It was not always possible to obtain the same pre-war quality groceries; coal, although not yet rationed, was in short supply. Briggs wrote of recovering at her parents' house in south-east London; a house which, although it was summer, was prone to damp if a fire was not lit regularly. She wrote of the difficulty they were experiencing obtaining good quality meat and the daily trials of making ends meet. Her sister had recently left service to take up a position in the munitions factory at Woolwich Arsenal; where she was able to earn three times the wage she was used to.

Briggs longed to be back nursing with Lady Julia, but had been told that she would need to spend a long time resting, as she had been exposed to the elements in the Mediterranean Sea for several hours and it was a miracle she had survived. Briggs had in fact amazed the medical staff at the military hospital she had been taken to; on top of the illness bought on from exposure, she had fractured her ankle and some ribs as she hit the ships side jumping into the sea. A few short months later she was walking using only a stick for assistance and was telling anyone prepared to listen, how much she was needed in France. Privately, her doctor had little doubt she would be in France by autumn at the latest; in the meantime she had to be content with helping out at the local convalescent home, which took some wounded.

Hadleigh was able to sense the frustration Briggs felt from the tone of the letter and hoped she would be cleared to return to France soon; the years they had spent nursing together had cemented a bond, which meant she missed her not being around.

Hadleigh got up from the pallet of bandages she had been sitting on and made her way back to the ward, hoping her ten-minute absence had not been noticed. Without Briggs to look after her, Hadleigh found it more difficult to escape the notice of Sister Blackstone, who seemed to delight in finding her in the wrong place at the wrong time. She was finding it difficult to concentrate at the moment; knowing that a major battle was imminent and that Captain Standish was likely to be involved in the thick of it.

Rounding a corner, Hadleigh was almost knocked over by Sister Standish hurrying in the opposite direction.

'Ah, Hadleigh, there you are! Can you come with me, please; we need to prepare Sutton and Clarke for the next hospital train. They've been lucky enough to get a passage to England, because we need the beds.'

'Of course, Sister,' Hadleigh replied. 'Sister Blackstone has just asked me to count some bandages, which I've done. If it's all right I need to report to her first with the figures.'

'That's fine. As soon as you've done that come and find me. We need to change their dressings and give some morphia, as the journey ahead of them will be arduous,' Standish replied.

***

Captain Max Standish turned over in his bunk and pulled his blanket up over his shoulders, attempting to cover his ears. The bombardment which had started earlier on in the day was both continuous and deafening. Recently he had attended a general briefing at headquarters and had been informed that he was to hold his section of the line for a few more days, but would then be relieved by one of the new Army battalions; which had been trained for this moment. His company would retire a couple of miles behind the line, to provide backup for the troops going over the top, on the first day of the spring offensive. At the same briefing he was informed of the plan to shell the German trenches continuously for days, so that when the attack happened there would be little, if any, resistance. This shelling was now disturbing his rest.

Although June, the night was cool; darkness had descended a couple of hours before and with it came a drop in temperature. The trench was full of men huddled together on the fire step trying to sleep. Beyond them the forward periscope positions were manned with men peering cautiously into no man's land, looking for any movement. It appeared as though the heavy bombardment was affecting the Germans in the trenches opposite, as the usual wire repair parties which came out every night were not in evidence.

Sergeant Major John Kennedy who was observing activity in no man's land was not happy; he could not understand if the wire was cut, why there were no repair parties in evidence and did not believe this was because the bombardment had been accurate enough to kill large numbers of Germans. Kennedy was new to trench warfare, after arriving from Australia three months previously; Sergeant Wilson had arrived with him, along with two hundred extra men; sent to replace some of the soldiers who had lost their lives at Gallipoli.

Moving along the trench, Kennedy came across Lieutenant Marshall who was discussing the feasibility of sending a party of men into no man's land, to assess the effect of the bombardment which seemed to have quietened down a little. Sergeant Wilson was arguing that the idea was too dangerous, as it was not possible to see where the shells were falling and that the chance of being hit was high. Seeing Kennedy arrive, Marshall turned to him.

'What do you think, Sergeant Major, should we assess the state of the wire?' Marshall asked.

'In my opinion it's too dangerous, sir. The bombardment may have eased off, but from the briefing Captain Standish received, that won't last. I don't think we'll be able to send out any sorties into no man's land in the near future, without huge loss of life,' Kennedy replied. 'We may have to leave checking the German trenches to the RFC observers for the time being,' he continued.

***

Shaken awake by his batman just before dawn, Lieutenant Guy Hadleigh was regretting the heavy session in the mess the night before. German aircraft were active at the moment and another pilot had been lost as he flew home the evening before. As always, the squadron marked the occasion with an auction of the pilot's possessions; the money from which would be sent to his young widow, who had given birth to their first child only a month before. It was impossible for most of the pilots to dwell for too long on squadron losses without thinking of their own mortality, most were grateful simply to have survived for another day, as for them life expectancy could be measured in weeks. For this reason, anyone who did not return was given a riotous send off. Some pilots, having crash landed, found their way back to the squadron only to discover they had no spare clothing and all of their possessions had been auctioned to the highest bidder.

Hadleigh drank the hot sweet tea his batman had left and then reluctantly got out of bed. Landing his plane a week ago, he had not immediately noticed the airfield was in the grounds of a considerably sized chateau. He soon learnt that the owners had left for the duration of the war, as they felt they were far too close to the front. They had agreed to hand over the chateau to the RFC; who were immediately taken with the long flat grassed area next to the house which would serve very nicely as a temporary runway.

Living in a chateau bought some advantages, the long gallery was a good space for the squadron to play cricket when the weather was too poor for flying. The adjutant had the foresight to order the removal of some of the more priceless antiques before the squadron moved in, so at least the damage was kept to a minimum. The dining room was also impressive, with portraits of French men and women, all related to the current owner, adorning the walls.

Walking rapidly downstairs Hadleigh finished dressing. As he walked he wrapped a long thick scarf around his neck and then started to pull on the leather gauntlets his mother had given him as a present, just before he left England.

Hadleigh was feeling nervous. Until now he had flown for very short periods in France. Captain Rochford had taken him up each day for an hour; to familiarise him with the trench landscape and get used to the guns below firing pot shots, as he flew overhead.

Hadleigh arrived at his aircraft before anyone else from the squadron. Cautiously and carefully he began pre-flight checks to make sure his kite was airworthy. He noted that a tear in the fabric had been patched since he last flew; he checked the wooden struts for cracking and any other obvious problems, before climbing onto the wing and into the cockpit. Just as he was settling into his seat other members of the squadron could be seen arriving to start their own flight checks. Lieutenant Percy Osborne arrived at a run, he had trained as an observer and was also about to fly on his first sortie. Climbing into the front seat of the plane, Osborne started to check the machine guns mounted at the front. Giving Hadleigh a thumbs up, he settled back in his seat, fastened his harness and then waited patiently for take-off.

The squadron took off in formation just as dawn was breaking. Captain Rochford led the way, ascending sharply and then turning to the north. After only five minutes of flying the Front was clearly visible below, snaking away as far as the eye could see. In the distance just behind the German lines were several observer platforms hanging below small balloons. As soon as the Germans became aware of the aircraft flying towards them frantic attempts were made to winch in the observer platforms, before they could be shot at.

The noise of flying in an open cockpit was loud but above this noise a rumbling sound could be heard and sporadic puffs of smoke could be seen, coming from the big guns pounding the German trenches. For twenty minutes the dawn patrol flew north, until with a wave of his arm, Rochford signalled it was time to return to the chateau. The time had been used fruitfully with photographs of the trenches below taken using cumbersome cameras attached to the side of the Sopwith's. Some of the observers also sketched rough pictures of what they saw. All of which would be sent to headquarters as soon as the formation returned to base.

For several hours after he landed Hadleigh felt a strange sense of elation; happy that he had survived his flight over enemy lines, but with a sensation in the pit of his stomach which had him dry retching as soon as the plane had come to a halt. Eventually he began to feel better, his pulse which had been racing since he took off, returned to normal and he stopped feeling light-headed. He was able to tuck into the bacon and eggs kept warm for him by a mess steward who was used to young officers who had flown on their first real sortie.

Chapter Twelve

July 1st 1916 – The Somme

In the final few hours before dawn the barrage had intensified; men in the trenches became used to the earth shuddering, from shells exploding close to the German lines beyond. The air was thick with smoke so that when dawn broke it was hazy; the smell of cordite was one which the few who survived that day would never forget.

The attack was planned for seven thirty in the morning; the men, who for days had delivered the bombardment, were ordered to stop firing an hour before. Briefly after the guns ceased there was a lull, the Somme became eerily quiet, the Coldstream Guards occupying the forward trenches stood still, acutely aware that any movement or sound, would bring a hail of shrapnel down upon them. On cue, the first of several mines was detonated, producing a terrifying explosion, accompanied by a cloud of earth, which could be seen several miles away.

Captain Hammond was grateful that his men had finally reached the trench, from which they were to climb out into no man's land and begin the slow walk towards the enemy guns. His company were to go over the top in the second wave of men, at the sound of a whistle blown by Major Cuthbert Chivers.

Chivers was a veteran, who had fought during the Boer War with distinction. He had managed to leave his staff job and re-join his old battalion, determined not to miss the show. Looking around, Hammond was able to count half a dozen men who had every right to be safe at headquarters, but were in the trenches, anxious not to miss the battle.

The night had been a long one. It was early evening when Hammond's company waved goodbye to the rear guard, who were to stay behind in the field next to the farm. The road to the front line was horribly crowded, with thousands of men attempting to find their way to pre-arranged rendezvous points. Supply wagons were still trying to move weapons and bullets forward to where they were needed. The road was poor and pitted with craters caused by earlier shelling. Frequently wagons became stuck; pushing them clear was time-consuming and caused long delays for the troops waiting behind.

Arriving in the communication trenches, Hammond and his men found progress slow. Despite many hours of planning there were problems with some people attempting to move against the general flow. Periodically, a call for stretcher bearers could be heard, as men were still being wounded closer to the front trench. One man slipped and caught his ankle between the duckboard and trench side, breaking it; this simple injury was responsible for a hold-up which lasted for more than an hour. Stretcher bearers found it difficult to extract him and then force their way back down the trench, battling the tide of men.

By the early hours of the morning Captain Hammond and his men were ready. They had arrived in the front trenches and immediately set about preparing themselves for the morning ahead. Crude ladders were resting against the parapet, spaced evenly along the trench; once the order was given the men would climb these into no man's land.

Sergeant Major Lewis was walking up and down the trench checking each guardsman to make sure they were properly equipped with full water bottles and that each man was carrying enough rations to survive for a period of time, until supply lines were established. Behind him Sergeant Davis was dispensing a small rum ration to cach man, to fortify them and make it easier to climb the ladders when the time came.

Some men were designated to remain behind when the order was given and were wearing red armbands to avoid being shot at as deserters. These men were to assist wave upon wave of men exit as smoothly as possible; they were also there to assist stretcher bearers looking for the wounded.

The nervous chatter which had accompanied the men on the march to the trenches had ceased, almost in tandem with the lull in the bombardment. Most men concentrated on writing one last letter home knowing they may not survive what was to come. Men sought out their pals; to give them special instructions about who to contact if they did not make it. Those who could write had left letters for loved ones with the orderly corporals, hoping to collect them on their return from battle.

As soon as the last mine was detonated and the sound began to die down, whistles could be heard up and down the line; the shrill sound signifying the Battle of the Somme had begun. The first wave of men left the trenches and started to walk towards the enemy. They had been ordered to walk not run; a military strategy devised by a team of generals convinced the bombardment would kill any Germans, who had not already run away.

The guns had concentrated on blowing gaps in the wire, to ease the men's passage through to the German trenches. Air reconnaissance suggested that this plan had succeeded and as a result the general mood at headquarters was optimistic. For the men on the ground exiting the trenches in the first wave, it was difficult to share this optimism; immediately German machine guns started raking across no man's land and they were cut down in their waves, collapsing and dying where they were hit.

The second wave immediately followed the first; without anyone being aware that the first wave was either dead or dying in the mud. Climbing out of the trench Hammond started to walk forward. Behind him his company were following as quickly as the makeshift ladder system would allow. Starting the steady walk towards the enemy lines Hammond glanced around; initially he wondered why some of the first wave appeared to have stopped moving forwards. Through the haze he quickly realised the men concerned were dead.

The machine guns started again and it became clear quickly, that they would not survive if they continued to walk. Seeing a couple of his men hit early on by machine-gun fire, Hammond broke into a run and dived into a shell hole up ahead, escaping the deadly bullets; he was soon joined by Lewis and a couple of guardsmen who had survived the terrifying start of the battle.

After taking a moment to recover, Hammond inched to the edge of the shell hole and looked over its lip. No man's land was full of dead and dying men, cut down together in waves. Up ahead it was possible to see the wire had been cut in several places; German guns were systematically raking the cut wire. Men, who by some miracle managed to get there, were wounded or killed by machine guns trained on the gaps. It looked as though crossing the wire was an impossible task and they were trapped in the shell hole for the time being.

Sinking back into the hole, Hammond turned to Lewis.

'We need to come up with a plan to get into their trenches,' he commented. 'We can't stay here; eventually a shell will find its mark.' In response Lewis nodded, removed a Mills bomb from a pocket in his tunic, pulled the pin and threw it as hard as he could at the German trench. The resulting explosion appeared to have found its mark as the machine gun stopped firing. Hammond stood and ran forward through the gap and then jumped quickly into the German front-line trench.

The hand to hand fighting, which followed was fierce; fortunately, Hammond and his men were soon joined by reinforcements who taking advantage of the gap in the wire, dropped into the trench beside him. It was immediately apparent why so many Germans had survived the bombardment which had taken place. The Germans had been occupying the sector for months and had taken the time to dig deep, comfortable dugouts metres below the earth's surface; the impact of the bombardment had been minimal and apart from some disturbed sleep the Germans were ready for the fight.

***

After five days of constant firing, the guns ceased before dawn; alerting Victoria Standish, who realised the start of the offensive, must be imminent. Several days earlier she had left the Casualty Clearing Station with Sister Blackstone, Major Chardingly and a handful of other nurses. They had been ordered to move closer to the front line to set up a Forward Dressing Station. If the battle proved costly, it was thought that basic dressing and rapid assessment, would assist with the flow of wounded towards the rear and keep the roads clear for much-needed supplies to be transported.

A few miles further behind, trains waited empty and idle, the interiors containing neatly made cots, with fresh linen, waiting to transport the wounded directly to the coast. Sister Brennan had been deployed to one of these hospital trains along with Major Strachan and was anticipating a busy few days. The nursing staff had spent the best part of a month rolling bandages and counting instruments. In the occasional spare moment Brennan could be found with her head buried in the *Modern Textbook of Anaesthetics*, a well-known guide she felt she should be familiar with in case medical expertise was scarce.

The wounded started to arrive at the Forward Dressing Station almost immediately; some men had been shot as soon as they climbed out into no man's land. One or two had fallen backwards onto men trying to scale the ladders behind them; they had been left propped up on the fire steps to wait for red-banded stretcher bearers to arrive.

By evening the trickle of wounded had become a flood. The noise of battle and smoke was intense and had not diminished at any time during the day. Standish was beginning to tire as she had been on her feet constantly for nearly twelve hours without anything to eat or drink. Standing up from a dressing she was applying to a soldier's leg she stumbled, suddenly feeling light-headed and very unwell. Her head started to throb, just as Sister Blackstone appeared beside her and led her outside.

'Sister, you must take time out to eat and drink,' Blackstone said. 'You will be no good to anyone at all if we have to look after you, as well as the wounded,' she continued.

Beckoning to an orderly, Blackstone asked for a pot of tea to be prepared and then presided over the ensuing tea party; incongruous though it was in the heat of battle. A few more nurses joined them, also on the verge of exhaustion.

Blackstone looked at the scene surrounding her and started to think. It did not seem as though the numbers of wounded arriving were starting to slow down. The original orders from headquarters had ordered she and her nurses were to provide temporary care for the wounded until the offensive moved on. No one had expected the battle to be bloody or prolonged; it had been anticipated that the combined allied force would quickly overpower the Germans and march onward to Bapaume at a rapid trot. The Forward Dressing Station would be overtaken by a Mobile Medical Unit following hot on the heels of the conquering army. In the event this battle was beginning to look as though far more casualties had happened than expected and she was going to have to start thinking of relief for her staff.

'Hadleigh!' she called to Lady Julia who was sitting on an upturned crate drinking a cup of tea. 'Go with Sister Standish and Nurse Forrest to the field down the road where the medical supplies are stored. We have asked the quartermaster to provide a couple of tents for us to rest in. Get some sleep and be back here to relieve us in four hours' time. I'm sorry I can't let you have longer, but we all need relief and we are going to have to stagger breaks until the Casualty Clearing Stations send us more nursing staff, which may not happen soon.'

Reluctantly, Standish set off with Hadleigh and Forrest. She was desperate to stay where she was, as there was so many wounded arriving, but recognised she needed rest to continue to work effectively. Arriving at the entrance to a large field the nurses were greeted by an RAMC quartermaster sergeant, who was standing in the middle of a pile of socks chewing on the end of a pencil, as he attempted to count the pairs; he appeared oblivious to the sound of the guns not so far away.

Seeing how tired the nurses were, he wasted no time in showing them a tent, which had been set up with a number of basic camp beds; to Standish they looked like the most inviting beds she had ever seen.

By late evening on the first day, twelve thousand wounded made their way from the trenches to Casualty Clearing Stations scattered around the region. In the late evening when Hadleigh and Standish returned to the Forward Dressing Station, feeling refreshed, they were astonished to see that every available piece of ground outside was occupied with men on stretchers as far as the eye could see; still more standing wherever there was space, waiting for medical attention. Ambulances were arriving rapidly and at the direction of Sister Blackstone were loading the wounded four at a time.

July 3rd 1916 – London

Violet Briggs pulled her VAD uniform off its hanger and looked at it critically. She had avoided examining the state it was in previously, as the sight reminded her of how she had almost drowned when the *Ariadne* sank. Limping over to the window and holding the dress to the light, she was able to see several seawater stains covering the main part of the dress. The arms were unaffected; Briggs thought they would not be noticeable once she put on a white starched apron over the top. Slowly she managed to dress, finishing the uniform off with a pair of starched white cuffs and an uncomfortable collar, the stud of which dug into the base of her throat. Several days earlier, Briggs had moved back into the household of Lord and Lady Hadleigh at their request; they thought they may have some light work for her while she convalesced and Briggs was conscious of a need to help her family make ends meet. Walking into the kitchen, Briggs found Mrs Trent sipping a cup of tea and reading stories of the Battle of the Somme, which had begun to be printed in newspapers a couple of days before. Mrs Trent looked at Briggs and sighed.

'If you are determined then, I'll see what I can do about getting a spare uniform from Salmons, it shouldn't take too long as they've still got your measurements,' Mrs Trent continued. 'Not that I think you are in any way ready to go back to this nursing business. Just make sure you take it easy and rest if you feel too tired.'

'I'm fine, Mrs Trent,' Briggs replied. 'I have to go; I think we can expect a lot of wounded. When I was enquiring at the hospital yesterday, they said they'd been asked to prepare another hundred beds by tonight and any help would be good. I said I'd help make some beds and write for some of the men who can't, to let their wives and families know they are safe. Nothing too strenuous,' she added.

Briggs left the house and climbed the steps into the street. Leaning on a stick she made steady progress to the end of the square and entered the large building at the end. Bedford House was a large Victorian building, owned by the University of London. In common with thousands of public buildings, Bedford House had been converted into a hospital for the duration of the war. During the day residents of Bedford Square were familiar with the sight of wounded men, wearing blue uniforms with a distinctive red tie, sitting in the centre of the square enjoying the warm summer weather.

The hospital was staffed by a number of civilian nurses and several VADs. The previous evening Briggs had visited the hospital and been interviewed by Matron Phillips. After explaining she was hopeful she would join her colleagues in France by the end of the year, she had offered her services for the interim period; an offer which had been accepted with alacrity. Phillips had spent the previous morning on the telephone to the War Office, requesting urgent assistance as she simply didn't have enough qualified staff to cope with the expected influx. Staff that volunteered and were trained at the start of the war, had long since disappeared to help nurse the wounded in France and Belgium. Briggs arriving on the door step, even in a limited capacity, was something of a godsend.

Briggs was met by an elderly porter, Arthur Jones, who had been persuaded out of retirement and was busy running the same sort of rackets he had for over thirty years as a porter at one of the larger London hospitals.

For a small fee he was happy to place bets for the incapacitated, as they were unable to do this for themselves. He was also happy to shop for personal items for the patients, and had come to an arrangement with some of the local merchants who were happy to produce a bill with a few extra pennies added on, in return for a slice of the profits.

Jones, escorted Briggs to an old creaking lift and pressed the button indicating they would be travelling to the third floor. As they stepped out into a long corridor, it became obvious that a previously unused area was in the process of being converted into a ward to receive the wounded. At the end of the corridor a considerably sized room ran the width of the building and was large enough to accommodate forty beds with ease. Several men were busy assembling iron bedsteads and placing heavy mattresses on them. The beds were then made with fresh sheets, by a couple of young looking VADs.

At one end of the room Matron Phillips was standing, sleeves rolled up, supervising the positioning of a grand piano. Seeing Briggs arrive she beckoned to her.

'We're almost finished here, Briggs. Off the main corridor are a series of rooms which we intend to set up to look after the seriously ill. They should all have a bed, linen and a bedside table in them. Can you please check them and report back letting me know what's needed?'

Matron Phillips said, before turning her attention to the men moving the piano.

By late afternoon the ward was prepared and additional beds were made; Bedford House was ready to receive men from the hospital trains arriving in rapid succession at Charing Cross Station. A procession of ambulances began to arrive in Bedford Square not long after five o'clock. The first few ambulances contained men capable of walking with relatively minor gunshot wounds. Under normal circumstances these men would have been treated at the nearest Casualty Clearing Station and would have convalesced in France before returning to their battalions, fit to re-join the fight. The sheer numbers of wounded, making their way off the battlefield in the first few days of the Battle of the Somme, changed that. First Aid Dressing Posts and Casualty Clearing Stations could not cope with the large numbers of wounded, so anyone that could be, was passed on down the line; until eventually they reached London and were sent to one of many hospitals, like Bedford House.

Briggs was starting to tire; her ankle ached from being constantly on the move, but she did not even contemplate going back to the welcoming respite of the servants' hall in Bedford Square. Most of the men arriving had not had their wounds looked at after the initial dressing was applied somewhere in France. They were all hungry, tired and anxious to let their families know they were wounded, but safe. Working in the methodical fashion she had been trained to, Briggs started sorting out the walking wounded one at a time. Many hours later she was tapped on the shoulder by Phillips who suggested she finish what she was doing and then get some much-needed rest, as she felt sure this was just the start and needed her fresh the following day.

***

Briggs arrived back at Lord and Lady Hadleigh's house just as Mrs Trent removed a kettle from the hob and poured boiling water into a large brown ceramic tea pot. Mr Buxton had removed his jacket and was sitting at the table in the servants' hall. Spread out in front of him was a map of France and the Somme; he was reading a newspaper trying to place the areas reported on by correspondents at the Front.

The newspapers were full of reports of fierce fighting around Albert, but spoke of a glorious allied victory, despite the sacrifice. It was too early for casualty figures to be published with any degree of accuracy, so they weren't published at all; for a few days at least, England and the Empire were happy in the knowledge that a decisive victory had been hard fought and won but were blissfully unaware of the appallingly high cost. Casualties which began as a trickle soon became a flood, with thousands and thousands needing treatment before the Battle of the Somme was finally declared over.

Almost every house in the country and its dominions was to be affected by the Battle of the Somme, with someone wounded or dead. In England's northern industrial towns, where men had been so keen to answer Kitchener's call, whole streets of men disappeared, killed on the first day of a battle that gained only a few miles of Somme mud.

The Pals Battalions that were left after the Battle of the Somme were merged, in an attempt to form a cohesive fighting force out of the remnants of those who had survived. Never again would men be recruited town by town to fight alongside each other; communities would suffer the effect of this one battle for decades, with a lack of men to marry and father children. A generation of women were destined to die spinsters, unable to find anyone of their own age to marry.

For Briggs, the Battle of the Somme marked the start of her return to the war and the colleagues she had come to love.

Chapter Thirteen

When the vision dies in the
dust of the market place,
When the light is dim,
When you lift up your eyes and cannot behold his face,
When your heart is far from him,
Know this is your War; in this your loneliest hour you
ride
Down the roads he knew;
Though he comes no more at night he will kneel at
your side
For comfort to dream with you.

May Wedderburn Cannan

July 1916 – The Somme

Major Gerald Hammond pulled the canvas sacking aside and walked down the stairs into the basement of the farmhouse, which was serving as Battalion headquarters. Sitting behind a roughly fashioned desk on a packing case, Colonel Chivers was attempting to write letters to the relatives of some of the men who had died on the first day of the offensive. The farmhouse was far too close to the Front to have many luxury fittings left; everything that could had been removed by the owners as they fled.

Hammond and Chivers were the only officers to have survived the initial assault on the German trenches several days before. Colonel Hugo Bannerman had climbed out of the trenches and led his men across no man's land, carrying the Union flag attached to a stick. He had immediately attracted fire from the trench opposite and collapsed forward into the mud, falling sideways, his sightless eyes staring up at the men passing him by. His men continued forward until most of them were also wounded or dead, some getting to within yards of the German front trenches, before being caught on the thick expanse of barbed wire protecting them.

The fighting had raged until darkness descended and it became too difficult to see the enemy. After jumping into the German trench, Hammond had gathered some men around him. Apart from Company Sergeant Major Lewis all other members of C Company seemed to have disappeared in the heat of the battle. Rapidly regrouping, Hammond had secured either end of the small piece of trench they had taken and had set about creating a safe area for them to continue to fight from.

It quickly became apparent why so many Germans had survived the barrage, which had rained down on them for over a week; the dugouts they had constructed were deep, with steps which turned at an angle. A Mills bomb thrown directly into a dugout was just as likely to explode half way down the stairs, leaving the men inside unharmed, but inflicting injury on the bomb aimer. Several Coldstream Guards were wounded after they thought they had cleared the dugouts of German life only to discover this was not the case.

With persistence, Hammond dug in and secured the position; several Germans were killed attempting to breach his defences. Overnight, machine guns fired sporadically. Very lights were fired upwards by both sides, to illuminate movement in no man's land. Eventually, he and his men were relieved and were able to slowly make their way back to the field they had left not so long before. When he arrived back at the farm, Hammond sat down and started to write a brief note by the light of an oil lamp. However tired he felt, Hammond was determined to let Margaret Brennan know he had survived the initial skirmish and was not wounded. After sending his batman to deliver his note to the railhead at Amiens, Hammond crawled into his camp bed intent on getting some rest.

The roll call the following day revealed the true extent of casualty numbers. Lewis had been injured when a Mills bomb he was throwing had hit the trench wall and exploded, throwing him backwards. A party of stretcher bearers had taken him to the Forward Dressing Station, where bits of shrapnel had been removed from his thigh and chest; heavily bandaged Lewis began the journey back to Blighty. For Lewis the road to recovery would be a long and arduous one with months of hospitalisation and rehabilitation ahead of him.

Chivers slowly read the roll call, most of the men from C Company were eventually accounted for; someone present having seen what happened to them, although a few had simply disappeared without a trace. It was to be several days before the last of the stragglers reached the farm and were crossed off the list of missing; it would be many months before factual casualty lists were able to be posted.

Hammond and Chivers had both been promoted almost as soon as they returned to the farm and established some kind of order. There were no senior officers left from the battalion, most having left headquarters determined not to miss the fight. A large proportion of non-commissioned officers had also been killed or wounded; leading to several companies being merged and men being promoted from the ranks, to create an effective fighting force. As Hammond and Chivers sifted through the lists of survivors they were both aware that within days they would be called on to relieve again in the front line, and that for the survivors the battle had only just started.

***

Captain Max Standish was starting to feel a little frustrated. The Battle of the Somme had started three weeks before and as yet showed no signs of being the decisive victory Allied Command expected. He and his men could be found living in tents, in the same field they had been living in for months; no closer to joining the fighting, but having to watch British soldiers marching off to relieve the front line every day. He and a few of his men had held the line just prior to the start of the main battle but had not been involved since and were beginning to wonder if they'd been forgotten.

Standish had seen his sister and Lady Julia only once during this time, although they were stationed quite close geographically. He and Lieutenant Marshall had walked to the Café Bleu early one evening for some supper; Victoria and Lady Julia had met them there, both looking exhausted.

Nursing the wounded in the initial stages of the battle had been hard work. The sheer volume of casualties in the first few days was incomprehensible, with some men taking hours and even days to arrive at the Forward Dressing Station; wounded at the very start of the battle. Work at the Forward Dressing Station was relentless. Major Chardingly operated for eighteen hours without a break on the first day and then pulled himself out of bed after only four hours sleep; to begin again when the build-up of wounded made it necessary.

During the first two weeks a pattern developed. Major Chardingly would operate until there were a few left to attend to and would then rest for four hours before starting again. Assisting him was Sister Standish and the padre who had been called to work as the anaesthetist. Between the three of them it was possible to operate on two patients at the same time, decreasing the length of time the wounded had to wait, but increasing the exhaustion they all felt. Standish was happy to be working in theatre as it gave her little time to think of where her brother was likely to be and if he was all right. It was to be almost two weeks before she discovered he was not involved in the initial assault and was safe behind the lines kicking his heels.

Max Standish nudged Marshall and stood up as his sister entered the Café Bleu with Lady Julia. He was happy to be snatching a meeting, but was not looking forward to telling them that his battalion was due to go into the trenches the following morning, as an attack had been planned on Pozieres. News was starting to filter through of an Australian led charge at Fromelles, where an attack had been launched with huge loss of life for very little gain. Standish had very little doubt that the fighting at Pozieres would be every bit as fierce and that many of the men he now called friends would die in the days to come.

'You look tired, Vic,' Standish commented. 'Was it awful?' he asked.

'Fairly grim,' Victoria responded. 'We've had so little sleep. The wounded just kept on coming, so we couldn't just stop and rest. We must have sent thousands through to the Casualty Clearing Station at Amiens, all of them so terribly badly wounded.' Victoria paused; seeing the expression on her brother's face, she quickly changed the subject.

'Anyway, let's not talk of the war; we've both got a glorious twenty-four hours before we return to Amiens. I plan a leisurely meal and then we're booked in to the Hotel Florence, which has the most divine baths. I feel as though its months since I was properly clean.'

'Sounds heavenly, let's start with a decent feed. Henri!' Standish called, nodding in the direction of an elderly waiter who was standing at the far corner of the room, behind the bar polishing glasses. 'A bottle of champagne, please.'

Over the next few hours it would have been possible to forget the war if not for the sound of the guns in the distance. As the evening wore on more tables filled with people desperate to inject some normality into their lives, in the short period of time they had left before war intervened. The piano was soon being played and popular songs were sung to the enjoyment of the people dining. As if by mutual agreement, aware that time was limited Captain Standish left the Café Bleu with Lady Julia to walk for a while, leaving Victoria and

Stanley Marshall to spend time alone. Somehow the war had managed to liberate some of the Victorian values held close by their parents' generation; making it possible to spend some time together without being chaperoned.

***

An old Roman road links the towns of Albert and Pozieres and then continues on to Bapaume. The Australians called on to fight in this area were barely able to pronounce the names, but were happy that at last they would be involved. The Australian Infantry Force veterans, who had been blooded at Gallipoli, wanted desperately to show the English that they were equal to the task before them.

The attack was planned for a little after midnight on July 23rd. The artillery had led with a sustained bombardment on the village of Pozieres, lasting for several days. It was hoped this would assist the Australians in attacking the town, which sat on top of a ridge of high country and was thought to be a difficult but achievable aim.

On the morning of the attack just after dawn the soldiers of C Company, along with the rest of the battalion paraded for one last time before their colonel; to be given last-minute orders and a few words of advice.

Captain Standish called his men to attention; stepping back from the hastily erected platform, he saluted Colonel Hathaway and stood to one side as he briefly addressed the troops.

'Men of the AIF, I am proud to have led you from Australia, fought with you at Gallipoli and trained with you here in France. In all of my years as a professional soldier I have never marched alongside such dedicated men. You have endured the sand, heat and flies of Egypt and the muddy, wet fields of France; already you have acquitted yourselves with honour. Australia is behind your efforts here in France and prays for her sons, that you may take up the fight for God, King and Country. My thoughts are with you all.' Hathaway then saluted quickly and left the parade.

Traffic out of Albert towards the front was heavy. The men marched in fours, singing until they got closer to the guns and could not be heard above them. Most men had additional kit on top of the heavy backpacks they carried, Standish carried a rifle and an extra water bottle; in London he had paid a trip to Bingley and Throckmorton and had bought extra pairs of warm socks as well as a more compact canteen with folding knife and fork.

As they marched towards the trenches, Major Smith-Barton could be seen riding up and down the line on a borrowed horse, shouting words of encouragement to his men. Despite the knowledge they were off to fight a bloody battle the mood was surprisingly good.

Closer to the line was a Company of Light Horse. Men were standing around with their horses waiting for the call to charge; most were disappointed that they had not really been involved in the war so far as both sides had dug in to trenches. The road ahead was straight and it was hoped that once the Australians had attacked the Light Horse would take care of the fleeing Germans. The aim was for the Australians to reach the Old German Lines, an area of two parallel trenches on the other side of the town, within the first few hours of the start of the battle.

Captain Standish and Lieutenant Marshall settled into a trench and shared a small tot of brandy just before the order to advance into no man's land was made. They were both lost in thought, thinking of home, which was half a world away and of the women they loved who were much closer. Each had given the other a letter in case they did not return, and in those few last moments was very conscious of their own mortality.

Once the order had been given, Standish and his company set off walking rapidly towards Pozieres. Under cover of darkness they drew less fire than they would otherwise have done, but several men were injured stumbling into potholes created by earlier shelling. Major Smith-Barton had managed to get rid of his horse and was jogging steadily towards the enemy trench to the right of Standish; Lieutenant Marshall was leading a group of men to his left, but gradually became separated from him. It was almost impossible to see what was happening, as the night was cloudy and no one wanted to light a flare; which would alert the Germans to the imminent attack.

The initial attack on the centre of the town ran smoothly. By morning the front-line German trench was mostly secured, with only a few pockets of fighting continuing. The right flank found advancing tougher, sustaining more casualties, but eventually they too achieved their goal.

The German trenches were impressive with substantial officers' quarters in the dugouts. It was immediately obvious that the German troops had retreated in a hurry. Half eaten plates of food were evident, as well as odd pieces of kit left lying around. In one corner, supplies of biscuits were neatly stacked alongside other non-perishable food. On a table next to an oil lamp stood a half full bottle of brandy; which if he hadn't needed his wits about him, Standish would have been tempted to take a swig out of.

Following Standish into the dugout Smith-Barton looked around and then sat down on an old packing crate.

'We need to spend some time regrouping,' he commented, 'Then we should be able to come up with a new plan of attack before first light. It's imperative we don't lose the advantage we've gained tonight.'

Looking round Standish noticed that Major Smith-Barton had been wounded. His arm was hanging uselessly at his side and there was a large patch of blood on the sleeve of his uniform jacket.

'Are you all right, sir?' he enquired.

'Yes, man, no need to fuss,' Smith-Barton responded. 'It's only a flesh wound. Perhaps you would be good enough to get hold of the field dressing in my pack and apply it.'

Standish did as requested and then, acknowledging that Smith-Barton was not about to seek medical attention, went with him to assess the situation and prepare for the morning.

C Company had secured several hundred metres of German trench, linking up with other AIF Companies who had also achieved their objective. Sitting on a fire step cleaning the muzzle of his rifle, Standish was relieved to see Lieutenant Marshall unharmed but very muddy. Standish was later to learn, that in the dark Marshall had stumbled into a large crater, caused by earlier shelling and rescued two men who were wounded early on; he had helped them both return to the Australian front line, dragging one from the mud, before continuing on.

The second phase of the battle for Pozieres began the following morning and lasted for several days. The fighting was bloody, with many soldiers who had survived the horror of Gallipoli losing their lives to gain a few yards of French soil; dying after the Germans launched a barrage, triggered by the initial Australian assault. Eventually the town of Pozieres was taken by the Allied Armies; but by the time this happened the town had ceased to exist, shelled to rubble in a German counter attack.

Stopping just short of the Old German Lines, Standish and his men dug in; preparing the area for the division relieving them.

July 1916 – Camden, New South Wales

Constance Standish stirred the large pot on top of the range and then turned to Agatha Marshall who had just arrived and was removing her hat and coat. Both women were concerned that it was now late July and they had not heard any news from the Western Front, although from reading the papers they knew a large-scale battle was being fought there.

'Good morning, Mrs Marshall, no news yet I take it?' Constance asked.

'No, I've just been down to the post office, because the train from town arrived an hour ago, but nothing yet. I had hoped by now there would be a letter for at least one of us,' Agatha replied. 'I sent to Sydney recently, to get a new pattern for a jumper that I want to knit for

Stanley, to keep him warm this winter; that has arrived, but no other news.'

'I'm surprised Victoria hasn't dropped anyone a line, really. She's usually so reliable. She must be busy looking after the wounded,' Constance responded. Turning to the large pot on the range, she than dipped a spoon in and tasted the stew she was preparing. 'This is just about done,' Constance said. 'Pass the pots from over by the sink, I'll fill them and then we'll allow it all to cool for a while,' she continued.

The stew which Constance Standish was preparing was destined for distribution to some of the labourers' wives living in Camden. The first flush of excitement when war was declared had long since gone and some families were beginning to experience the problems associated with the main breadwinner fighting a war half a world away. It was inevitable that some families were suffering financial hardship as a result; the Camden War Society set up to assist with comforts for the AIF, had recently turned its attention to the welfare of families who had men away fighting; the distribution of nourishing meals being a part of several initiatives agreed to by its members.

After Constance and Agatha had brewed and drunk a cup of tea, Constance called for Hector to help get the pony and trap ready. Until very recently, the stables to the rear of the house were looked after by a young groom and his father. Old Bill Reardon and his son Billy cared for the family horses and looked after the rest of the grounds surrounding the house; growing a variety of vegetables for consumption by the family. The call of war had finally affected Oakfield House, with both men enlisting at the recent Camden Show. Old Bill Reardon had lied about his age, before a recruiting sergeant who was keen to win points for enlisting the most men at the Show. Both had long since disappeared to the local AIF training camp, leaving Hector to look after his own horses.

Once the trap was loaded Constance and Agatha climbed in and started off in the direction of Camden. The day was sunny but cool, with a breeze blowing, which they felt all the more after leaving the warmth of the kitchen. Turning into the road, which would take them up past the hospital, they both noticed the Reverend Sharpe riding towards them. Constance pulled on the reigns bringing the pony and trap to a halt.

'Good morning Reverend Sharpe,' Constance called. In response the vicar applied the brakes to his bicycle and dismounted.

'I was on my way to Oakfield House to see you,' the Vicar replied. 'I have just received some dispatches from the Western Front, such sad news. The Hendersons have lost their son on the Somme. Mrs Randolph has lost her husband and the Goodwin boys are both missing believed killed.'

'That's terrible news,' Agatha gasped. 'We were on the way to see Mrs Randolph, as we thought some of the stew we have made might be needed there.'

'Take it anyway, Mrs Marshall. The family will be glad not to have to think of preparing meals at this time.' The Vicar responded. 'I'm just off to visit the Hendersons now and am not sure they have been told the news yet. Sometimes I think people must dread me arriving at their door.'

With a nod of his head the Reverend Sharpe re-mounted his bicycle and rode away from Camden, towards the Henderson's farm.

Chapter Fourteen

There's a rose that grows in no-man's land, And it's
wonderful to see, Tho' it's sprayed with tears It will
live for years
In my garden of memory, It's the one red rose the
soldier knows, It's the work of the Master's hand; In
the War's great curse, Stands the Red Cross nurse
She's the rose of no-man's land

Popular Song, World War One

August 1916 – London

Violet Briggs was worried about her family. Gladys, her sister, was working full time down at the Woolwich Arsenal making shells, which were desperately needed by the troops at the front. The Battle of the Somme had been raging for six weeks with no sign that either side was about to capitulate. The disastrous decision to make the men walk towards the enemy, killing wave after wave of British youth was somehow swept under the carpet, with no one shouldering the blame. The true scale of the slaughter was not immediately apparent as in the aftermath newspapers reported a glorious allied victory. Slowly it became obvious that almost every street in the land had suffered casualties; telegrams to wives and parents in England started to arrive almost immediately and continued for months.

Briggs arrived back in Bedford Square after a visit to her family. Her sister had been at home and Briggs was shocked to see she was bright yellow. Seeing her sister, she could understand why munitions workers were called 'canaries'; the sulphur used in shell-making had left its mark.

Briggs was concerned about the number of explosions which were reported frequently. She was worried her sister was doing such dangerous work and had gone home to see if she could persuade her to return to service, as friends of Lord and Lady Hadleigh were looking for an under house parlour maid. Her sister wouldn't entertain the suggestion as she was making a great deal of money and was not constrained by any of the restrictions inherent for a young maid in service.

For Briggs the visit to her family was the first since leaving them to return to Bedford Square in June. She had been fully occupied nursing the wounded from the Somme at Bedford House, with no time spare to visit. Train after train continued to arrive at Charing Cross every day. Some men did not survive the long journey from France and one or two died of wounds on the station concourse, while waiting to be allocated to a hospital. Hospitals in London and the Home Counties filled with the wounded, rapidly reaching capacity; soon it became necessary to send casualties further afield. After years of rolling bandages and kicking their heels VADs in the north of England were finally given real patients to practice their skills on.

Although exhausted, Briggs was finding the injuries she had sustained when the *Ariadne* sank were healing more each day. She had managed to abandon using a stick as she walked around the ward, finding she had gained confidence as time wore on. The dull ache which she had suffered for months had disappeared at last, making her less tired; she could sleep, without being woken by a throbbing pain in her ankle.

Coming out of the linen store Briggs could see Matron Phillips walking towards her.

'Good morning, Matron.'

Good morning, Briggs,' Phillips replied. 'I have been meaning to have a chat with you. How have you been managing with the influx of wounded?' she asked.

'It's been very tiring, ma'am. But I have been managing to get around without a stick and I don't think I'm limping as badly. I still take a stick with me outside, as the pavements are just so uneven,' Briggs replied.

'I suppose you will be thinking of going back out to France shortly? We have been very grateful for your help over the offensive; but I understand we were only ever going to have you working here while you became fit. If you need a reference from me, I will be happy to supply one,' Phillips continued.

'Thank you, ma'am, if a reference is not too much trouble I would appreciate that. I had planned to visit Devonshire House to discuss my future on my next afternoon off,' Briggs replied.

On the next day possible, Briggs finished work at lunch time and caught an omnibus the short distance to Devonshire House in Piccadilly. She had deliberately left her stick behind, not wishing to give anyone the impression she was not fully fit. In her hand she carried a very complimentary reference, written the previous evening by Matron Phillips.

Briggs had arranged an appointment with the sister in charge of recruitment for overseas service. Sister Marjorie Austin had served with distinction in the early stages of the war, working first in Belgium during the retreat from Mons and then later in Cairo. After witnessing first-hand, the shambles which seemed to occur whenever nurses' movement orders were issued, Austin had requested a posting to Devonshire House to attempt to inject some sense into the system. She now presided over several women who dealt with everyday requests from members of the VAD and was adept at sorting out postings with a minimum of fuss.

Briggs made a concerted effort to climb the steps into Devonshire House without limping. She was determined that she would be successful in applying for service in France without further delay; the last letter she had received from Lady Julia had outlined in detail how grim the situation was closer to the Front, and how desperately more nurses were needed.

Sitting behind a desk in the entrance hall was a formidable looking lady who glanced up briefly as Briggs entered and then bent her head to continue writing. After several minutes, she carefully blotted the communication and looked Briggs up and down.

'May I help?' she asked.

'Yes ma'am, I have an appointment with Sister Austin,' Briggs replied.

With a sigh, the lady stood up and muttering under her breath marched off in the direction of a corridor to the left of her desk. Briggs was unsure if she was meant to follow her, so in the end stayed where she was. A few minutes elapsed before the lady returned.

'Third door on the right, she'll see you now,' the lady said, before sitting back down and picking up her pen.

Briggs set off down the corridor, acutely aware that she was being watched and feeling a little embarrassed that the coat she was wearing was not of a slightly better quality. Knocking on the door, she then entered as requested.

Sister Austin was standing over by the window watching what was happening outside on the street; turning at the sound of the door opening she smiled and moved forward to shake Briggs by the hand.

'Nurse Briggs, I have very much wanted to meet a survivor from the *Ariadne*,' she said. 'I trust you have made a full recovery. We were all very distressed here, when we heard a hospital ship had sunk. I returned to England from Cairo about a month before it happened and was very aware of the danger to shipping, but to sink a hospital ship is unforgivable.'

'Thank you, Sister. I have recovered slowly,' Briggs replied. 'Recently I have been working at Bedford House, looking after the wounded from the Somme. Some have been horribly injured and need a lot of nursing. I have managed quite well and think I should be fit enough to return to France. Matron Phillips has given me a reference for you.'

'Thank you, Nurse. I shall see what we can do and will be in touch. Nurses are needed out there so desperately. I do not see a problem.'

***

Lord and Lady Hadleigh were enjoying a rare evening at the theatre together. London was in the grip of renewed Zeppelin fever with many people staying away from the centre of the city. At the end of July, over a couple of nights, an attack had been launched over the south-east; on the whole unsuccessful, but enough to frighten many Londoners into staying at home. The streets were deserted and although friends had made an effort to attend the gala opening night of the revue organised by Lady Hadleigh, disappointingly the theatre was not quite full.

Lord and Lady Hadleigh had booked their usual box at the Theatre Royal and were then planning a light supper at a restaurant in Soho with a number of their friends and members of the cast.

The evening had been a roaring success with a large amount of money raised for the comfort of wounded troops; after a pleasant evening meal they had returned to Bedford Square, only to find the household awake and in a state of excitement. Major Gerald Hammond had returned from the Front unexpectedly and was waiting in the drawing room sipping on a glass of brandy.

'Gerald it's so good to see you. When did you arrive?' Lady Hadleigh asked.

'On the leave train this evening, Mama,' Hammond responded. 'They've sent me for staff officer training, apparently the Somme took care of everyone capable of doing a staff job at battalion level, so they are keen to train me. I was not happy about being pulled away from the men, but a few weeks in England are very much appreciated, I can tell you.'

'It's good to have you home for a while,' Lord Hadleigh replied. 'I hope once you are settled and have caught up with everyone you wish to, you will do me the honour of joining me for luncheon at my club. There are many acquaintances there who will want to talk to a man who has been so close to the offensive.'

Hammond was exhausted after days spent on his guard in the trenches unable to sleep for any prolonged period of time. Immediately he arrived home he removed his worn, dirty uniform and asked Buxton to arrange for it to be cleaned. He then put on a second newer uniform, which felt soft and clean and did not smell of a combination of sweat and cordite.

He intended to see his tailor first thing in the morning; lately young officers posted to the Front were wearing a newer style of service dress, with their rank attached to epaulettes on the shoulders, instead of on the sleeves. In Hammond's opinion this was a sensible change. Along with carrying a rifle instead of his service revolver, the change made it harder for enemy snipers to pick off officers as they crossed no man's land.

Hammond had come home with a list of items, which he needed to purchase, either to make his own life or that of his fellow officers easier, during the long weary hours spent in the front line. A visit to Bingley and Throckmorton was planned to pick up several items he had been asked for. He needed to buy a greatcoat with a shorter skirt; the current design being long enough to become encrusted with mud as soon as it started to rain. At the risk of being charged with damaging military property, several of the men hacked off the bottom section of their greatcoats with a knife, to decrease the weight of the coat, which could be considerable in wet weather. Stories were rife of men who, hampered by the weight of their greatcoats, were unable to move quickly around no man's land and had paid the ultimate price as sitting ducks.

A week after his return home, Hammond reported for staff officer training. Unhappy that he was away from Margaret Brennan he was determined to complete the course in as little time as possible; he wanted to return to France and continue the strange life he was leading there, which although dangerous was where he felt most useful. His leave had been a frustrating one. Increasingly as the week wore on and he was asked to accompany his parents to meet various London dignitaries, Hammond was struck by the unrealistic view of the war held by many. A number of his father's friends appeared either unwilling or unable to believe the campaign on the Somme had been a disaster. Some still believing that a slow walk towards the enemy was a reasonable military tactic.

As the week wore on, Hammond became increasingly more withdrawn as it was apparent that everyone in London had become an expert, with set opinions on how the war should be fought and won, without ever setting foot on the Western Front.

Brennan, for her part, was happy that Hammond was safe for the time being and she could continue working without worrying that he may be injured or killed in the fierce fighting; which did not seem to have lessened for months now.

September 1916 – Near Amiens

Lieutenant Guy Hadleigh was colder than he thought he had ever been and wondered how he would manage in winter. His squadron had taken off earlier in the morning and after dodging the guns had flown deep into enemy territory, intent on a reconnaissance mission to assess movement behind the German lines.

The squadron had flown in formation until they reached the German lines and were fired at from below. B Squadron was led by Captain Rochford, with Hadleigh flying on his wing. Early on the squadron lost Lieutenant Fitzgibbons who flew far too low over no man's land and was hit by a stray shot from the trenches below. The shot caused a considerable amount of damage to his left wing, which buckled causing the plane to start to spin and then stall. With the War Office refusing to acknowledge that the RFC should be equipped with parachutes Fitzgibbons went down with his plane, crashing into the ground just behind enemy lines.

Hadleigh considered he was lucky, if not blessed, as he had survived beyond the average lifespan of a new pilot in the RFC. He had seen a number of his squadron die, and still more simply hadn't returned from flying.

Once a pilot was gone an auction was held for their possessions; after which tradition dictated they were not mentioned again.

Captain Rochford always spent some time writing to the family of the pilot to point out how brave they had been and how much they were likely to be missed. He did this alone in the Squadron Office, with a glass of malt whisky at his side.

Osborne had been assigned permanently as Hadleigh's observer, much to his delight. They both shared common friends in London and had attended the same school. Recently they had started to spend the majority of their time off together, enjoying the food, wine and young French ladies at the Café Bleu; Hadleigh had persuaded his father to ship across his motorcycle, giving him mobility; unlike the majority of the squadron who had to beg a lift from the maintenance truck if they wished to go into town.

Osborne straightened up from leaning over the side of the cockpit, where he had been taking reconnaissance photographs. Half turning in his seat he waved to indicate that he was happy with the photographs and it was all right to head for home. Looking around the sky Hadleigh was able to see that other members of the squadron were also turning to fly back, having completed the required task.

The attack when it came was unexpected, with the German planes taking advantage of the sun. Three

Albatross D1 aircraft suddenly appeared behind Hadleigh settling on his tail. The first bullets from their machine guns strafed the side of the Sopwith 1 ½ Strutter, creating several holes in the canvas, but fortunately missing Hadleigh and his observer; Hadleigh pulled hard on the control column causing the Sopwith to rise sharply, he then manoeuvred the plane diving away to the left. A fierce dogfight ensued as other planes from B Squadron became aware of the German presence and arrived to help Hadleigh escape.

With every possible manoeuvre he could think of, Hadleigh spent several minutes throwing the Sopwith around the sky to try and shake off the Albatrosses. Eventually he emerged high above the clouds, with the sun behind him. It appeared that he had been successful as there were no German aircraft anywhere near. Osborne recovered quickly from the excitement and took over the watch for Germans, allowing Hadleigh to fly the plane. Within seconds he was gesticulating wildly and pointing below, to where the three planes were flying together, creeping up on Rochford and Horton who were oblivious to the danger.

Diving towards the first Albatross, Osborne concentrated on capturing the German plane in his gun sights. Waiting until the very last minute possible, he then let out a burst of fire from the machine gun mounted in front of him. The result was spectacular with some of the bullets piercing the engine cowling of the

German plane, which then burst into flames. Hadleigh watched as the stricken plane fell rapidly, spiralling into a fatal spin before hitting the ground.

Before either man had time to become complacent about this victory, Hadleigh became aware of an altered engine tone, which seemed to indicate that perhaps they had not escaped damage from the Albatross earlier. Almost immediately the plane's engine began to stutter, sounding as though it might stall; a trail of black smoke could be seen pouring from the engine. Hadleigh looked below to see where they were. No man's land could be seen snaking away into the distance; rapid assessment showed they were on the British side of the trenches and within range of several fields which appeared flat with only a few trees.

Hadleigh managed to steer towards the fields, coming in low over some tall hedges, before the engine stalled. The landing was bumpy, with the plane bouncing several times before the right wheel got caught in a rut bringing the plane to an abrupt halt; the wing immediately crumpled causing the plane to flounder in the mud. Hadleigh and Osborne quickly unbuckled their harnesses and jumped clear, running away from the plane before it burst into flames.

With nothing left to salvage the two men walked to the nearest main road and on into the nearest town. They had crashed not far from Albert and were able to persuade a transport officer they met to arrange for their return to the chateau.

***

Sister Brennan was feeling pleased with herself. She felt that after the hell of the last two months she had earned a rest and was planning to take one soon. Shortly after midnight the day before, she had arrived on an empty train at the railhead in Amiens; she was expecting to take on some of the hundreds of wounded who had been lined up waiting on their stretchers for several hours. After transporting them either to Calais or Le Havre, she planned to spend a couple of days in an upmarket hotel, sleeping, eating decent food and of course bathing.

With the train waiting in the station, Brennan expected to supervise the loading of the wounded so was surprised to be summoned to see the station transport officer instead.

'Ah, do come in, Sister; I have a small proposition for you,' Major Creswell said. 'How would you feel about taking your days off in London?' We may even be able to arrange a couple of extra days, if that would suit?' he added. 'I need you to accompany a wounded man to London.'

Brennan was delighted to accept the proposition, after it was explained she would be nursing a staff officer, wounded in some heavy isolated fighting a couple of days previously.

General Sir Peter Rushworth was a valued tactician, brought in by the War Office to attempt to organise the British Army, which was in disarray after the attack on the Somme; he had unfortunately sustained shrapnel wounds to the leg and abdomen while inspecting a forward listening post. It was thought that he stood more chance of survival if he was rapidly evacuated from France; arrangements were made for a distinguished surgeon to be waiting at St Thomas's Hospital in London, ready to operate.

General Rushworth was loaded onto the train after everyone else was settled. Brennan carried out an initial assessment as the train started to move slowly away from the station, making sure he was comfortable for the first part of the journey. Rushworth's bandages were bloodied but dry. Brennan made the decision not to disturb the bandage on his thigh, as it looked to have contained the bleeding and she did not want him to haemorrhage if she disturbed it. The abdominal bandages were a different matter though. They had been hastily applied and had small amounts of serous fluid flecked with blood oozing through. The bandages had been applied quickly with little thought given to the dirt surrounding the wound.

If she was to prevent infection, or worse gas gangrene, Brennan knew she needed to clean and redress the wound. Standing up and swaying to the motion of the train, Brennan made her way to the small treatment area at the end of the carriage. Looking up, she was surprised to see Major Chardingly standing at the door watching her.

'How is he, Sister?' Chardingly enquired. 'I've agreed to accompany you to London; we need to try to get the general there alive.'

'I'm glad you're here, sir,' Brennan responded. 'I think his thigh is all right and we should leave those dressings, but I'm very worried about the abdominal wounds. Perhaps you would be good enough to help me take the dressings down?' she continued.

In response, Chardingly took off his uniform jacket and hung it on a nail behind the treatment room door. After rolling up his sleeves he started to sort through some of the instruments Brennan handed to him and then set off towards the patient.

Carefully removing the dressings which had been applied many hours before, Brennan held a lamp while Chardingly looked into the abdominal wound; grabbing a pair of forceps he started to probe around until eventually he triumphantly lifted out a large jagged piece of shrapnel.

'Getting rid of this should make him feel better, Sister,' he commented. 'Can you draw up some morphia? No more than ¼ of a grain, to help him rest,' Chardingly added.

Brennan administered the morphia and then settled down for the long night ahead. She had been ordered to take sole care of the general on the trip across and felt a little guilty that her colleagues would be working so hard caring for the rest of the wounded, in carriages on the other side of the treatment area.

Major Chardingly remained for the first few hours of the journey, sitting in the treatment area at a small desk, writing notes. Throughout the war he had kept a diary of his day-to-day experiences hoping that if he did not survive, the diary may be a lasting reminder of the horror he had encountered.

In the end the journey passed without incident. On arrival at Charing Cross Station an ambulance was parked on the platform. With some very careful manoeuvring, General Sir Peter Rushworth was taken from the train and loaded into the waiting ambulance, which then sped off in the direction of St Thomas's. Sister Brennan remained on the platform, having agreed earlier with Major Chardingly that he would accompany Rushworth, allowing her to surprise Gerald Hammond with her sudden return to England.

Chapter Fifteen

*They were summoned from the hillside, they were
called in from the glen,
And the country found them ready at the stirring call
for men.
Let no tears add to their hardships, as the soldiers
pass along,
And although your heart is breaking, make it sing this
cheery song:
Keep the Home Fires burning,
While your hearts are yearning,
Though your lads are far away they dream of home.
There's a silver lining, through the dark clouds
shining, Turn the dark cloud inside out, 'till the boys
come home.*

Popular Song World War One

October 1916 – France

Violet Briggs checked again to make sure her suitcase
was secured in the luggage rack and then sat down next
to the window of the railway carriage. The train was not
due to depart for over half an hour, but terrified of
missing it, she had insisted she was brought to the

249

station in plenty of time. Her movement orders had been hand delivered by Sister Austin the previous week; she was to travel by train to Amiens and re-join her colleagues from Lemnos, at the Casualty Clearing Station they had set up. The week had gone swiftly with a last shift to be worked at Bedford House, before preparing for the journey. Briggs had paid a visit to Salmons and purchased the items required on a uniform list given to her by Devonshire House. She was wearing a new coat on top of her VAD uniform, paid for by Lady Hadleigh, who was proud of the way she had recovered from her injuries sustained earlier in the year and did not appear daunted by the ordeal.

Briggs was pleased that after so many months recuperating she had been passed fit for a return to active service and was on her way to the Western Front. She realised in the long months at home that she not only missed the camaraderie but also missed the nursing, seeing soldiers bought in from the battlefield, looked after by her and leaving for home gave an immense feeling of satisfaction; knowing in some small way she had contributed to their recovery.

Briggs only regret was that she would not be around to take her sister in hand. She was unhappy that she continued to work at the Woolwich Arsenal in the munitions factory and that she would not be there to try and influence her decision to move jobs. Her sister had recently been promoted to supervisor and had lost some of her yellow pallor, as she no longer handled the sulphur used to make the bombs. Bomb making was a dangerous business though and several of her friends had been injured in minor explosions. With London experiencing an increased number of Zeppelin raids, there was a real concern that along with the real danger of working in such a place, munitions factories were also a target for German bombs.

Looking out of the window Briggs could see activity on the platform was increasing as the train's departure time approached. A couple of elderly looking colonels with red tabs indicating their status as staff officers strode past, followed by two railway porters, wheeling a mountain of kit after them. Stopping a couple of carriages away they entered the train, barking orders to the porters as they did so.

Although still early in the afternoon, Briggs could see several of Lady Hadleigh's friends, dressed in evening clothes, handing out cups of tea and cigarettes to soldiers waiting to board the train. Over on platform eight it was apparent that a hospital train was expected. Stretchers were piled at one end of the platform; ready to replace those taken off the train once it arrived. Ambulances had begun to pull up and were forming a queue; the drivers gathering in groups for a smoke while they waited. Briggs knew that the hospital train would not be allowed to enter the station before the leave train she was on departed; to avoid frightening troops leaving for the Front for the first time.

Briggs watched the station master step onto the platform with his flag and whistle. After a few short blasts on his whistle to indicate the train was about to depart, he began to walk rapidly toward the front of the train. Seconds before he got there the door to her carriage was flung open; Briggs looked round to see a young lady dressed in the uniform of the Australian Army Nursing Service throwing her bags into the carriage, before climbing in after them. Briggs closed the carriage door and then helped stow the bags before sitting down opposite the woman.

'Hello! My name is Daisy McMaster; I didn't think I would make this train,' the woman gasped.

'You certainly look flustered, Sister, is everything all right?' Briggs asked. Uncapping a flask, she poured some lemonade into a cup and handed it across to McMaster, who drank quickly before replying,

'I got caught up on the way to the station. There was a lorry which had crashed into an omnibus on the Tottenham Court Road; I think the omnibus driver had a heart attack at the wheel, because he was dead by the time I got to him. Some of the passengers on the top deck were badly injured, so I felt I needed to stay until ambulances arrived.'

As she finished speaking the train suddenly jerked and with a screech of wheels began to build up momentum as it left the station; neither woman had heard the final shrill whistle blasts which announced the train's departure.

'You must have some more lemonade, Sister. If you are hungry, I have some biscuits that cook made in case I became hungry on the journey. I've heard it's such a tedious trip!' Briggs offered the flask to McMaster.

'Where are you posted to?' McMaster asked. 'A friend of mine from back home is working close to Amiens and I have orders to join her. At least someone I know will be there to show me the ropes,' she added.

'It looks as though we are bound for the same place, Sister. I also know people there. We all survived the sinking of the hospital ship *Ariadne* at the beginning of the year. It took me a little longer to recover than most because I broke my ankle jumping into the sea.' Briggs began to look distressed as she recalled the events in the Mediterranean. 'To tell you the truth I am a little anxious about crossing the Channel today. I have not been near the sea since I was pulled out of it,' she continued.

The journey to Dover was punctuated with frequent stops for prolonged periods, mostly for no apparent reason. Unusually, the train was fairly empty. Briggs and McMaster were the only people in their small section of carriage, but could hear the sound of men talking beyond. Briggs was nervous and as the train crept towards Dover she tried to quell her fears by talking about mutual friends with Sister McMaster.

As the train drew into Dover Station, McMaster could see Briggs was becoming a little more anxious at the prospect of boarding the leave ship for the voyage across to Calais. German submarines were still active in the area and although no boats had been sunk in the English Channel recently, there had been plenty of activity in the North Sea.

Summoning a young porter, McMaster took control; she supervised the loading of their trunks onto a trolley and then led the way up the gangway. Briggs seemed to hesitate at first, looking around as though wishing to make her escape; but tapping into some deep inner reserve, with a sharp intake of breath she lifted her skirt and strode up onto the deck.

Once they left the confines of Dover Harbour a slight breeze blew up causing the boat to roll a little; but on the whole the crossing was uneventful. Briggs soon discovered she did not like being inside but felt better looking at the sea; both women spent the crossing on the upper outside deck, retiring inside only when they were about to disembark. Briggs was grateful she had met someone prepared to sacrifice the warmth inside to remain with her.

December 1916 – France

As she walked over to the wood-burning stove Sister Blackstone thought the weather was far too cold to be living in a tent; opening the door of the cast iron wood burner she added another log to the fire. The ground outside was frozen as overnight temperatures had dropped to below zero two weeks previously and showed no sign of changing for the better. The winter sun struggled to melt the frost each morning, making the ground treacherous to walk on; the previous evening a sister working over in the medical area had slipped and broken her arm, when hurrying to the dispensary. Matron Gillespie posted several warnings asking her staff to be careful, but acknowledged privately with a certain degree of pride, that concern for the wounded often caused her staff to act in haste.

Blackstone picked up the latest copy of *Women at War*; a magazine dedicated to nurses and other women serving overseas. Although a little trite and written by people clearly not on the front line, it was nice to be able to spend an afternoon away from the wounded, with her mind otherwise engaged. Blackstone intended to occupy her time with a cup of hot tea and her magazine.

The Casualty Clearing Station had recently moved to a village school, long since abandoned by the fleeing French, who did not think it safe to remain. The school was far more comfortable for the wounded than the tented area they had all worked in during the summer months; with space to set up proper wards and store supplies. Although the school was substantially sized, the area was not large enough to accommodate the nursing staff as well as the wounded. The nursing staff still lived in large tents erected in the grounds. A recent campaign, fought in the newspapers by Lady Hadleigh and several other influential society mothers had led to a slight improvement in the quality of their accommodation.

The scandalous conditions nurses were forced to endure in France had come to national attention after two nurses died of pneumonia attributed to the freezing temperatures. Boards had been laid, creating paths between the tents, so the nurses themselves were less likely to suffer from injuries bought about by the icy conditions. An area had been set aside as a lounge, with a wood-burning stove and comfortable chairs for them to use in their off-duty hours. Although minor, the improvements had a marked effect on morale; as the nurses realised that they were not forgotten back home.

Sitting down and taking a sip of her tea, Blackstone soon became engrossed in an article complaining of conditions for nurses and comparing the relative merits of two types of vanity chest. Available from Salmons, they contained hard to come by items, such as soap and perfume. The article suggested that relatives of nurses on the Western Front should buy a chest, to bring a little luxury into their lives. Blackstone intended to send her elder sister the article once she had finished with it.

The tent flap opened letting in a draft of icy cold air. Stamping her feet as she entered, Victoria Standish walked over to the wood-burning stove to where the teapot was and poured a cup. Choosing an empty seat as close to the stove as she could, she spoke to Blackstone.

'I cannot believe how cold it is in this country.'

Blackstone lowered her magazine and thought before replying. 'I suppose you are not used to it,' she replied. 'It may still get colder though. We haven't really seen too much snow this winter,' she added. 'At least we're not in the trenches, fighting in puddles of water. That's something to thank God for.'

Standish picked up a spare magazine, becoming engrossed in a crossword puzzle, a relatively new form of relaxation, which was rapidly becoming her main escape from the chaos occurring around her.

After ten very satisfying minutes, Standish quickly finished her tea and stood up. 'I must get back. There are several young men who need dressings doing and a number of men to get ready for evacuation. Enjoy the rest of your afternoon.'

***

Recently the Casualty Clearing Station had seen a marked increase in the number of soldiers presenting with trench foot. The weather had changed suddenly, becoming much colder; this combined with the freezing puddles found all over the trenches meant men often stood knee-deep in cold water for hours on end. Although all of them carried a spare pair of dry woollen socks, most were reluctant to sit down in the cold weather and change them; dreading the necessary exposure of cold wet feet to the freezing air. The damage they were doing to their feet was often not apparent until they finally removed their socks back at their rest area after leaving the front line.

Trench foot started in soldiers' feet, which looked white and swollen and to begin with were completely numb. As the feet warmed up, feeling returned, causing excruciating pain. As the disease progressed the feet became red and hot to touch; the symptoms then spread to the lower legs. Sister Blackstone and her VADs had become masters at looking after trench foot, often managing to save toes and whole limbs from amputation.

Lady Julia Hadleigh had been dressing the wounds of soldiers presenting with trench foot for several days. She was tired, but not at the same point of exhaustion she had been at during the Battle of the Somme. As autumn turned to winter the fighting had lessened; with both sides preparing for the long winter months. The nearby English and Australian troops were determined to make the trenches they were in as comfortable as possible and were more concerned with this than killing the enemy. After months of constant work, the Casualty Clearing Station was experiencing a lull in activity, giving the nursing staff a welcome break and an opportunity to take in their surroundings. Away from the fighting the countryside was very pretty, dotted with villages unaffected by the war.

Hadleigh wheeled a trolley to the storage area at the back of the ward. She needed to replenish supplies of cotton wool, 1% picric acid solution and paraffin wax; all three being standard treatment for trench foot. Sister Standish was away at the dispensary obtaining further hypodermic injections to guard against tetanus, which seemed to accompany the disease in many cases.

Hadleigh re-entered the ward and wheeled her trolley to the first bed. Sergeant Murphy was a career soldier with the Coldstream Guards and had been admitted the night before after spending two weeks in the pouring rain in trenches near Beaumont Hamel. Both of his feet were badly affected by trench foot and had gone from being cold and lifeless with no feeling, to causing severe pain within the last few hours. Hadleigh was hopeful that Murphy would eventually recover and that by careful nursing his feet could be saved from amputation. As Hadleigh approached the bed she let out a squeal of delight, as standing next to Murphy's bed was her brother.

Hadleigh had not seen her brother for several weeks. Completing the staff officer training course, Major Hammond had been posted to headquarters to work as a strategic planner. After several years of fighting with a group of men who had become friends, he was not happy that he no longer shared the same day-to-day living conditions and was relatively safe behind the lines.

Headquarters had been set up several miles away and although close enough to hear the shelling was safe from any German attack. Major Hammond found it tiresome to be working with a group of staff officers who didn't really appreciate the depravation and hardship suffered by men in the trenches on a daily basis.

Looking up as Lady Julia approached, Major Hammond spoke.

'Julia! It's so good to see you. I've spoken to Matron and she has agreed it's all right for you to come out to lunch and spend the afternoon with me.'

Julia grinned before replying, 'That sounds really good. I can't remember when I last had a decent meal. I am due for an afternoon off; give me half an hour to finish here and change into something a bit cleaner and we'll go.'

I thought maybe a quick trip to the Café Bleu would be good? It's so long since I last saw you. I'm sure there's lots to catch up on.'

Lady Julia and her brother had just been seated for luncheon and were scanning menus when they heard the sound of a number of aeroplanes overhead.

'It sounds very busy up there,' Lady Julia commented. 'I wonder if Guy is involved. I have not seen him for absolutely ages. He spends so much time flying.'

'I should say so,' Hammond responded. 'He's been flying every day the weather is good enough. The squadron has taken a battering recently; I think several of his colleagues have been killed, some as soon as they arrived from England. Young Guy is becoming something of a veteran.' As he finished speaking the distant sound of several explosions could be heard, causing most diners present to stop speaking in mid-conversation. Whatever had just been bombed, it sounded serious.

Violet Briggs and Victoria Standish were doing a dressing round when their world came crashing down around them. The first bomb the German plane dropped hit the storeroom Lady Julia had been collecting stock from not long before. The blast reduced the corridor to rubble and destroyed everything in the immediate area. On the ward, Briggs and Standish had just finished massaging Sergeant Murray's feet with oil and were looking at how red and swollen they were. Between themselves they were trying to decide if wrapping his feet in cottonwool would be of any benefit, or would simply induce more pain. The force of the blast from the corridor blew them both off their feet; both lost consciousness momentarily.

Sister Blackstone almost spilled her tea at the sound of the first explosion. Although she was used to loud bangs, having spent the early part of the Battle of the Somme at a Forward Dressing Station, nothing could have prepared her for the sight which greeted her as she left her tent. Several bombs dropped from the German planes flying overhead had devastated the hospital. The main ward block and storage areas had been reduced to piles of rubble. Blackstone started to run towards the area, not sure of what she would find.

The smoke and brick dust woke Standish first. Opening her eyes and looking around she was able to make out what she thought were the soles of Briggs' shoes. They both appeared to be lying in a small cavity created by the iron bedstead Sergeant Murray had been lying on; which had saved them from being crushed when the roof fell in. Briggs also woke quickly and sat up dazed.

'Are you all right, Briggs?' Standish asked.

'Yes, Sister, I don't think I've broken anything,' was the muffled response.

Looking around it was possible to see a shaft of light penetrating the rubble. Within minutes, Standish could hear Sister Blackstone ordering stretcher bearers to start digging and within a short period of time she and Briggs were dragged from the rubble.

***

Captain Max Standish was sat in the adjutant's office at the farmhouse, completing some of the endless amounts of paperwork that seemed vital to staff officers at headquarters, when he heard planes overhead. Stepping outside, he looked up to see a dog fight occurring high above the fields to the left. The German planes involved were obviously trying to distract the British planes from several bombers flying at a steady pace towards their objective.

As he watched, one of the British Sopwith's attached itself to the tail of an Albatross and chased it across the sky, guns firing rapidly until they found their mark. The stricken Albatross fell, smoke streaming from its tail; then started to spin faster and faster until it ran out of sky and crashed into the fields beyond. The RFC pilot turned his attention to the remaining Albatross which was poised to strike another Sopwith and was so intent on the kill it failed to notice him creeping up behind.

Standish could not help wondering if Lady Julia's brother was involved in the fight, as he knew he was stationed close by and had been flying in the area since the Battle of the Somme earlier in the year. By all accounts, young Guy Hadleigh had started to make a name for himself, with half a dozen confirmed kills, and so far only one occasion where it had been necessary to ditch the plane.

Standish had not yet met Guy Hadleigh, despite courting his sister, but hoped to meet at the Café Bleu soon. Recently he had been sent to attend a number of training courses and had been away from the area for a considerable period of time. After the intense fighting at Pozieres during August the Australian Imperial Force was in disarray, needing to regroup. Colonel Hathaway had been declared missing during the battle as had Captain Crowley. Both men were almost certainly dead, but as no one was able to confirm their deaths, they remained on the list of missing men; a list which had grown steadily over the summer months.

Standish missed them both; after serving with them on the Gallipoli Peninsula earlier in the war. Much that he had learnt about the art of soldiering had come from Captain Crowley. Standish wondered if he would be able pass on the skills he had learnt to a new group of soldiers due out from Fremantle any day soon.

In consideration of his length of service, time in the trenches and VC, Standish had recently been summoned to headquarters and asked if he wished to return to Australia to assist with recruitment. The Australian Army had suffered heavy losses at Pozieres and new blood was desperately needed.

After the first frenzied burst of recruiting at the start of the war the number of men volunteering had decreased and was now only a trickle. For some time, the government had been concerned about the number of fresh troops available to replace those wounded on the Western Front. Recently the country had been asked to vote to conscript all young men of a suitable age, who were not already performing a service vital to the war effort.

Standish had politely declined the offer to become a roving ambassador, wishing to remain with his company fighting in France.

Standish stood up and stretched. The dogfight was long since over, but he had been lost in thought wondering how his parents were managing without him or his sister at home. He hoped his father was managing to keep the farm running and his mother did not spend too much time worrying about him and his sister. Taking one last look at the empty sky above him, Standish started to walk back inside. In the doorway he almost collided with the orderly room corporal who had been sent to find him.

'Sir, the Hun has bombed the hospital,' he exclaimed breathlessly. 'I haven't heard how many casualties there are, but the building has collapsed and help is needed to pull people out of the rubble.'

Chapter Sixteen

*Lord, who once born your own Cross shoulder high to
save mankind, help us to bear our Red Cross banner
high with clean hands unafraid.
To those who tend the wounded and sick give health
and courage, that they of their store, may give to those
who lie awake in pain with strength and courage gone.
Teach us no task can be too great, no work too small,
for those who die or suffer pain for us and their
Country. Give unto those who rule a gentle justice and
a wisely guiding hand, remembering "Blessed are the
Merciful." And when Peace comes, grant neither deed
nor word of ours has thrown a shadow on the Cross,
nor stained the flag of England*

Rachel Crowdy, Commandant VADs France

Christmas 1916 – France

A few days previously the hospital had suffered
substantial damage after being hit in a German bombing
raid; despite the large red crosses painted on the roof.
Following the disaster, the surviving wounded had been
moved and the hospital temporarily de-commissioned
as the damage was too large to continue to effectively

care for the wounded. Most of the nursing and medical staff were sent on local leave while preparations were made to repair the damaged buildings and produce an operational hospital.

Victoria Standish and Violet Briggs had both been exceptionally lucky. The bombs which hit the hospital did not land directly in the ward area where they were attending dressings, but had landed in the storeroom on the other side of the building. The ensuing blast caused walls to collapse, killing several nursing staff and some of the wounded. Briggs and Standish had been thrown sideways and were safe in a cavity created by remnants of a bedstead which protected them from the falling rubble. Sergeant Murphy was not so lucky, as he was crushed beneath a wall which collapsed. Apart from an understandable amount of shock at what had happened and a few minor cuts and bruises, Briggs and Standish survived the bombing unharmed.

Once the dead were accounted for, it was recorded that one hundred and twenty-three wounded had been killed, along with nine of the nursing staff caring for them. Amongst the dead was Sister Daisy McMaster, who was killed when the main hospital corridor collapsed, as she rushed to theatres to assist operating on casualties from an earlier attack on the front line.

Standish was devastated to hear this news; it seemed such a long time since Kelly had died during the Gallipoli Campaign and even longer since the three women had shared the night shift at Victoria Barracks in Sydney. She was suddenly very aware that she was the only survivor out of the three nurses who had left Australia so full of hope and excitement for the journey ahead. Australia felt like a faraway dream; recently she had begun to wonder if the war would ever end and if she would return to the peace and tranquillity of Camden.

The funerals of the nursing staff that died took place in the early evening. Soldiers of the Coldstream Guards, who were resting away from the Front, formed an honour guard, supporting the coffins as they were carried to an orchard at the back of the hospital where permission had been granted to bury the dead. The mournful notes of the Last Post rang out as surviving medical and nursing staff bowed their heads, acutely aware of the sacrifice their colleagues had made.

As each coffin was lowered into the mass grave Padre Bertram North moved forward, preparing to address the men and women present.

'I believe we should take time to reflect awhile,' he started. 'These nurses we have lowered to their rest were brave women. From all walks of life and from the Dominions they came, to serve their King and take care of our soldiers engaged in the defence of the realm. Repeatedly, we have seen them sacrifice comfort and safety to tend to the wounded. It was inevitable that eventually some would pay the ultimate price and lay down their lives. Let us leave here clear in our minds that the greatest memorial to their sacrifice we can offer, is to carry on the fight for God, King and Country, ceasing only when the battle is won, secure in the knowledge that these your colleagues did not die in vain.'

As the padre concluded his address Matron Gillespie moved forward and on behalf of the nursing staff dropped a handful of earth into the grave. The nursing staff then made their way slowly back down the hill to the tented area they were living in, determined to heed the padre's words and continue to come to the aid of the sick and wounded.

Christmas 1916 – Camden, New South Wales

Hector Standish stood up and mopped the sweat from his brow. The day was a hot one with almost no breeze, making it hard work cleaning out the stables.

The war had brought about changes to the lives of everyone in Australia. Although conscription had never been introduced, by the end of 1916 there was a lack of young men working on farms and apprenticed to other trades.

The Camden District had lost a number of men during the Gallipoli Campaign and still more during the Battle of the Somme. It would take almost a generation before the youth of Australia could be found in the same numbers as before 1914. For Hector Standish this translated into a lack of assistance around his property, which was why he found himself cleaning out the stables prior to making the trap ready to take Constance into Camden for the Christmas Day service.

Only two days previously, Hector and Constance had been delighted to receive a letter from Victoria. The letter was full of news from the Front describing their rather strange day-to-day lives. Victoria had announced, rather casually Constance thought, that she believed she was in love with Stanley Marshall; who had recently been promoted to captain and was away on one of the endless training courses that seemed to accompany quiet periods in the trenches. The letter also hinted that her brother Max had found romance and was courting an English Lady. Constance Standish was excited at the prospect of imparting this news to Mrs Marshall when they met at St John's Church later in the day.

Harnessing a horse to the trap, Hector Standish climbed in and then drove round to the front of the house. As early as 1912 the Standish family had owned a motor car. As a young man Hector had business dealings with a man called Herbert Austin, who had left for England some years previously to become involved in the production of motor cars. On his advice Hector had arranged for delivery of an Austin 7, which arrived after many weeks at sea.

The original car turned heads as they drove into Camden, being one of the first to be seen in the district. The family retained a young man with an interest in motor cars to look after their acquisition and were happy to be seen chauffeured around the district at such rapid speed. Early in 1915, with a sense of regret, the young man departed for Sydney intent on joining up and leaving for Europe; determined not to miss out on the global adventure the whole world appeared to be involved in. Unable to maintain his pride and joy, Hector was reduced to using a horse and trap for transportation.

Constance bustled out of the house carrying a large wicker basket containing several jars of marmalade and various other preserves she had made earlier in the year; she intended to distribute these to friends and acquaintances after the morning service, as a small Christmas gift. She had been up since first light, preparing the pork and goose which she would help their elderly cook to roast for a late luncheon. Even at seven o'clock in the morning the kitchen was stiflingly hot, causing her to wonder why a hot meal was necessary to celebrate the occasion.

The war had been raging in Europe for over two years now and was beginning to affect food production in Australia. Traditional Christmas fare, which had been obtained in previous years without any difficulty, was now scarce; Constance was aware that this Christmas would not be as lavish as in the past.

Climbing into the trap, Constance indicated she was ready to leave for the church, where the Reverend Sharpe would give his Christmas address. The sun was already strong but as the trap picked up speed Constance was grateful for a slight breeze. Hector steered the trap up on to the road which wound past the hospital. Several young men could be seen sitting outside, enjoying the morning sun. Constance observed that several of them were recovering from wounds, having served in France at an earlier stage of the war. As they rode past she half wished that her son Max could have been amongst them, instead of continuing the fight half a world away.

Christmas 1916 – London

Lady Hadleigh stood still for a moment, to allow Buxton help her into her coat. The weather had turned bitterly cold during the previous week, leading many to speculate snow would fall on Christmas morning. When Lady Hadleigh had risen earlier, Bedford Square was layered with a thick covering of frost, making things look as though snow had fallen already. Taking no chances, she had ordered her thickest, heaviest coat to ward off the cold.

Lady Hadleigh was on her way to Victoria Station. Although it was Christmas morning the leave trains would continue to arrive and depart without respite; she and her ladies were determined that no soldier arriving over the festive season would do so without appropriate fanfare and she had organised a roster to make sure every expected train was met. Leaving Bedford Square, Lady Hadleigh settled back on the soft brown leather seat of the carriage, which before the war the family had all but stopped using in favour of a motor car. With all spare fuel needed over in France, Lord Hadleigh had ordered the return of two horses from their country estate; to pull a small family carriage short distances around town, while fuel was in such short supply.

The Hadleigh family planned a quiet Christmas. Major Gerald Hammond continued to work several miles behind the lines in France, planning for the New Year and spring offensives. Over the last couple of months, he had tried pulling every string possible to return to his regiment, but so far without success, much to the relief of his family. Kicking his heels at headquarters, Hammond was beginning to feel the war was passing him by; at headquarters he had become known for his willingness to carry dispatches to the front line whenever possible.

Guy Hadleigh also remained in France; with nine confirmed kills he had become known as an Ace in the Royal Flying Corps. Several months before, his family had been approached by a local cigarette company who asked for a recent photograph to include in a series of cigarette cards depicting heroic fighting men.

Roberta Hadleigh had returned home from school a few days earlier and had spent almost every available moment attempting to persuade Lady Hadleigh that her life at school was not only too dull but was being wasted. Her best friend at school, Nora Kingsley, had an elder sister, who was a commander in the First Aid Nursing Yeomanry and was drumming up support from her friends; she hoped to gather together a group of ambulance drivers who would travel to France and form a unit. Word from the Front suggested that transporting the wounded was a somewhat haphazard affair. The sheer numbers of wounded on the Somme overwhelmed the transport service available, with people available to drive the transport in short supply.

Lady Hadleigh was of the opinion that Roberta had probably learnt everything she was ever going to at school and was on the verge of consenting to her request; reasoning she would learn far more useful lessons outside of the cloistered boarding school she had so far attended. Once Christmas was over she intended to investigate the First Aid Nursing Yeomanry to see if it was at all suitable as an organisation to entrust with the welfare of her daughter.

When her carriage arrived at Victoria Station it was still only half light and very cold, Lady Hadleigh dismounted quickly leaning on Buxton's arm for support; the pavements were slippery and wet where the frost had started to melt but had not cleared. After making sure Lady Hadleigh was safely inside the station, Buxton turned to the back of the carriage where he had secured several large canvas baskets with rope, he began to untie them. Standing huddled around a brazier was a group of soldiers, clean and spruced up, preparing for the long journey back to the trenches. Lady Hadleigh raised an arm in their direction and acknowledged the cold.

'If you give me a hand, boys, I'll have a warm cup of tea ready for you in no time,' she called, before unlocking the entrance to the small canteen at the end of the station platform. Within minutes the canvas baskets had been stacked neatly in the kitchen. Bustling around inside she filled a large urn which was placed on a gas hob to boil. The first canvas basket was quickly emptied of the dozens of mince pies it contained; these were stacked on trays ready to be heated in the large ovens, so that the troops passing through Victoria that day would at least have a little Christmas cheer to speed them on their way.

Before long half a dozen other members of the Red Cross joined Lady Hadleigh to spend a few hours handing out cups of tea and other Christmas gifts, which the ladies had spent many hours assembling into small parcels for the men returning from leave. Following the morning service, the Vicar of St Andrew Undershaft also arrived with a small choir, to sing Christmas carols under the Christmas tree which had been erected close to the canteen.

Lady Hadleigh had a satisfying Christmas morning. As the leave trains began to pull out of the station, full of young men who may not be lucky enough to return, she was happy in the knowledge she and her ladies had done what they could to make those last few moments bearable. A great many soldiers had joined in the festive spirit and waved cheerfully from their carriage windows as the trains left the station.

The second part of the afternoon was expected to be more difficult with several hospital trains due to arrive. The war in Europe had quietened down over the winter months with fighting reduced to a war of attrition; the wounded arriving on hospital trains were not all gravely injured and were less likely to die in transit. For some to be taken back to Blighty after receiving a wound which would normally be treated in France was the best Christmas gift possible.

The first hospital train drew in slowly. Ambulances were parked next to the platform, ready to transport the wounded to the nearest hospitals able to accommodate them. Lady Hadleigh and her team wheeled a large trolley with a tea urn and cups onto the platform and started to pour tea as the train drew to a halt. As soon as the train was emptied it was moved to a siding to be cleaned. It was followed by a second then a third hospital train.

With a belch of steam and screech of metal wheels the third hospital train arrived beside the platform. The carriages closest to the barrier contained stretcher cases looked after by a number of nursing staff, who were busy making sure the wounded were all right after being moved from the carriage to the platform.

Lady Hadleigh was handing out tea and cigarettes to walking wounded further down the train; it was to be several minutes before Lady Hadleigh noticed that her daughter and the young Australian nurse, who had stayed after the Ariadne sank, were amongst the nurses caring for the more seriously wounded as they were lowered onto the platform.

As soon as she spotted her, Lady Hadleigh walked down the platform to her daughter.

'Darling, what on earth are you doing here?' she asked, after kissing her on both cheeks.

'I might have guessed you would be here, Mama,' Lady Julia replied. 'We were asked to escort the wounded at short notice. The hospital is out of action after the bombing, which left us with time on our hands. We were both offered a few days off, if we escorted the wounded. It all happened too quickly to send a wire.'

'What better Christmas present? By the time you have delivered the wounded to St Thomas' I will be home. I will ask Buxton to prepare some champagne and also draw you both a bath. I am looking forward to hear what you have both been up to.'

Christmas 1916 – France

Guy Hadleigh landed with the smooth precision of a veteran pilot and steered his aeroplane towards the hangar. He was tired, after being shaken awake by his batman before it was light and was looking forward to some strong French coffee to help stimulate his nerves. The mess would be full of his Flight, returning from a reconnaissance mission that had started as dawn broke and had lasted several hours. Two pilots and their observers had been seen to crash land after a short dog fight with three Albatross' who came from the German sector early in the mission. It looked as though they had survived the encounter, although their aircraft had not; Hadleigh had managed to pinpoint the crash site for one of the aircraft and had dispatched a tender to assist with retrieval as soon as he landed.

Entering the mess, Hadleigh became aware of how hungry he was. The smell of bacon frying permeated throughout the room and did nothing for the slightly nauseated feeling he had in the pit of his stomach. He still had a hangover from the night before, after drinking far too many glasses of whisky at the Café Bleu in memory of Lieutenant Woods who had crashed on take-off. Sitting down at one of the long refectory tables he ordered strong coffee, bacon, eggs and kedgeree before picking up the latest edition of *Punch* which his mother sent to him.

'Hadleigh, old chap, the CO wishes to see you as soon as you've had breakfast.' Hadleigh looked up to see his navigator standing beside the table.

'Right-oh. I'm nearly finished. Any idea what it's about?' he asked.

'Sorry, no idea,' was the response.

Hadleigh finished his breakfast and then walked out of the mess down the corridor to his CO's office. Rapping loudly, he opened the door at a request to enter, marched to the centre of the room and saluted Major Rochford who was seated behind a large ornate desk looking at flight plans.

'Ah, Hadleigh! I've had a request to carry out a mission from headquarters, which may appeal to you,' Rochford said. 'Headquarters need a man to carry some urgent dispatches to the War Office in London. Sending these dispatches by land will take too long with current train and shipping delays, so I've been asked to spare a pilot and a plane. You'll need to be ready within the hour. Pack for a few days away and plot a course for Brooklands. You can leave the kite there. There's a new Sopwith Triplane being made, which so far only the Navy have been lucky enough to try out. I've arranged for delivery of a couple, so would like you to bring one back,' he continued.

'That will mean Christmas at home, Mama will be delighted, sir,' Hadleigh replied. 'Is there any chance of taking Osborne to navigate?'

'Unfortunately not, the other seat will be occupied by a man from headquarters. They are sending someone who needs to attend an urgent planning meeting.'

Rochford stood up and walked over to a drinks' cabinet on the other side of the room. Pouring two large tots of brandy he approached Hadleigh and handed a glass to him along with an envelope. 'This came through as well, the King wishes to meet you on New Year's Day to award you the Military Cross; apparently some of your exploits have been advertised in the popular press, he must have got to hear about them. Well done! Oh, and with it goes promotion to captain.'

Guy Hadleigh was so surprised by this turn of events that he didn't think to enquire as to who his travelling companion might be.

After packing a small valise to take with him, he walked out to his aircraft and was pleasantly surprised to see his brother Gerald was to accompany him on his journey.

Chapter Seventeen

The Florence Nightingale Pledge

*I solemnly pledge myself before God and in the
presence of this assembly, to pass my life in purity and
to practice my profession faithfully.
I will abstain from whatever is deleterious and
mischievous,
And will not take or knowingly administer any harmful
drug.
I will do all in my power to maintain and elevate the
standard of my profession,
And will hold in confidence all personal matters
committed to my keeping and all family affairs coming
to my knowledge in the practice of my calling.
With loyalty will I endeavour to aid the physician in
his work,
And devote myself to the welfare of those committed to
my care.*

Mrs. Lystra E. Gretter 1893

January 1917 – London

Gladys Briggs was enjoying life; the war had bought about a freedom previously not known by her or any of her acquaintances. As a munitions worker she was earning money that before 1914 she could only dream of. She could not understand why her sister seemed content to work as a volunteer, living off the benevolence of the Hadleigh family, when she could easily obtain a job down at the arsenal with large financial rewards on offer.

The previous evening had seen out the old year and welcomed in 1917. South-east London had been a lively place with most public houses putting on a party for any troops on leave; everyone was determined to welcome in the New Year sure in the knowledge that this year the war had to end. The Railway Tavern across the road from Forest Hill Railway Station had been preparing to host a party for several days. Patriotic red, white and blue bunting had been hung wherever there was space and an area at one end of the bar had been cleared to accommodate a small band and singer.

Revellers began arriving early, intent on squeezing the maximum enjoyment out of the end of a year which had been exceptionally bleak. Gladys Briggs and Cecil Watkinson had been walking out for a year, but had spent very little time together, as Watkinson was an ordinary seaman in the Royal Navy and had spent most of the year at sea. They had met before the war one sunny afternoon in Greenwich Park, after Gladys had taken the omnibus there to walk along the river. Initially fearing parental constraint, they had met in secret. More recently, acutely aware of how precious time was, they had started to meet in public and had even invited Gladys's mother to celebrate with them that evening.

The evening had been an outstanding success. The Ambrosia String Quartet performed most popular songs, accompanied by Lilly Lane, a well-known local singer. 'The girl I left behind me' was a particular favourite which was sung three times over the course of the evening, with almost all of the men in uniform joining in loudly. As time drew on and midnight approached the requests made to the band became more sentimental, 'Keep the home fires burning' was sung with some vigour; everyone present hammering out the words.

***

Gladys Briggs was still thinking about the magical evening she had enjoyed as she made her way to the Woolwich Arsenal for an evening shift the following day; Watkinson had left her to re-join his ship in the early hours just before dawn, after an evening of fun and laughter. Briggs had been happy that her mother appeared rather taken with Cecil and was looking forward to sending a letter to Violet telling her all about the evening.

As the omnibus she was travelling on drew closer to the factory, Briggs began to think about the shift ahead. She was proud of her achievements as a shift supervisor, but had been concerned for a while about the way TNT was sometimes stored and worried that it would take very little for an accident to happen.

The railway servicing the factory terminated next to the melting-pot shed. Unstable TNT was offloaded directly into a small cobbled yard and was then transported into the shed to be refined. Some supervisors had taken to storing bags of refined TNT in the melting-pot shed itself until close to the end of their shift, believing it to be a time saving measure. Briggs often arrived to see large amounts of TNT being moved at the end of the day. She was concerned that on several occasions she had noticed some bags stored in the yard had split, exposing the TNT they contained to the elements. Briggs felt more care needed to be taken to prevent an accident and had decided she would discuss the matter with the factory manager before starting her shift.

As the omnibus negotiated Shooters Hill, Briggs looked at her watch but remained seated. She often got off and walked for the last part of the journey, keen to breathe in some outside air before starting a long shift in a chemical environment. As she was planning to see the factory manager she did not move, but continued to look out of the grimy omnibus window.

As the omnibus reached the top of Shooters Hill, the sound of an enormous explosion ripped through the air; some of the windows shattered with the force of the blast, causing shards of glass to fall inward. Almost as soon as the sound of the explosion began to die down two passengers started to scream, although neither appeared injured. Other passengers stood up, keen to leave the confines of the omnibus, worried they were somehow under attack; however, the majority of passengers travelling were on their way to the munitions factory and knew immediately where the explosion had come from, as an orange glow could be seen lighting the sky.

When she recovered from the shock of what had happened, Briggs became aware of a warm sticky sensation. Gently feeling her scalp, she cut her finger on a piece of glass protruding from her head. Without thinking she pulled out the jagged splinter, which had caused a superficial cut above her left ear. Blood gushed through her fingers, making her feel a little dizzy. Taking a handkerchief from her bag she applied pressure to the cut to staunch the bleeding and then looked around to see if there was anyone else needing urgent assistance.

The omnibus driver had no desire to continue towards an explosion, fearing that this may be the start of a chain of blasts. He stopped the omnibus, applied the handbrake and turned off the engine.

'This is as far as I go, ladies and gentleman,' he announced. 'Anyone wishing to return to town is welcome; I'll be leaving within ten minutes.' He then climbed down from the driver's seat and lit a cigarette before looking towards the glow. Briggs returned home on the same omnibus, terrified for friends and colleagues she knew to be working, but recognising it would not be helpful to continue travelling into the factory, where those that had survived would be attempting to quickly leave.

Later Briggs learnt the munitions factory was almost completely destroyed by the explosion. Where the melting-pot shed and train yard had stood there was nothing left but an enormous crater; all thirty people working in the immediate vicinity died instantly. Gladys Briggs, who before her promotion had worked as part of the melting-pot team, lost a great many friends.

In the aftermath of the explosion the government were quick to compensate the victims and play down the enormous amount of devastation that the explosion caused. Questions asked in the House as to why a munitions factory was to be found in such a built-up area, were quickly squashed without explanation, the simple fact being that to move the factory would be prohibitively expensive and might even hamper the war effort.

It did not take long for Cecil to persuade Gladys that she should leave the munitions factory and take up a less dangerous occupation. She found work out at Brooklands, attaching canvas to aircraft frames at the Sopwith factory, much to her sister Violet's relief.

February 1917 – France

The Casualty Clearing Station was on the move. As the Battle of the Somme had eventually fizzled and died in the winter mud, the need for the number of hospitals currently in the area had been discussed at headquarters; the Belgian Sector although quiet did not have much medical support and with an offensive at Passchendaele planned for the summer months, it was decided to move the hospital

As soon has he heard of the decision Major Hammond borrowed a motorcycle and set off for the Casualty Clearing Station, wishing to speak to his sister. Arriving behind a group of ambulances, Hammond wondered if closing the hospital was such a good idea after all.

Hammond parked the motorcycle and walked towards the entrance of the building. Standing in the doorway Victoria Standish was looking a little flustered at the arrival of more ambulances, when she scarcely had room for the wounded already there. Noticing his arrival, Standish spoke.

'Good morning, sir. Is there anything I can do for you?' she asked.

Hammond looked at the Australian uniform Standish was wearing. 'I need to speak to Lady Julia Hadleigh urgently, she's a nurse here do you know where she is?' Hammond replied. 'I say! Are you the Australian nurse my sister has become friends with?' he asked.

'You must be Gerald,' Standish responded. 'I will go and look for her. I think she is off duty at the moment, but you will need permission from Matron if she is to leave the hospital. We are on alert at the moment to take all wounded; sometimes it is necessary to recall off-duty staff if a lot of wounded arrive.'

'Thank you, Sister, I am hoping to take her out for some afternoon tea at the Café Bleu. I have some news which will affect both of you. Perhaps you would care to join us?'

***

Before long, orders were posted about the impending move and Hadleigh found herself caught up in the chaos that any move entailed. She was pleased to have been given advance warning by her brother and had prepared Max Standish for her imminent departure.

Hadleigh spent endless hours helping to catalogue and pack medical supplies ready to be moved to the new hospital. After being clearly labelled, supplies of bandages and dressings were packed in large wooden crates, only to be needed when a fresh batch of wounded arrived from a small night-time sortie.

The order in which hospital staff should leave and travel to Belgium was discussed over and over again by Matron Gillespie and the commanding officer. Both undecided on how many staff should remain behind to deal with remnants of wounded. In the end they both agreed it would depend on the severity of the wounded that were left on the day of the move, so all medical and nursing staff were ordered to prepare to leave at short notice.

Once she was satisfied that most of the preparation for the move had been accomplished, Matron Gillespie and a small party of nurses went on ahead to prepare the new buildings they were allocated and create a functioning hospital.

Violet Briggs and Lady Julia Hadleigh were amongst the nurses left behind, in the charge of Sister Blackstone, to clear up and see the last of the wounded onto hospital trains. As with any planned move, things did not run smoothly. News had been sent to medical officers in charge of Regimental Aid Posts advising that the move was imminent and the hospital had stopped taking casualties. Stretcher bearers were asked to transport any wounded to No' 26 Casualty Clearing Station a mile further down the line. Some stretcher bearers did not receive this instruction so for a while the wounded continued to arrive.

The departing medical and nursing staff included Victoria Standish who managed a quick word with Hadleigh just before she boarded the transport taking her to the station.

'Hadleigh, if you see my brother before you leave, can you let him know where I am and tell him I'll write as soon as we are settled?' she asked.

'Of course, Sister,' Hadleigh replied. 'I am hoping to meet him at the Café Bleu, after we have cleared the hospital of the remaining wounded; although Sister Blackstone may well have other ideas. The clerks down in the orderly office tell me his battalion of the AIF came out of the line first thing this morning,' she continued.

'Good! Do what you can,' Standish replied. 'Captain Marshall may be with him; can you give him this letter if you see him?'

***

Two days later, Hadleigh watched as the last of the wounded was loaded into an ambulance and taken to the station. The hospital was eerily quiet after their removal. With most of the equipment gone and the beds dismantled, it was difficult to tell that the empty rooms had been used as operating theatres and wards. Somehow, the buildings looked far more suited to their original purpose as school rooms.

Hadleigh walked slowly through the building and out into the grounds, pausing for a moment to look at the point in the corridor where Daisy McMaster had died. After a minute's reflection she carried on walking, up to the small cemetery where the dead from the bombing had been buried, making her way to the medical staff graves. Placing flowers on McMaster's grave she said a brief prayer and then turned, preparing to retrace her steps. She immediately saw Sister Blackstone walking briskly up the path towards her; she was carrying flowers, clearly intent on paying her respects.

'Glad I caught you, Hadleigh,' Blackstone commented, as she drew close. 'The train leaves at any time after six o'clock tomorrow morning. I presume you wish to apply for a leave pass until that time?' she asked.

'Yes, Sister.' Hadleigh drew a deep breath, before deciding that honesty was probably the best way to discuss her plans. 'I promised Sister Standish that I would try and meet her brother, who has been fighting in the area and let him know she has been posted,' she added.

'Providing you are at the station by six o'clock I am prepared to ignore where you may decide to go tonight and what you may decide to do. God knows! I think it's time you younger nurses had some enjoyment in life, after everything you have endured since joining,' Blackstone replied. 'It's only the endless amount of red tape involved in closing the Casualty Clearing Station that prevents me from joining you.'

Leaving Hadleigh gawping in stunned silence, Blackstone swept on towards the graveyard.

***

The Café Bleu was busy that night. Hadleigh had taken Briggs with her to the café in case Captain Standish and Captain Marshall failed to make the rendezvous. Briggs had made Hadleigh promise she would be able to leave as soon as the officers appeared, as she was unused to socialising with the upper classes and did not wish to feel out of place. She was nervous enough to have discovered that Lady Julia had booked them both into the Hotel Florence for their last night in France and that she would not have the safety and security of the nurses' accommodation to sleep in. Briggs was not at all sure she liked the idea of staying in a foreign room, even if the towels and bed linen were as good as any she had seen in all her years in service.

Standing on the steps leading down into the café's basement, Hadleigh looked at the crowded tables. She was happy to see that she and Briggs were not the only nurses present who were due to leave on the six o'clock train. Scanning the tables, she was initially unable to see the two officers, so led Briggs to a vacant corner table and ordered a bottle of white wine. With the wine on the table Briggs warmed to the café atmosphere and started to feel more relaxed; casting her eyes around the room she was able to make out several people she knew, each alone in the company of an officer. She could not help reflecting that war had changed everything and for the first time began to question her life in service once the war was over. Maybe she would be allowed to train as a proper nurse? Turning to Hadleigh she began to discuss her thoughts.

'Do you think the war will change things for good?' she asked. 'I would never have imagined sitting somewhere like this before the war. It's all so strange.'

Lady Julia thought for a moment before she replied. 'I can't imagine life will ever be the same again,' she replied. 'With luck we shall see a new order; not quite so stuffy and bound by convention. I really don't think my parents' world will ever be important again. Look around this café, the nurses are from all walks of life and from the four corners of the earth. I don't know that any of us would want to go back to living such a restrictive life.'

'I do hope you are right, Hadleigh. You see I am considering doing my training after the war is over. One day I would like to be as confident as Sister Blackstone, she always stays calm no matter what we are facing; I think a lot of nurses will still be needed, to look after some of the men so hideously wounded out here,' Briggs replied.

'Oh, I say! You must do that if you can. I shall miss you horribly of course, but I really can't see you scrubbing out fireplaces again. It would be such a waste having been through this.' Hadleigh finished speaking and looked up in time to see Captain Standish and Captain Marshall weaving their way through the café tables to join them. Standing up she waved to the approaching men intent on attracting their attention.

The evening was a great success; the Australian men entertained Briggs and Hadleigh with tales of life in Australia. They talked of living on the land and how harsh the summers were with the unrelenting heat, and of bush fires which tore through the land with frightening speed and ferocity.

Society in Australia seemed more relaxed with people socialising, regardless of station in life, at various events throughout the year. Clearly, Standish and Marshall were best friends, growing up in the same area. Listening to their stories it was obvious that Standish came from landed gentry and that before the war Marshall had worked for his father; but these circumstances had not created a division with their friendship surviving regardless. Hadleigh hoped one day to travel to the places the men talked of and see for herself what things were like.

Briggs found it difficult to comprehend, as they sat in front of a log fire, that on the other side of the world it was daylight and stiflingly hot in a place called Camden; a place the men mentioned often, with affection. The idea that men of the Australian Imperial Force had willingly travelled for weeks to fight in France, defending England's honour was hard to understand; it did not feel as though the outcome of any European conflict could possibly affect Australia. Blooded in Gallipoli and at Pozieres both men could not explain why they were there and not having a quick beer with their mates down at the Plough and Harrow.

The evening wore on with everyone keen to forget the war and extract every last ounce of pleasure before leaving for a different front. Hadleigh said goodbye to Captain Standish with a heavy heart, not sure if they would meet again.

March 1917 – France

Captain Guy Hadleigh was bored. The weather had been too poor to fly for several days now, with driving rain and strong winds. Several reconnaissance missions had been planned for the early weeks of spring and he was eager to complete the task. He was experiencing the same level of disinterest in his surroundings as he had in London at Christmas, when he had last spent a few days away from the squadron.

Decorated by the King, with his parents and elder brother present, Hadleigh was unable to share the enthusiasm they all had for the number of enemy planes he had shot down, and had spent the ceremony wondering what it was all for. Guy Hadleigh felt as though he had entered a disjointed, unreal world. The relatively safe lives most Londoners were leading disconcerted him. Friends from school who had drifted into secure, reserved occupations at the War Office, seemed to understand nothing about the reality of life on the Western Front; after several days he gave up trying to explain what it was like to face mind-numbing fear each day, as he took off looking for enemy aircraft to attack, knowing he may not survive to see nightfall. In the end he had returned to France several days early, after convincing his parents he had been recalled prematurely.

The war had changed Hadleigh, he was no longer the fresh-faced school boy who had joined up so willingly, determined to avenge the deaths of the people who had died in the Zeppelin raid. He was beginning to realise that he experienced a heart stopping adrenaline rush only when he was in pursuit of someone fearing for their life or fearing for his own.

Turning over in bed, Hadleigh looked across at the naked woman asleep beside him. He had paid her for the whole night and was over the road from the Café Bleu, staying in what appeared to be an upmarket hotel, but in fact was a brothel for officers. The previous evening, after the squadron was stood down with no prospect of flying in the morning even if the weather did clear, Hadleigh had made the trip into town.

Hadleigh looked at his watch and decided that despite his exertions the previous night; he had time to carry on where he left off and make the girl in the bed earn her money. For an airman in France with time on their hands there was little to do other than drink or visit the local brothel.

Prostitution was a thriving industry, with brothels set up in every major town. Some were legal with stringent, regular medical checks carried out on the women, to make sure they were not spreading disease to the fighting men who frequented them. Hadleigh made sure that he only went to this type of establishment, as he had no desire to end up discussing an embarrassing medical problem with the squadron doctor.

***

Several hours later, feeling slightly less frustrated than he had twelve hours before, Hadleigh mounted his motorcycle and returned to the chateau. The weather was beginning to clear. The rain had stopped and the wind had died down a little. The ground was still very wet and on a couple of occasions Hadleigh's motorcycle became bogged in mud; cursing he managed to push the wheels clear. Arriving back at the chateau Hadleigh parked his motorcycle, strode into the building and down the corridor to the mess, where he knew his Flight would be waiting with news of how soon it was forecast the weather would improve.

Chapter Eighteen

For all emotions that are tense and strong,
And utmost knowledge, I have lived for these.
Lived deep, and let the lesser things live long,
The everlasting hills, the lakes, the trees,
Who'd give their thousand years to sing this song
Of life, and Man's high sensibilities,
Which I unto the face of death can sing.
O death, thou poor and disappointed thing.
Strike if thou wilt, and soon; strike breast and brow;
For I have lived: and thou canst rob me now
Only of some long life that ne'er has been.
The life that I have lived, so full, so keen,
Is mine! I hold it firm beneath thy blow
And, dying, take it where I go.

Ernest Raymond, *Tell England*

May 1917 – England

Major Gerald Hammond looked at his watch for the tenth time in five minutes. He was nervous and could not help feeling that what he was about to do was furtive and slightly un-English. He had fought bravely for nearly three years, giving everything to his regiment and his King, but now felt it was time to do something for himself and the woman he loved.

By chance a few weeks earlier, Hammond had seen listed the movement orders and postings for members of the QAIMNS remaining in France. Sister Brennan was scheduled for a couple of weeks leave, before being posted to Belgium, where she would join a hospital barge transporting wounded men to the coast. Hammond had immediately arranged to meet her at the Café Bleu. After they were both seated and had ordered from the menu, Hammond spoke.

'Margaret, I have something to ask you,' Hammond said before removing a small box from his jacket pocket. 'I have been in love with you from the very first moment we met and cannot imagine what life would be like without you. Will you do me the honour of becoming my wife?' he asked. He then opened the box and removed a diamond ring which had been in the family for centuries.

Brennan looked at Hammond and thought for a minute before she replied.

'Gerald, I would marry you tomorrow if I thought I could continue working here in France. As things stand I would have to resign and give up nursing. I doubt very much I would be able to nurse the wounded anywhere really. All of the hospitals I know will not allowed married women to nurse. I wonder if it may be better to wait until the war is over?' Brennan speculated.

'I understand that you could no more sit at home knitting socks for the troops while I'm out here, than I could take a permanent transfer to the War Office,' Major Hammond replied. 'We both need to see this through. Leave everything to me and I'll see what can be arranged. If we can marry without anyone knowing, you may be able to carry on as before; if this proves too difficult we may have to wait until the war is over.'

Gerald Hammond set about arranging a secret wedding in the remote village of Blythburgh in Suffolk. His family had an estate close to the town of Hadleigh, where centuries previously they had been feudal Lords of the Manor, answerable only to the King. They owned a large amount of land in the area, but had in more recent times built a house further north, between Blythburgh and the sea. In between social engagements the family usually spent a portion of the summer months there. Winds coming from the North Sea blew in over the flat marshlands making the climate in summer more bearable than London.

Holy Trinity Church at Blythburgh was a large imposing building, known as the Cathedral of the Marshes; the church had a chequered history, but had been on the site since the seventh century. A thousand years later a puritanical parliament had set about destroying the ornate, heavily decorated angels in the roof, believing that such ornamentation was anathema in the eyes of God. The surviving angels were peppered with bullet holes, which somehow seemed a fitting witness to the marriage about to go ahead while war raged in Europe.

Hammond felt that although they were to marry in secret the least he could do was ensure the venue was appropriately grand. His family attended matins at the church every Sunday when they were staying at Hadleigh Hall, leaving Holy Trinity the natural choice for his wedding.

The Reverend Archibald Posselthwaite had been vicar at Holy Trinity since Viscount Hammond was a small boy and was now in his late seventies. He had hoped to retire in early 1915 but had been unable to do so once war intervened. Most young clergymen had eagerly joined the war in France within months of the declaration, keen to give succour to the wounded and dying. With no successor to train it looked unlikely that the Reverend Posselthwaite would be able to put his feet up much before the end of the war.

The Reverend Posselthwaite was delighted to receive a telegram in early April from Hammond requesting he be available to preside over his marriage in May. The telegram announced a letter was to follow with more comprehensive details for the marriage ceremony; but also advised that of necessity there would be some secrecy surrounding the wedding.

Hammond was now standing in the central isle of Holy Trinity church wearing his Coldstream Guards dress uniform, complete with ancestral sword, nervously awaiting the arrival of his bride. In front of him the Reverend Archibald Posselthwaite was also waiting. The only other people present were Lord and Lady Hadleigh and his sister, Roberta, who had been collected from school and sworn to secrecy about what she was about to witness.

Roberta was still unhappy that in the end her age had prevented her joining the First Aid Nursing Yeomanry and that with nothing better to occupy her time, Lady Hadleigh had insisted she return to school until the end of the school year.

At the sound of a slight commotion coming from the back of the church, Hammond turned to see Margaret Brennan start her slow walk down the aisle towards him. She was accompanied by Buxton, who had linked arms with her and was to give her away in the absence of her late father. Gerald Hammond gave a gasp of surprise; Margaret Brennan looked beautiful in a wedding dress of the finest English lace, originally worn many years before by his mother, who had the dress handed down to her by her mother. Natural light poured in through the large windows which ran down either side of the nave, the sight that greeted him was breathtaking.

**

With the service over and the register signed, Viscount Hammond accompanied his wife to the family motorcar, which was parked beyond the church gate. He had managed to obtain a few gallons of petrol and intended to take his wife somewhere special, where they could forget all about the war and the horrors of France. They had three more days before his brief spell of leave was over and he intended to make the most of them. Engaging the clutch, Hammond waved to his parents and sister before driving off in the direction of Southwold.

The Crown Hotel in the centre of Southwold was a busy place. Almost all of the male guests were officers in uniform. The guest lounge was full of couples engaged in conversation, oblivious to things happening around them; all intent on extracting the last moments of enjoyment from their leave.

Viscount Hammond ordered their bags be delivered to the suite of rooms he had booked; once inside he poured a glass of whisky, while he waited for his wife to change out of the wedding dress she had arrived wearing. For many months he had dreamt of marrying Margaret Brennan and was scarcely able to believe the day had arrived and that they were now man and wife.

It was a beautiful May evening. The day had been warm and there was only a light breeze drifting in from the ocean. Walking down from the hotel the Hammonds arrived at the sea front, where several couples were strolling along the promenade towards the pier and back. At the end of the pier the Belle Steamer was tied up after journeying from London Bridge; the following day it would continue on to Great Yarmouth, before returning to London.

The pier had been constructed at the turn of the century and had opened fifteen years previously to provide entertainment for visitors to the town. On the pier itself it was possible to visit a fortune teller, enter into the amusement arcade, listen to a brass band or have a cup of tea in the Daffodil Tea Rooms.

Hammond and his wife opted for a glass of beer and a cup of tea, along with a light supper before strolling back to the hotel. The lamps in their suite had been lit while they were away making the room look inviting and a welcome retreat from the noise of the guest lounge downstairs. The bed had been turned down and the curtains drawn, shutting out the last of the day as the sun started to set.

Viscount Hammond moved across the room and poured two glasses of champagne, from a bottle which he had asked to be put on ice while they were walking to the pier. Handing one to Margaret he then raised his glass to her.

'Darling, here's a toast to many long and happy years together. I hope that once this war is over we will be able to spend our days pottering around the estate doing nothing more strenuous than deciding where to plant the next lot of roses and talking about which school we should enrol the children in. I long for the day when the guns finally fall silent.'

'I also long for that day,' his wife responded. 'I feel very fortunate to have found you. The war for us has been kind, as we would not have met otherwise. I thank God every day that I was there the day you came looking for a gassed sergeant I never thought that I would love like this again.'

Putting his glass down, Hammond took Viscountess Hammond in his arms and began very slowly and very carefully to remove her clothes, layer by layer. Carrying her across the room he lay her down in the centre of the large four poster bed, before removing his own clothing and joining her.

June 1917 – Belgium

The weather had been shocking for June; cold and wet there was no sign of any let up in the rain which had been pouring down for several weeks. The makeshift roads and tracks leading into the trenches at Passchendaele were becoming more bogged down with every passing day.

Even before the Battle of the Somme, military planners in London began to plot an offensive in Belgium. Unhappy with the results of the first two battles at Ypres a third was planned. At the start of 1916, when winter frosts were still present, and the ground was as hard as iron, men of the Royal Engineers began to dig. Now, more than a dozen tunnels were slowly taking shape, edging closer each day towards the German front line.

The work was arduous; skilled miners were rapidly inducted into the Royal Engineers to assist with construction. Given only the very basics of military training, miners from the North of England and Wales were posted to Flanders, where they were paid almost six times as much as men fighting in the trenches. It was predicted the tunnels would herald a turning point in the war once they were detonated in the forthcoming spring offensive.

The work was not without problem; although the main excavation was through clay there were patches of sand and underground water, prone to collapse unless shored up quickly. Deep in the Flanders earth the clay took on a bluish hue, which unless disguised when excavated attracted German interest. Germans in the trenches lining the Messines Ridge were not averse to shelling any area below which looked unusual as dozens of miners found out to their cost.

***

Captain Standish was a frustrated man. Three weeks previously he had been summoned to headquarters and had been advised that his company was to move with the rest of the battalion to an area near Ypres. The spring offensive in Flanders was a poorly kept secret, with most men aware that something big was planned in the area. For the small number of men who had survived Gallipoli and Pozieres the knowledge was not very welcome. A couple of men with appropriate skills had taken the opportunity to transfer to the Machine Gun Corps, to learn how to drive a tank. Tanks had until now been largely experimental, but were to figure heavily in the planned offensive.

As soon as he was able, Standish sent a wire to his sister advising he was on the move and should be able to meet up shortly. Censorship ruling had until now prevented him from finding out her exact location, but he was not concerned, confident he would be able to find out her whereabouts once he was in the area. He had not seen his sister since February; both had taken leave, but it had been at different times and they had failed to meet up.

Despite being known to clerks in the orderly office, Standish had extreme difficulty finding out the location of the Casualty Clearing Station. At first, he was told that the information he was requesting was classified; then it seemed that none of the maps accompanying the battalion from France were sufficiently up to date to contain the necessary information. In the end he waited on the road until an empty ambulance passed by and stopped the driver who was able to tell him where the hospital was.

The Casualty Clearing Station had set up in a small village close to Essex Farm, a couple of miles behind the front-line. Unlike earlier in the war, care seemed to have been taken in the selection of the site used. A vacated factory had been commandeered and a number of its buildings had been converted into wards for the wounded. The factory kitchens had been thoroughly scrubbed and prepared to provide nutritious meals. The factory was alongside a canal with direct access to hospital barges, which utilised the canal system to deliver the wounded to the coast.

When Captain Standish arrived at the front gates he was surprised to see things appeared quiet. The semi-circular driveway had only one ambulance parked on it; used to chaotic hospital conditions in France he initially wondered if he had arrived at the right place, but was relieved to see a group of nurses emerging from the front entrance. With a cry of recognition one of them saw him and detached herself from the group, walking quickly towards him. Lady Julia Hadleigh looked very pleased to see him.

'Max! It's so good to see you,' she exclaimed as she drew close. 'I have missed you so much. When did you arrive here? Does Victoria know you are in the area? Sorry, I'm talking too much; tell me what's been happening,' she continued excitedly.

'I sent a wire several days ago to tell Victoria we were on the way but have heard nothing since. Is she working at the moment? She didn't say she was going on leave,' Standish replied.

'She may not have received it. For the last few weeks she has been working on the hospital barges which are transferring the wounded to the coast. The trips take days; on this latest one she has been away for almost a week. We are expecting her to return later this afternoon though. Perhaps we could both meet you at the Wild Poppy Hotel later? It's in the main street, close to the church, I'm not sure what its name is in Flemish, but everyone knows where it is.'

***

Sister Victoria Standish straightened up and walked over to her desk. The barge was empty of any wounded at the moment, as they had been offloaded a couple of days earlier. Standish had spent the morning preparing each bed and the area in general, for a fresh batch of wounded, which she anticipated would be waiting once the barges arrived back at the Casualty Clearing Station.

Work on the barge was a welcome change from the frenetic activity after the Somme. Standish was lucky enough to spend most of her time working with Sister Brennan, who had recently returned from a spell of leave, which seemed to have done her a power of good.

She appeared relaxed and happy; the strenuous nature of nursing in general did not seem to have the usual tiring effect on her. Standish and Brennan worked on separate barges, linked together with rope; each looking after an area containing beds for thirty men. Assisted by another sister and a number of orderlies, they managed to provide round the clock care.

The two barges were towed through the canal system by a steam tug, with an engineer and an assistant making sure all ran smoothly. At the start of the war barges had been commandeered from ordinary transport vessels, used mainly for coal. They had been painted with large red crosses on their grey hulls, to make sure they were not mistaken for ammunition barges and accidently bombed by the German Air Force, which was becoming more sophisticated with each passing week. The barges Standish and Brennan travelled on had been custom built the previous year and were marginally better designed than the original hospital barges; although the intent was still to sell the barges to haul coal at the end of the war.

The hold, where the wounded were accommodated, had no windows so remained very dark. In fine weather it was possible to lift a few of the hatches to take in some natural light, but for the rest of the time lighting was artificial and reliant on a generator powered by the tug's engine. Sleeping accommodation for the nursing staff was not terribly satisfactory; a small cramped cubicle was located at the end of the ward, with only a thin wall separating the two areas. Sleep was often impossible during the day as normal ward activity was quite loud. At night the plaintive cries of the wounded also made sleep difficult.

It took a little while to become accustomed to working on a barge. The decks were often slippery after a spell of rain. At the start of the journey Standish watched in horror as a colleague lost her footing while supervising the loading of wounded men, slipping off the roof and into the canal below. Fortunately, the sister concerned was able to swim and managed to find her way to the canal bank, where she was hauled in by the tug engineer, with nothing more than her pride dented.

On top of the neatly made beds and stacked all around the ward were supplies of every description to be delivered to the Casualty Clearing Station. It was obvious from the nature and amount of the supplies that a large battle was planned. The amount of morphia and fresh dressing material they were carrying would under normal circumstances last for several months.

Sister Standish entered the amount of morphia she had counted into a register on her desk. Looking at her watch she reached over and rang a bell. An orderly appeared and then scurried off at her request for a pot of tea. Standish figured it would take only an hour or so to reach the mooring and was looking forward to a proper bath, some sleep and a change of uniform. She often dreamt of a world where it was possible to wash as often as she wanted; where clean clothes were not a luxury and sleep was plentiful. She felt sure that, as had been the case last year, the coming summer months would be very busy indeed and these basic desires would be difficult to obtain.

Chapter Nineteen

Thus are commemorated the many
Multitudes who during The Great
War Of 1914 - 1918 gave the most that man can give
Life itself
For King and Country
For Loved Ones, Home and Empire
For the sacred cause of justice and
The freedom of the World
They buried him among the Kings because he
Had done good toward God and toward
His House
Tomb of the Unknown Warrior, Westminster
Abbey, London

June 1917 – Belgium, Messines

Standish and his men marched into the trenches two
days before the battle was due to commence. He was
happy that he had managed to catch up with his sister
and Lady Julia two days previously and was wondering,
not for the first time, if Lady Julia would consider
moving to Australia at the end of the war. On leave in
London a couple of months previously he had visited

Paget's of Bond Street, where he had arranged for a large opal, found years before on some family land, to be fashioned into a gold pendant attached to a chain; he now kept it in a small box inside his uniform pocket.

Originally, Standish planned to ask Lady Julia for her hand in marriage the very next time he saw her, but had not been able to as she arrived for dinner accompanied by his sister and a couple of their nursing colleagues; he felt the proposal should wait until they were alone.

The evening had been celebratory but a little constrained as everyone present was aware of another looming offensive and the possibility that not all of them would survive. The longer the war continued the more fatalistic some of them became, as it seemed the charmed life they led could not continue forever and injury or death was inevitable.

Several bottles of wine had been consumed and the limited wartime menu sampled when towards the end of the evening Captain Marshall arrived. He had just completed a stint as orderly officer which he had tried desperately to wriggle out of. He had been unable to arrange a swap as everyone seemed hell-bent on sampling the delights Ypres had to offer, keenly aware that it may be for the last time. Marshall was flustered and very concerned he might miss Victoria, after spending several hours sucking on his pen composing a letter for her; to be opened in the event of his death.

***

The mines which had been dug over the previous year, with a certain amount of difficulty, were detonated simultaneously at ten minutes past three in the morning. The sound of the explosions was deafening, leaving Standish with ringing in his ears and feeling disorientated for several minutes.

Standish had been instructed that he and his company were to leave the trenches once the debris from the explosions had settled and run towards Messines Ridge. The plan was to take both Messines Ridge and the town of Wytschaete as quickly as possible, to gain the high ground and the advantage, for further planned fighting around Passchendaele.

Captain Standish and Captain Marshall both called to their men, climbed quickly onto the fire step and then up out of the trench. The sight that greeted them was hell on earth. High on the ridge the sky seemed to be on fire, with several pockets of flame burning everything in the immediate vicinity. The explosions had caused several huge craters, around which hundreds of dead German soldiers were littered. Thousands of Germans had died as a direct result of the mines being detonated, when the ground was blown from beneath them. The intricate series of trenches which they had modified to perfection and occupied since 1914 ceased to exist.

Resistance was almost non-existent. Within a couple of hours Messines Ridge was taken and efforts turned to Wytschaete. The Australians prepared to dig in while the Fifth Army passed through their ranks, intent on consolidating the favourable position gained so easily.

Captain Stanley Marshall lost his life midway through the battle. There had been some sporadic resistance from a few German soldiers not injured in the initial explosions. On top of the ridge was a solid concrete pillbox manned by troops with a machine gun. Unaware that the concrete bunker contained uninjured men, Marshall led his platoon towards it. Visibility in the area was poor, as the dust and debris from the explosions had not quite settled, making it impossible to work out where resistance was coming from. As he ran towards the bunker a single spray of machine-gun fire hit him in the chest, killing him instantly.

Captain Standish was close by and watched him fall. Seconds later he saw Sergeant Major Kennedy throw a Mills bomb in through the slit in the pillbox that the machine gun was firing through. The ensuing explosion killed everyone inside. Once the bunker was cleared the risk to men running to the top of the ridge diminished considerably, enabling them to pause and take stock.

Up ahead a tank was bogged down, the thick mud preventing it taking any further part in the battle. Tanks were a new innovation being used for the first time; some of the men present had never seen anything like the huge metal monsters, driven through the battlefield on large caterpillar treads. The mud around Messines was treacherous, decreasing the effectiveness of the tanks as they regularly became stuck needing to be dug out by their occupants, or pulled out by another tank. When moving their sheer size did prove useful as protection for the troops on foot, who were easily able to walk alongside as they traversed the ridge, maintaining an element of surprise.

By the days end the Australians were able to say with pride, they had taken part in one of the most decisive battles of the war. For the first time in years significant ground had been captured and all objectives had been taken. However, Stanley Marshall would have no known grave and would be commemorated with a headstone declaring he was "Known unto God", along with thousands of others lying in Flanders fields. His name would in due course be etched on the Camden Memorial; erected by local families, as a reminder that the war was not worth the enormous loss of life, hopeful that such a tragedy would never happen again.

***

Victoria would never forget the morning she heard of Stanley Marshall's death and the heart wrenching grief that came with the news.

The wounded had been arriving at the Casualty Clearing Station for a number of hours. Although reports were trickling in that the Allies had taken Messines Ridge and, with it, vital ground, the gains were not without cost; a steady stream of wounded had arrived keeping all of the nurses occupied since first light. Standish had been working with Violet Briggs, assessing men as they arrived and advising Sister Blackstone who was in most need of urgent treatment. Most of the wounded had walked in, as stretcher bearers were encountering extreme difficulty recovering the men. The ground which the stretcher bearers had to negotiate was treacherous; the large number of troops moving into the trenches combined with the appalling weather had turned the ground into a quagmire, doubling the number of stretcher bearers necessary to move a single man.

At first Standish did not see her brother standing there. She was bent down examining a gaping wound that a sergeant in the AIF had sustained to his right leg. His femur had been exposed from his groin to his knee cap by a piece of shrapnel; luckily the bone did not appear broken, but some urgent surgery was needed to save the limb.

'Briggs, can you let Major Chardingly know that Sergeant Joseph will need exploratory surgery as soon as he is able?' Standish asked.

'Yes, Sister, I'll do that now,' Briggs replied. Both nurses turned and saw Captain Standish standing at the entrance to the ward. His demeanour implied something serious had happened. His shoulders were hunched and he looked weary, he was covered in mud which was beginning to dry. He had removed his hat and was playing nervously with it; the expression on his face was one of utter devastation.

Victoria was almost at his side, before he looked up sorrow deeply etched on his face.

'Vic, I have the worst possible news,' Captain Standish spoke. He then stepped forward and hugged his sister, which prevented her from collapsing to the floor.

July 1917 – Camden, New South Wales

Constance Standish lifted the latch on the church gate and walked hurriedly on to the road where her trap was waiting. She had been surprised when she arrived at St John's to find that Mrs Marshall was not sitting in her customary pew on the left-hand side, three from the front. Thinking retrospectively, she should have realised something was amiss, as the fresh flowers Mrs

Marshall placed on her husband's grave every Sunday were not there, indicating she could not be in church.

Her worst fears had been confirmed when the Reverend Sharpe drew her to one side before the service started and told her he had been the bearer of the worst possible tidings, about half an hour earlier. Not having time to drive out to Oakfield House before matins, Sharpe was relieved to see the trap pull up and Constance arrive. Hurrying out from the vestibule he quickly informed her of the situation allowing her to go straight to her friend.

On the short drive out to Mrs Marshall's house, Constance wondered how her friend would have reacted to the news. Many years before when her husband was killed in a mining accident out at Picton she had been stoic, pouring all of her energy into bringing up their only son. Now that he had gone, Constance could not begin to imagine her grief; but knew that if anything happened to either Max or Victoria she would be inconsolable.

As the trap drew up outside of her cottage Constance could see that Mrs Marshall was not alone. A grey horse was tethered to the white picket fence surrounding the property. Constance knew the horse was owned by Matron McNally, as she was often seen riding around the district to attend on patients who, for whatever reason, needed to be visited in their own homes. She was pleased that, despite her brusque manner, Matron was present; as she knew she would have dealt with many grieving relatives in the past and felt sure she would be able to offer the right degree of empathy.

Walking around to the back of the house, Constance Standish knocked on the kitchen door and entered the small room which served as both a kitchen and dining room. The small table, where until recently Stanley Marshall had eaten his meals was set for tea, with a teapot, milk jug and a plate of biscuits which looked freshly made. Next to the plate of biscuits lay an open telegram; it was not difficult to imagine what it contained. Catherine Marshall was standing by the wood-burning stove, watching a kettle as it started to boil. Looking up she saw Constance standing in the doorway and spoke.

'Ah, Constance, I thought the Reverend Sharpe may send you, although there really was no need for you to miss matins. As you can see Matron McNally has been kind enough to sit with me for a while.'

'Agatha, I am so sorry to hear of your loss,' Constance replied. She paused before adding, 'Is it definite?' she asked.

'Yes, it would seem so. Have a look at the telegram. Max sent it; he saw him fall,' she responded. 'He was trying to capture some high ground to cover the rest of his platoon, who were following, when he was hit by machine-gun fire. I think a letter with more detail may be on its way.'

Constance could see that Mrs Marshall appeared to have switched to an automatic mode. Without thought she poured water into the teapot, moving back to the stove with the kettle. Performing routine tasks seemed to be comforting her, as though helping her cling to normality.

Matron McNally turned to Constance.

'Of course, she'll need someone to stay with her tonight,' she said; speaking as though Mrs Marshall was not present. 'I've given her a mild sedative already and have some Sydenham's Laudanum made up for her to take, so she will sleep. Will you be able to stay with her?' she asked.

'Yes, of course. Hector will be here directly and will collect some clothes and some of the casserole cook prepared earlier. We will be quite comfortable,' Constance replied.

Hearing Constance speak, Catherine Marshall looked up.

'I wonder how Victoria will cope with my son's death,' she commented.

July 1917 – France

Captain Hadleigh was delighted to see a break in the weather which had kept his squadron grounded for

323

several days. The summer was not looking very promising with far too many showers which prevented flying. At first, some of the squadron members had defied local rules and taken off despite the recommendation they did not. After a few needless deaths, where pilots crashed in poor visibility, an absolute ban on flying had been issued until the weather improved.

The sector had been very quiet for a number of months. A few battalions had been transferred to Flanders where a big push was happening; they had been accompanied by all of the support they needed, including medical personnel, stores and transport. The Somme was having a quiet time with only sporadic fighting; soldiers on both sides were happy that the intense fighting of a year ago seemed to have passed them by, at least for the time being.

When the weather was clement, Hadleigh spent his time trying to destroy barrage balloons, which were winched into position behind the German lines. Swinging from each balloon was a basket, containing an observer, who from his high up position was able to take notes of troop movements behind the Allied lines and report back to the German High Command. Hadleigh enjoyed playing a dangerous cat and mouse game. His aim was to destroy the balloon before the winch men on the ground realised he was in the vicinity and tried to frantically wind in the observer.

A couple of weeks previously Hadleigh visited a small group of men responsible for manning a balloon behind the British lines. He was sure that their balloon deployment tactics would mirror those of the Germans and wanted to plan a series of attacks with maximum success.

Osborne had accompanied him on the back of his motorcycle, keen to learn a little of the dangers that men observing from a static balloon faced. The road was muddy and difficult to negotiate with several large shell craters and lots of tree stumps, left from fighting the year before. Some trees were beginning to show early signs of regrowth with small shoots emerging from the stumps.

Towards the Front, noise became more intense. The shriek of occasional shells and rapid machine-gun fire was a little nerve-wracking for two men used to fighting their war high above the clouds. With a measure of relief, Hadleigh found the dirt track he was looking for and turned away from the trenches up ahead, riding towards a relatively undamaged wooded area.

Deep in the woods a clearing had been made to accommodate the largest balloon either man had ever seen. Filled with hydrogen, the balloon was straining at its moorings and looked ready to be launched. As Hadleigh dismounted from his motorcycle a lieutenant in the Royal Engineers strode across, came to a halt in front of him and saluted.

'Glad you could make it, sir. My name is Frost. We are about to take her up, to check out what Fritz has been up to. I can take one of you at a time, if you fancy a trip.'

Cautiously, Hadleigh climbed the ladder into the wicker basket suspended from the balloon. Frost climbed in beside him and then started barking orders to the engineers below. Gradually the balloon was freed from its moorings, until the only thing holding it was a steel hawser connected to a large winch.

Slowly the balloon rose above the tree tops and Hadleigh was able to see the trenches snaking through the landscape, as far as the eye could see. The ground was much closer and the detail much clearer than it ever was when he was flying, giving him an idea of how valuable the reconnaissance gained from balloons must be. In a corner of the balloon a field telephone was mounted giving Frost the capacity to communicate with the ground, without being winched down.

Hadleigh learnt that Frost was only able to deploy his balloon in favourable conditions. There could be no appreciable wind and although light rain was not considered an issue the accompanying poor visibility was. The balloons were expensive to manufacture, so great care was taken when they were launched and retrieved.

The biggest danger for any observer was enemy attack from the air, as the hydrogen used to inflate the balloon ignited easily; choosing to sit out the war behind the lines as an observer was seen at the best as foolhardy, with the prospect of a fiery death an ever-present reality.

***

Captain Hadleigh was excited that weather conditions were perfect and made his way to the hangar to make sure his kite was ready to go. Recently he had flown several missions without Osborne, in a single seater plane. The Sopwith Camel had been around since the start of the year, as a prototype, but had only recently arrived in France.

Hadleigh wanted to command a squadron of Camels, as he believed they would shortly dominate the war in the skies. April had been a terrible month with many pilots losing their lives at the hands of Baron von Richthofen, who managed to hunt down dozens of English planes because he had a superior class of aircraft.

The Camel was a highly manoeuvrable plane which could perform in extreme conditions. Unfortunately, it was also very sensitive with many pilots misreading the Camel's centre of gravity, causing them to crash on take-off. Hadleigh thought that anyone who survived a first outing in a Camel was welcome to join his squadron.

Hadleigh walked into the hangar and shouted for Sergeant Flynn.

'Sergeant, where are you?' he called. 'Is my kite operational? The weather is just about perfect for some balloon strafing,' he continued.

Flynn stepped out from behind the engine of a Triplane he had been servicing. 'The Camel is airworthy, sir, but this Triplane is much easier to control. Are you sure you don't want to take this for a spin? You'll get closer to the balloon, without needing to worry about stalling.'

With a dismissive wave Hadleigh walked across to the Camel which was parked just outside of the hanger on the close-cut grass. The day was cool with a fine haze present and not a breath of wind. Walking round the aircraft Hadleigh quickly performed his pre-flight checks. Everything seemed in order so he leapt up onto the wing and then climbed into the cockpit. Sergeant Flynn walked out of the hanger wiping his hands on an oily rag as he did so. Stuffing the rag into his trouser pocket, he walked to the undercarriage and pulled away the chocks, which had been keeping the aircraft from moving. He then moved to the front of the plane and stood waiting for the command to swing the propeller.

The Camel roared quickly into life; Flynn stood back and watched as Hadleigh taxied to the end of the field, turned back towards the chateau and took off. His take off was the smoothest Flynn had witnessed so far.

Clearly, he had got used to having an engine, a full fuel tank and his own weight located in the first seven feet of fuselage and was able to compensate accordingly.

The stillness of the day and the early hour combined to make flying exhilarating. Grateful for his leather flying jacket and the scarf knitted by his younger sister, Hadleigh climbed rapidly above the sparse cloud, scanning the sky to make sure no German aircraft were around.

Turning his plane to the east, Hadleigh started to fly to where he knew the Germans had been operating an observation balloon. High above the area he began to dive, steeper and steeper; straining every strut and wire supporting the Camel's wings. Coming out of the thin cloud cover he almost collided with the balloon. Grabbing the forward mounted machine gun, he raked the balloon with gunfire, using incendiary bullets provided for the purpose. The bullets tore through the balloon's material igniting the hydrogen beyond; the fire from the ensuing explosion engulfed both the observer's basket and the Camel, which was not flying quickly enough to avoid it. Hadleigh and the balloon observer both died instantly.

That evening Major Rochford asked all of his pilots to attend the traditional auction for Guy Hadleigh's belongings. The night was a long one with several toasts drunk to Hadleigh's fearless reputation and ability to dodge the Hun until his luck finally ran out. Rochford retired to his office to open a bottle of aged malt whisky. In silence he raised a glass to one of the bravest pilots he had ever had the privilege to fly with. Once Hadleigh's mess bill was paid little remained to send back to his parents, although in due course they did receive his Military Cross and a few other personal effects.

Chapter Twenty

Bent double, like old beggars under sacks,
Knock-kneed, coughing like hags, we cursed through
sludge,
Till on the haunting flares we turned our backs
And towards our distant rest began to trudge.
Men marched asleep. Many had lost their boots
But limped on, blood-shod. All went lame; all blind;
Drunk with fatigue; deaf even to the hoots
Of gas-shells shells dropping softly behind.
GAS! Gas! Quick, boys!-- An ecstasy of fumbling,
Fitting the clumsy helmets just in time;
But someone still was yelling out and stumbling
And floundering like a man in fire or lime.--
Dim, through the misty panes and thick green light
As under a green sea, I saw him drowning.
In all my dreams, before my helpless sight,
He plunges at me, guttering, choking, drowning.
If in some smothering dreams you too could pace
Behind the wagon that we flung him in,
And watch the white eyes writhing in his face,
His hanging face, like a devil's sick of sin;
If you could hear, at every jolt, the blood
Come gargling from the froth-corrupted lungs,

Obscene as cancer, bitter as the cud
Of vile, incurable sores on innocent tongues,--
My friend, you would not tell with such high zest
To children ardent for some desperate glory,
The old Lie: Dulce et decorum est
Pro patria mori.

Wilfred Owen, 1918

July 1917 – Flanders

Lady Julia Hadleigh wondered if this current push would ever be over. For six weeks now, the fighting around Ypres had been fierce, with no respite. She had been tested to the limit during this time; often called on to perform tasks which in peacetime would definitely be the preserve of senior physicians. Suturing was a skill she had picked up quickly, frequently being congratulated on her neat approach. Her mother would have found this surprising, after reading school reports from the Prudence Bradford College for Young Ladies which had almost made her hair curl.

Hadleigh had been summoned to see Sister Brennan, who was in charge in the absence of Matron Gillespie; Gillespie having taken a chill a month earlier, which still kept her incapacitated and convalescing at a small hospital just outside of Dover. Hadleigh did not know Brennan terribly well, as she had spent very little time since the war began working in the same place. She was vaguely aware that Brennan may have met her brother, but beyond that did not know if they had ever seen each other again.

Standing outside of her office waiting for the command to enter, Hadleigh could not think of any reason she may have been called away from the dressings she was attending to. Entering the office, she was mildly surprised to see it looked as if Brennan had been crying; her hat was awry and her eyes were red, disturbing her usual immaculate appearance.

'Nurse Hadleigh, please sit down. I am afraid I have some very bad news,' Brennan said.

***

Twenty minutes later, Hadleigh left Sister Brennan's office. She felt quite calm, as though for some odd reason she had been more in control of the situation than Brennan had. Brennan had been very tearful as she delivered the obligatory condolences and poured a glass of brandy to help with the shock, informing Hadleigh that her brother had died flying earlier that week.

The fact was, Hadleigh didn't know her brother Guy very well. For most of their childhood, one or other of them had been away at boarding school. The school holidays were punctuated by visits to stay at friends' houses, meaning they spent only short periods of time together. Hadleigh felt closer to Gerald, as before he was packed off to school, they had at least spent some time closeted in the schoolroom with a governess. Later, when she sought out Briggs and gave her the news, she couldn't help commenting on the disproportionate amount of sorrow she felt Brennan had exhibited as she delivered the news.

Hadleigh did not immediately return to the ward, but took Brennan's advice and went for a walk. Following the canal path, she did not have to walk far before arriving in open countryside. About a mile from the hospital was a small lock; the last one to be negotiated by hospital barges on their way to deliver supplies. When she could steal a few brief hours away from the hospital, Hadleigh often walked as far as the lock, happy to be out in the open air for a short time. Recently she had made friends with the lock keeper and his wife. Her schoolgirl French and time spent on the Continent meant she could speak enough French to be understood by Henri Defort and his wife Marie.

Henri was in the garden when she arrived; as soon as he saw her he started to wave and called for his wife. Within minutes they were all seated around an ornate iron garden table drinking a glass of lemonade Marie had made. In halting French Hadleigh explained about her brother and the reason for her sudden time off. The tranquillity of an afternoon spent in the sun speaking about her loss, made her feel better and more inclined to return to the unrelenting workload at the hospital.

Finishing her second glass of lemonade, Hadleigh stood up and prepared to take her leave; glancing along the canal she could just make out a barge in the distance and hoped it would be carrying her friend, Victoria Standish, who was due to arrive at the hospital any day soon.

During the Battle of Messines, Standish had been assigned briefly to the Casualty Clearing Station, which was where she heard the terrible news of Stanley Marshall's death. Following a short period of leave she had been posted to the hospital barges for a rest. Hadleigh had missed her, she felt as though they were closer to each other than anyone else she had ever known, having survived the hell of Lemnos and the tragedy of the *Ariadne* together.

As the barge edged closer Hadleigh was able to see Standish sitting on the deck in a comfortable chair. She was drinking a cup of tea, poured from a pot which had been placed on a small table beside her. In her other hand she held a small fishing rod, which was trailing lazily over the side of the barge. She was pleased to see that despite the trauma of the past few weeks, Standish appeared to be recovering. Hadleigh very much hoped that she would return to hospital work quickly, certain that the summers fighting was not yet over and that all the skill and expertise available would be needed at the Casualty Clearing Station.

July 1917 – France

Fiona Moncrieff flipped the sign round on the door to the Union Flag Café, indicating it was closed for cleaning and walked over to the service area. Pouring a cup of tea, she walked to the nearest table and sat down next to Lady Hadleigh and her daughter, who were already passing around a plate of sandwiches. Trade for the last couple of months had been brisk; it was obvious that an offensive was planned as most battalions had sent men on leave. Troop trains arrived in the port in unprecedented numbers, disgorging hundreds of men at a time. Moncrieff had been working as many hours as she could, to keep up with demand from men tired of a diet of tinned meat and hard biscuits. On the point of exhaustion, she was happy that this would be her last working day at the café. After a month in England and a little training, Moncrieff was off to drive an ambulance.

Roberta Hadleigh had at last left school and had been working at the café ever since. She was rapidly learning the war was not quite as glamorous as she thought it would be and that for the most part the soldiers she came into contact with were tired and filthy; wanting simply to go home to their families and sleep without the fear of being buried alive, or blown to pieces. Lady Hadleigh was happy her daughter was doing something useful and was no longer costing the family money gaining an expensive education, which she believed would not prepare her for life.

Lady Hadleigh had taken her son's death in her stride. When the telegram arrived, she and her husband were entertaining a group of London bankers and some old family friends to luncheon. The luncheon had been a productive one with several of the men present persuaded to donate funds to Lady Hadleigh's branch of the Red Cross; the money was vital to allow continued operation of the café in France and the one at Victoria Station.

After a knock at the front door Buxton entered the room and asked Lord and Lady Hadleigh to leave their guests as something urgent had cropped up. Walking into the morning room, Buxton gestured to a side table where the telegram was sitting on a small silver salver.

'I did not think you would want me to deliver this to you in the dining room, sir,' he stated, by way of an explanation.

'Quite right, Buxton,' Lord Hadleigh replied. He then stepped over to his wife and put his arm around her. Opening the telegram, they both read the contents. With a small gasp Lady Hadleigh sat down on the sofa and buried her head in her hands. Lord Hadleigh cleared his throat and spoke.

'Buxton, it would appear that Captain Guy has been killed while attempting to destroy an enemy balloon. We will need a few moments alone. Can you please explain what has happened to our guests and ask that they forgive us but the luncheon is over? Let them know we will be in contact shortly.'

'Of course, sir; I will bring Lady Hadleigh some brandy and a cup of tea,' Buxton replied.

Lady Hadleigh did not allow the household to be consumed with grief for long. The news seemed to strengthen her belief that everyone should be assisting with the cause, however slight their contribution. After another visit to Teddy Moncrieff at the War Office, she managed to obtain permission to travel to France with Mrs Trent; essentially to check on the Union Café and see if she would be able to buy the building next door. Expansion of the café was desperately needed to accommodate the larger then ever numbers of soldiers passing through. She also intended, if the opportunity arose, to travel closer to the front line.

Reports in the *Times* continued to decry conditions women working as nurses and ambulance drivers were expected to endure. Having obtained funds, Lady Hadleigh hoped to create a rest area not too far behind the front line, for nurses and ambulance drivers to experience a little luxury when they could get away. She intended to recruit local staff to assist in looking after their needs and had a list of buildings set in pleasant surroundings. She felt sure she would be able to report back to the Red Cross Committee with positive news, after visiting a few places and having duly considered all options.

Finishing her tea, Lady Hadleigh stood up.

'Roberta, I shall let you know how things are once we reach the Front and will of course see you on my return. Good luck, Fiona, I hope you do not find ambulance driving too arduous. I'm sure Teddy will keep us all informed of your progress.'

September 1917 – Belgium

Lieutenant Colonel Gerald Hammond was happier than he had been in months. After what seemed like a lifetime as a staff officer, working from the relative safety of headquarters, he had finally been rewarded with his own battalion and promotion to lieutenant colonel. Throughout July and August, he had been driving his men hard, training them for the impending attack.

From the sidelines they had all watched and heard the bombardment which took place at the end of July, before action involving the 8th Division. Hammond was confident that his battalion would acquit themselves well when called on to relieve the men involved in the initial assault.

The weather had been wet and cold, despite being summer. August was to be the wettest August on record. Troop movements had reduced the already muddy fields around Ypres to a bog. Towards the end of the first week in August it became impossible to move artillery without spending a considerable period of time digging out the guns, as they were easily bogged down. Reports filtered down from headquarters of men drowning after stumbling into shell holes filled with water. Orders were immediately posted telling the men to take extreme care, especially at night.

Casualty Clearing Stations were full of men suffering a range of medical conditions brought on by the appalling weather; after spending hours up to their waists in water when in the front line.

Hammond and his men marched into trenches close to the Menin Road, ready for one of the smaller battles of the offensive; he was understandably nervous, after being away from the fighting for so long, but very happy to be back with his men. Just before he left, he managed to contact his wife at the Casualty Clearing Station and arrange a clandestine meeting. He was pleased no one seemed to have discovered their secret and that she was occupied with preparing for the forthcoming offensive, so had little time to fret.

The bombardment started before dawn and was much more effective than a year before on the Somme. A far higher proportion of shells landed in the German trenches, clearing the way for the Allied Forces to take the ground with relative ease. The Germans had been preparing for the fight for months, knowing that the area around Ypres was where the Allies were concentrating large numbers of troops. They had spent a considerable period of time strengthening their front line, intent on making it impenetrable. Concrete pillboxes overlooked the trenches which were themselves far better constructed than previously. Dugouts were more permanent, with some containing a back exit to prevent troops becoming trapped if under attack.

The battle when it started was chaotic. As night became dawn and then finally turned into day, Hammond's men left the trenches and started towards their objective. The rain which had plagued the area for the whole of summer had stopped, but had left behind mud and deep craters filled with freezing muddy water. A fine mist hung over no man's land causing men to stumble; some got caught and started to sink into the mud, others walked on quickly, only to fall into the deep shell holes full of water.

The bombardment and months of shelling had left the woods surrounding the Menin Road devoid of trees. As the Germans waited for the attack to begin they launched a barrage of mustard gas onto the unsuspecting Allies; aware that it was unlikely the gas would kill but hoping to disable the attacking force.

Mustard gas was more pervasive than the phosgene gas used earlier in the war. Heavier than air the gas settled on the ground where it was effective days and sometimes weeks after it had been launched with devastating effect on the advancing armies. Knowing that the Germans were likely to launch a gas attack, Hammond had ordered that all of his men carry the most up to date respirator, his quartermaster sergeant was able to obtain. The respirators provided were cumbersome and difficult to deploy quickly. Often as the gas descended men were still trying to pull tight the straps.

B Company bore the brunt of the gas attack; Captain Jerome Green and Company Sergeant Major Wilkes were standing together and smelt the faint aroma of gas. Shouting an order, Green pulled on his rubber gas mask before looking towards his men. Guardsman Richard Pringle appeared unable to pull his mask tabs tight and was beginning to be affected by the fumes. Staggering around trying desperately to fit the mask he eventually slumped to the ground. The air was thick with gas and had taken on a yellowish tinge; it rapidly became difficult to see anything as a thick fog descended.

***

The Casualty Clearing Station was prepared for the men arriving down the line, but had not banked on the delays the mud would cause. The mud was treacherous, with double the number of stretcher bearers needed to transport each casualty; it was to be a long time after the battle started before the first of the wounded began to arrive.

Hadleigh was having a break; recently she had begun to smoke, finding the activity gave her the time to calm down and take stock of her current situation. She lit a cigarette and inhaled deeply before sitting down on a bench situated close to the hospital, on a pathway which led to the canal. Earlier, Blackstone had ordered her to take twenty minutes off before reporting to Sister Standish to help with any new arrivals.

As Hadleigh finished her break and stood up intending to return to the ward, five ambulances arrived with seated wounded on board. The ambulances had wheels which were caked in mud and looked as though they had driven hard through impossible conditions to reach the hospital. The first ambulance had steam billowing from its bonnet and was clearly in need of some urgent mechanical attention.

Each ambulance contained six walking wounded; all but the first man emerged with heavily bandaged eyes, needing assistance to negotiate the steps leading from the truck. Once safely on the ground, the five men with bandaged eyes stepped forward, each placing a hand on the shoulder of the man in front; the sixth man who had a minor injury and did not appear to have suffered any adverse effects from the gas, then set off leading them all to the hospital entrance.

Realising she was needed, Hadleigh began to walk quickly towards the hospital. Skirting round the wounded men she arrived back in the ward, slightly breathless.

'Sister, there are about thirty men arriving, who are all blind,' she announced when she found Standish.

Standish looked up from the supply inventory she was attempting to get to grips with and stood up quickly. 'Thanks for the warning, Hadleigh, can you please fetch a trolley containing bicarbonate of soda and the cocaine solution we prepared earlier? We will also need plenty of dressings. While you do that I will get some oxygen cylinders from the orderlies. You will need to be quick; it looks like the lull is over. Report back to me once you have done this.'

The nursing staff worked in teams to settle the gassed men as quickly as possible. Clothing was removed cautiously and was taken away by orderlies to be burnt. Despite taking every precaution, some orderlies began to feel the effects of gas exposure themselves. The constant handling of men who had been exposed to mustard gas took its toll, with men reporting mustard burns to the hands and face. Nurses were only able to work for short periods of time without complaining of sore throats and irritated eyes; a roster was quickly developed to give adequate time away from the area.

The Casualty Clearing Station staff had never come across the debilitating nature of mustard gas injuries. Men exposed to the gas were often blind, which fortunately in most cases only lasted for several days. The pain was excruciating and was accompanied by large yellow blisters concealing chemical burns. The worst part of it all was, that those who had inhaled the gas felt unable to breathe and cried out constantly. Hadleigh and Briggs worked together moving down one side of the ward replacing dressings and administering oxygen in ten-minute cycles. Time became meaningless as hour after hour they continued to work, stopping only when their own symptoms became so difficult to put up with it was necessary to rest for a while.

***

The battle had been raging for several days when Lieutenant Colonel Hammond was brought in. His battalion had become temporarily disorientated during the mustard gas attack, but recovered and continued on towards their objective. Hammond was leading from the front with Company Sergeant Major Wilkes on one side and Captain Green on the other. They were all inching forward slowly, keeping an eye out for shell craters when the fog started to lift.

Rapid machine-gun fire started almost instantly with the Germans concentrating fire on men emerging from the fog. Hammond was hit twice in his thigh with one bullet shattering his femur, close to his kneecap. Seeing him fall, Wilkes arrived quickly by his side and pulled out a large field dressing, which he applied to the wound creating a compression bandage.

'Leave me here, Sergeant Major,' Hammond ordered. 'There should be some stretcher bearers along shortly who will get me back to our lines.'

'Are you sure, sir? I think you are too exposed here. Perhaps I should try and move you to where those tree stumps are on the right. It looks a little more sheltered,' Wilkes replied.

Slowly Wilkes began to drag Hammond sideways to a less vulnerable position. Propping him up against a tree stump he gave him a sip of water from his bottle, before running off to re-join his company.

It was to be almost a full day before Hammond was picked up by stretcher bearers, who then began the torturous journey down the line. Drifting in and out of consciousness he was unaware at times of the painfully slow progress made toward the Casualty Clearing Station. The stretcher bearers staggered through the mud, cautiously testing the ground at each step to make sure they didn't all sink. Eventually they arrived at the Regimental Aid Post, where a cursory examination was made, before Hammond was loaded into one of the roadside ambulances; parked waiting to take on the wounded.

Fiona Moncrieff finished her oil and water checks, pulled down the heavy ambulance bonnet and while attempting to clean her grease stained hands with an old rag, walked around to the back doors to supervise the wounded being loaded. She gasped as she recognised Hammond lying semi-conscious on a stretcher.

Growing up Fiona Moncrieff had admired Lady Julia's elder brother from a distance, hoping that one day he may become aware of her existence. Unfortunately, the war had intervened before she was old enough to join his social circle through the long dreamt about London Season. Now standing in a very different world and looking at the shattered remains of his right leg Moncrieff hoped only to get him safely to the Casualty Clearing Station, without him dying before they got there.

After supervising the loading of five more wounded, Moncrieff got behind the wheel and started to move off slowly towards Essex Farm.

Chapter Twenty-One

If I were fierce, and bald, and short of breath,
I'd live with scarlet Majors at the Base,
And speed glum heroes up the line to death.
You'd see me with my puffy petulant face,
Guzzling and gulping in the best hotel,
Reading the Roll of Honour. 'Poor young chap,'
I'd say – 'I used to know his father well';
And when war is done and youth stone dead,
I'd toddle safely home and die – in bed.

Siegfried Sassoon

September 1917 – Flanders

The Casualty Clearing Station was at capacity. As soon as men were patched up and evacuated either by hospital barge or by train, their beds were filled with a fresh batch of wounded. Lieutenant Colonel Hammond was brought in by ambulance at dusk. Moncrieff had driven carefully, skirting each pothole on the road to the Casualty Clearing Station, acutely aware that the smallest jolt may lead to an uncontrollable haemorrhage. She was driving a Rover-Sunbeam ambulance, converted by a London firm and donated by her father;

after lessons in its operation, she had joined a group of private ambulance drivers working in convoy to transport the wounded.

Driving into the hospital forecourt Moncrieff gently applied the brake bringing the ambulance to a stop. Climbing out of the cabin she walked to the back and opened the doors. She was happy to see Hammond did not appear any worse for his ordeal; his face was drawn with pain and he remained semi-conscious, but the bloodied bandages covering his thigh had no new stains on them.

Within seconds, an orderly and a VAD nurse she was unable to place but vaguely recognised, arrived at the ambulance. The nurse saw Lieutenant Colonel Hammond and immediately gave a shocked cry of recognition.

Briggs looked at Moncrieff. 'I must warn Lady Julia, before she sees him like this,' she said, starting to walk quickly towards the building.

Moncrieff recognised her retreating back as Briggs, a former ladies' maid and couldn't help thinking she seemed far more self-assured than she had been in service.

Hammond was carried into the main assessment area, where Major Chardingly was called and rapidly arrived to inspect his wounds. Slowly an orderly cut away at his uniform jacket and trousers, which smelt strongly of mustard gas. He had a couple of small blistered burns where the flesh on his wrists had been exposed, but in general appeared to have been lucky; his gas mask had clearly worked and he was not suffering any respiratory or optical complications.

His right leg was covered from mid-thigh to knee cap with a large padded field dressing, which had not been disturbed at the Regimental Aid Post; for fear he may bleed. Spots of dried blood mixed with mud crusted on top of the dressing. Major Chardingly addressed Sister Blackstone who was standing with a group of people gathered around the stretcher.

'Sister, I intend to take these bandages down to look at the extent of the damage underneath. We must do that quickly if there is to be any chance of saving his leg. We should go straight to theatre, where we can look at the wound under anaesthetic and can sew up any bleeders as we find them.' He paused for a moment, to examine the outside of the bandage before continuing. 'He has been lying in such appallingly muddy conditions his leg will have started to fester and may be gangrenous. Can you make sure there is plenty of Eusol to hand, to clean the exposed flesh?'

'As you wish, sir,' Blackstone replied. 'I believe this young man is Viscount Hammond. His sister, Nurse Hadleigh, is a VAD on the staff here. She will of course be relieved of any duties she may have, to be close to him. We will need to stabilise Viscount Hammond and get him out to England as soon as possible. I believe his presence here may disrupt the smooth running of the hospital, with so many of the nursing staff knowing him,' she continued.

Before Major Chardingly was able to express any kind of an opinion, Sister Brennan arrived almost running. To the astonishment of the staff gathered around the stretcher she came to an abrupt halt at his side, looked down at the muddy, wounded body lying there and promptly burst into tears

Blackstone quickly took control of the situation. 'Briggs! Please take Sister Brennan to the office and make her a cup of tea. There is a small flask of brandy in the top drawer of the desk, on the left-hand side. As soon as I am able I will come there. In the meantime, do not leave her alone. Clearly this has been a great shock for her.'

Briggs gently led Brennan away, taking her to the Matron's office where she sat her down.

'Are you feeling all right, ma'am?' she asked, at the same time as she poured a generous measure of brandy into a crystal glass. 'Viscount Hammond is Hadleigh's brother. We need to find her to let her know he's here. I've been looking but she's not on any of the wards,' Briggs continued.

Brennan lifted her head and sighed. 'She is down in the dispensary making up some more of the cocaine mixture for the gas cases. I must speak with her urgently. Please can you send an orderly to find her?

She will be anxious to see her brother, but he will be in theatre for some time and what I have to tell her won't wait.'

***

Hadleigh left the dispensary and walked as quickly as she could to Matron's office. She was puzzled as well as being a little unhappy that she had been ordered to report to the acting matron before being allowed to see her brother; although she acknowledged she would not be able to enter the operating theatre and it was better to occupy herself with whatever trivia Brennan was likely to ask her to do than sit around waiting and thinking.

Knocking on the door she entered as soon as she was asked to do so. Brennan had regained her composure and was busy reading a letter which Hadleigh quickly realised was in a hand she recognised as her brother's. Brennan looked up and beckoned her to be seated in a chair which had been placed in front of her desk. Folding the letter carefully she put it back in an envelope and spoke.

'Hadleigh, what I'm going to say will come as something of a shock to you but I'm hoping that the explanation will help you to understand why you have not been a party to this news before now,' Brennan said. 'There is no other way to break this, Viscount Hammond and I got married in May of this year, at the

Holy Trinity Church in Blythburgh. We honeymooned in Southwold before returning to France in early June. Your parents and younger sister were all present.'

Without waiting for a response, Brennan stood up and walked over to the window. Gesturing towards the courtyard, where a stream of ambulances was rolling through the gates, she continued.

'We both agreed that I should nurse until the end of the war and not leave all of this. There are precious few trained nurses available to work at the Front. The war has taken its toll here as everywhere, but as each month passes more nurses are needed at home to look after the long-term wounded, if not to help with their families. It seemed such a selfish thing to give up nursing just because we got married, despite the regulations which say I must. We couldn't tell you because of your position here, which would have been compromised; you would have been honour-bound to inform the hospital commandant of my position.' As she spoke tears began to roll down her cheeks. 'I will be so sad to give all of this up.'

Hadleigh stood up and walked over to the window. Standing beside Brennan she reached out and hugged her. 'This is a lot to take in. I knew you had both met, but had no idea you had developed such a close relationship. I am glad for you both, no one will hear about your marriage from me although you may have given yourself away earlier. He will come through this you know; the Hadleigh family is a tough one. I think we should go and wait close by, in case there is some news.'

***

Major Chardingly would afterwards describe the surgery he performed as the most intricate and painstaking of the war. He was used to patching people up; amputating limbs and sending the wounded rapidly on. Acutely aware that Hammond was not only related to Nurse Hadleigh, but had also been courting Sister Brennan, who he had loved and lost, Chardingly was determined to do the best possible for the man.

In the assessment area when Chardingly carefully removed the bandages, copious amounts of blood poured from the wound, causing him to wonder if the bullet had torn through the femoral vein. Quickly he reapplied the bandages before wheeling the man into theatre for exploratory surgery.

Chardingly started to prepare himself for the operation ahead, by scrubbing and disinfecting his hands, prior to donning clean surgical gloves; Sister Blackstone entered the room.

'We have found Hadleigh, sir. She's outside waiting with Sister Brennan,' Blackstone reported.

'Great, can you please bring her in here? I may need Hadleigh to give some of her blood to her brother, if he is to survive this.'

Hadleigh arrived in the operating theatre and was asked to give a blood sample for serum testing. Sitting her down, Chardingly applied a tourniquet to her arm and extracted a small sample of blood after introducing a needle into one of her veins. Giving the blood-filled syringe to an orderly, he spoke.

'Take this as quickly as you can to Colonel West in the laboratory and ask that he tests to see if it matches the blood sample we have taken from Lieutenant Colonel Hammond. Let him know that if it does I intend to perform a transfusion as soon as possible.'

Turning to Hadleigh, Major Chardingly gently explained that her brother had lost a great deal of blood and may not survive surgery, but if they were a match, some of her blood would possibly improve his chances. She agreed immediately to the proposition and sat down in a corridor close by to wait. Hadleigh had heard of the lifesaving effects transfusions had earlier in the war, but had not so far witnessed it first-hand. A short time later Chardingly called Hadleigh back into theatre; next to her brother another theatre table had been set up.

'The match is positive Hadleigh. If you can lie down here we'll transfuse Lieutenant Colonel Hammond before I undertake the more delicate part of his operation.'

Major Chardingly reapplied a tourniquet to Hadleigh's arm. Making sure she was comfortable he then inserted a large-bore tube into a vein in her arm and attached it to a piece of tubing. The other end of the tubing was then fed through the neck of a small bottle, into which her blood ran freely. A piece of tubing ran from the bottle straight to a vein in her brother's arm. Strapping the needle and tubing to Hadleigh's arm Chardingly produced a rolled-up bandage which he placed in her hand, asking her to squeeze on it at regular intervals to increase blood flow. Once the transfusion was complete Hadleigh was told to lie still for a few minutes, before being given a cup of hot sweet tea, to help with any possible shock she may be feeling.

Hammond survived the initial exploratory surgery Major Chardingly performed. His wound had been cleaned and debrided with as much Flanders mud as possible washed out; his femoral vein was repaired using intricate little stitches. For several days following the operation, Hammond drifted in and out of consciousness, with high fevers indicating his wound may be infected. Hadleigh and Brennan took turns to nurse him round the clock, giving morphia when they felt he had become restless with the pain and introducing a regime of cold sponges to bring down his temperature.

His thigh was dressed several times a day and had Eusol injected into the silver drainage tube poking through the bandages. Initially the wound discharged large amounts of yellow pus, but slowly the drainage became clearer and clearer until the only fluid returning was the antiseptic which had been injected in. Major Chardingly inspected the wound himself every day. Each time he looked at the wound he withdrew the drainage tube a fraction, until eventually the tube fell out.

***

Lady Hadleigh took the news that her eldest son had been injured and was gravely ill badly. She had come to terms with the loss of her younger son gradually, keeping herself busy with the Red Cross Committees she organised and by trying not to dwell on the tragedy. The prospect of losing her eldest son as well was too much to accept in such a short space of time.

When the telegram arrived advising that her son Gerald was wounded and unlikely to survive, she immediately tackled Teddy Moncrieff at the War Office, to see if anything could be done to hasten his return to England. She was aware that several eminent London families had dealt with the news that a relative was injured by sending a private ambulance to collect them. However, this practice imposed an enormous strain on already harassed transport officers, with increased road traffic and an increased demand for transport to ferry private ambulances across the Channel.

Teddy Moncrieff could only advise Lady Hadleigh to wait in the hope Lieutenant Colonel Hammond would be transferred to England soon. Not content with this advice Lady Hadleigh booked a passage to France, advising the War Office she was travelling to France to work for a few weeks with her daughter at the Union Flag Café.

September 1917 – France

The crossing from Dover had been rough. Lady Hadleigh had been invited to dine with the captain on the voyage across and was happy that her appetite was not affected by the rolling motion of the ship. The food was well prepared and nourishing, a welcome change from the standard of food currently available in London, where legislation was in place to conserve the best supplies for the war effort.

England had begun to suffer at the hands of the German Navy. Throughout the war England continued to rely on food supplies imported from the United States and Canada, with merchant ships regularly crossing the Atlantic. The German Navy had recently perfected the art of submarine warfare and had taken to torpedoing merchant shipping in the Atlantic, significantly impacting on the quality of food available for general consumption. Much to her embarrassment Lady Hadleigh found herself having to offer meagre portions to guests at dinner parties, often with minimal meat content. The lavish dinner parties she and Lord Hadleigh had hosted before the war were long gone; the last time they had hosted a dinner party with enough guests to fill the dining room table was a distant memory.

Initially the seas were too rough for HMS *Stapleton* to negotiate the harbour walls and dock. The ship spent several hours wallowing outside the safety of the harbour, waiting to cross a treacherous sand bar at the port entrance. A midshipman kept a weather eye out for submarines; scanning the sea continuously for signs of activity with a pair of binoculars. Lady Hadleigh and the other passengers waited nervously for news that it was safe to enter the harbour. Eventually the captain declared it was safe to take the ship in, docking without incident in the wind and pouring rain.

Lady Hadleigh arranged for her luggage to be delivered to the hotel she intended to base herself at and strode down the gangway to the Union Flag Café. Opening she door she entered into the warm steamy atmosphere of the café. Her daughter was in the middle of dishing up plates of hot sausage rolls, which made the café smell like the kitchen in Bedford Square after cook had been baking. Lady Hadleigh sniffed appreciatively before walking over to greet her daughter.

***

Over the last eighteen months Lady Hadleigh had got to know almost everyone of any importance, working to supply the trenches and smooth the progress of the war. Major Creswell, the Area Transport Officer was possibly the most important man in France. Responsible for troop movements in and out of the port he was the only person who could arrange passage for her to the Ypres Salient. The evening after her arrival in France, Lady Hadleigh could be seen entertaining Major Creswell, having arranged a dinner engagement when she got off the ship the afternoon before.

'I appreciate this must be a busy time for you, Major,' Lady Hadleigh stated. 'I must see my son though. I've heard how some people are causing problems bringing across private ambulances to collect their wounded; I've not done that, but I do need to go to him, to make sure he is receiving the very best of care. He is the only son we have left now,' she continued.

'I shall see what can be done, ma'am. I'm sure we can arrange something. My concern is for your safety though. We can get you to the front line, but cannot look after you once you get there. Would it not be better for you to remain here until your son is well enough to travel?' Major Creswell asked.

'No, if transport is at all possible then I must go. Do not worry about my comfort; as you will be aware, Major, I bought a small chateau not far from Ypres a couple of months ago and have been preparing it as a rest area for nursing staff working close to the Front. The rooms have just been finished and I believe the staff move in this week; the plan is to open by the end of the month. I shall be quite comfortable there while I wait for my son to recover enough to travel,' Lady Hadleigh replied.

The journey to the Front was tedious in the extreme. Lady Hadleigh was lucky enough to travel in the first-class part of the train, with a carriage full of officers returning to their battalions after short spells of leave. She was well prepared for the inevitable delays which accompanied every trip and had brought adequate provisions. In a small wicker hamper she was carrying freshly baked sausage rolls, sandwiches, a fruit cake and a large ham and veal pie. The hamper also contained several bottles of French wine and a bottle of champagne; which she intended to drink with her daughter once she had been assured her son was on the mend.

At last the train drew in to the station closest to the Ypres Salient. Lady Hadleigh alighted from the train, found a station porter to assist with her luggage and set about finding her way to the chateau. The war felt very close, with sporadic explosions and the sound of gun fire ever present, as the trap took her to the chateau. Lady Hadleigh found it difficult to imagine what it must be like for her son and daughter to live with the constant fear that they could be killed or wounded at any moment.

October 1917 – Belgium

Lady Julia Hadleigh removed the last of her brother's dressings and peered closely at the wound beneath. The wound looked clean and appeared to be healing nicely with granulating pink flesh. Over the years she had spent nursing, she had observed that when a wound turned green and pus started to pour from it, amputation soon followed. She was proud of the effort she and Sister Brennan had made to save his leg and pleased it seemed to be working. The previous evening Major Chardingly had spent a considerable period of time examining Hammond's wound and had then announced he was fit to travel to England on the next available hospital train.

'Well, Gerald, I reckon this may be the end of the war for you,' Hadleigh announced to her brother. 'With luck it'll take several months before you are fit to do anything at all. Mama may pull some strings and get you a safe job at the War Office,' she continued.

'I hate to disappoint, but as soon as I am fit I hope to get back here, old thing!' Hammond replied. 'I feel as though every minute I'm away I'm letting the battalion down. My men have come to trust me. Some of them have been fighting with me since 1914. I don't pretend to know what we are fighting for any more; but win or lose I want to be here with them at the end. I would feel as though I'd failed if I'm not. But enough of this gloomy talk; have you any idea what has happened to my wife? She went to pack a suitcase hours ago.'

Hadleigh finished bandaging her brother's leg and pulled the bed covers back over the metal frame protecting him. Turning around, she was happy to see her mother had arrived and was standing waiting patiently for her to finish.

'Mama, as always, Gerald is being impossible. You may need to talk some sense into him. I'm off to find his wife, to say goodbye.'

Sister Margaret Brennan was struggling to close the locks on her suitcase when Hadleigh entered. After several years at the Front she was taking home far more than she had arrived with. The regular requests for essential items to be bought by her family at Salmons and sent out, added up to a suitcase she now had trouble closing.

Following the revelation that she had defied all rules and regulations and was married, Brennan had, after deliberation, been allowed to stay and nurse her husband; providing she went with him when he was moved to England. She was leaving now with some trepidation, unsure that her new life as Viscountess Hammond would be as satisfying as the one she was leaving. Although frustrated beyond belief at times with military protocol and the hospital hierarchy, Brennan had never known anything else. She was about to leave a familiar world for one of privilege; where she would not be expected to do anything more exacting than decide on what she wished prepared for dinner.

Hadleigh crossed the room and hugged Brennan.

'I'm going to miss you, Margaret,' she commented. 'We must get a move on though. I think the ambulances are almost ready to leave. They were being loaded with wounded as I walked here. I have just done Gerald's dressing and Sister Standish gave him a small injection of morphia.'

'Promise you will write to me?' Brennan asked. Wiping back a tear she walked over to her suitcase, picked it up and quickly left the room.

With a great deal of care, the stretcher carrying Lieutenant Colonel Hammond was loaded into the back of an ambulance, to begin the long slow trip home to England where months of convalescence awaited him.

Chapter Twenty-Two

Here dead we lie because we did not choose
To live and shame the land from which we sprung;
Life to be sure is nothing much to lose;
But young men think it is and we were young.

A.E. Houseman

March 1918 – Sydney

Constance Standish finished arranging the display of flowers and stood back to look at her creation. With a contented sigh she looked around the church at the three other displays she had already completed and positioned at various points close to the altar. Flowers were at a premium this year, with every available piece of land utilised to grow crops for the war effort. Constance had managed to maintain a small garden close to the kitchen at Oakfield House, which produced some seasonal flowers for just such an event as Easter Sunday, due to be celebrated the following day.

Much had happened in the lives of the Camden community over the past year. Mrs Marshall was the first in a long line of people to feel the loss of a loved one. Stanley Marshall's death was followed by several skirmishes involving Australian divisions. By the end of the European summer and autumn almost every family in the district had been directly affected by the war, losing sons, brothers and fathers to the cause. The casualty list read out by the Reverend Sharpe at each Sunday service seemed to grow in size every week, as did the number of families who attended wearing black mourning clothes.

Christmas was a sombre affair with very few celebrations taking place as each family braced themselves for yet another year of war. For the first time at the start of the New Year no one was predicting the war would be over by Christmas, with a glorious allied victory. The newspapers had given up speculating on an outcome to a World War which had finally attracted American involvement in April of 1917 and looked set to continue for many years to come.

Constance and Hector were both relieved to have received a letter from Victoria two days before. She appeared to be coming to terms with the loss of Stanley Marshall nine months before, by throwing herself into her work. Her letters home described a world of unrelenting pressure where every small push produced multiple casualties. Day after day, she and her colleagues were woken at all hours to help deal with the long line of ambulances waiting to discharge their wounded.

She wrote of a close friend who worked alongside her and appeared to have fallen for Max. Difficult as it was in war-torn Belgium, with restrictions on movement and strict chaperone arrangements for nursing staff, somehow the romance had flourished. Victoria even hinted a wedding may be the end result, if her brother survived the war.

Constance was secretly delighted by this news believing that her son needed to settle down and produce an heir for Oakfield House. She was intrigued that her son appeared to have fallen for a member of the English aristocracy and wondered how she would settle at Oakfield House if the pair ever married. Constance decided to make enquiries of Burkes Peerage to find out more of the family she may soon be related to.

Hector Standish bought the trap to a halt outside of St John's Church and strode inside eager to collect his wife. Hector was planning to spend the greater part of the afternoon updating his map with the latest information the Sydney papers could provide, before discussing in detail troop movements and possible battle plans with Colonel Runcorn, who had retired from the Light Horse several years before and was something of an authority on any military subject. The meetings between the two men had become a regular early evening occurrence each Sunday, with the war discussed over a glass of the finest malt whisky.

'As always you have produced a spectacular Easter display, my darling,' Hector commented as he entered the church.

'Thank you,' his wife replied. 'We have had some nice flowers in the garden this year. I still have some left for a few displays at the hospital, if you could take me there. I promised Mrs Marshall I would drop by and perhaps help with some letter writing for the men who cannot do it themselves. There are a few recently returned soldiers unable to write because of their injuries.'

March 1918 – Belgium

The Wild Poppy Café was slowly coming to life. The evening was still young, with the majority of patrons not expected for at least an hour. Sitting in a secluded corner of the café, Lieutenant Colonel Chardingly lifted up the bottle of champagne and refilled the two glasses standing on the table. Seated opposite him Judith Blackstone raised her glass and spoke.

'Congratulations on your promotion, sir. This is definitely not before time. I believe you have been responsible for saving countless lives over the last few years. There are many men who should be grateful to you.'

'Nonsense, Sister! We have all played a part,' Chardingly replied. 'I may have been able to patch men up before sending them back to Blighty, but my war has been boring in comparison to yours. I have spent most nights, when away from the operating theatre, relatively safe in my quarters. I cannot imagine what the fear must have been like when the *Ariadne* sank and when they bombed the hospital. It seems to me that I work amongst some very brave women, who should be recognised for their heroic deeds.'

Taking a sip of champagne Chardingly continued. 'It is good to get away for an evening though and if I may say so it's a pleasure to be with such charming company.'

'That's very kind of you, sir. I have been looking forward this evening for a while. I think everyone needs a break from the pressure,' Blackstone replied.

The truth was that while he was pining for Margaret Brennan, Lieutenant Colonel Chardingly had not looked at any of the nurses other than in a professional capacity. After Viscount Hammond was wounded, he had at last acknowledged that unless the man was killed, he was unlikely to ever feature as a romantic contender in Margaret Brennan's eyes and if he wanted a wife would need to look elsewhere. A practical man, Chardingly had plans for when the war was over; he hoped to live a quiet life as a family doctor, close to the sea if possible. With such plans he thought it may be beneficial to find a wife who would bear him the children he desired, sooner rather than later.

Lieutenant Colonel Chardingly proved to be an entertaining and witty companion. He regaled Blackstone with stories of the days spent learning his craft. For years he had studied medicine at St Mary's in London, before moving to King's College Hospital just prior to the start of the war. At St Mary's he had been lucky enough to work for a short period with Alexander Fleming, who as a young man was a driving force behind innovative medical treatment; some of the desire to find modern medical solutions had unwittingly been passed on to Joseph Chardingly, who was seen as something of a risk taker by his peers.

Judith Blackstone had always thought that Chardingly was a charming man. She admired his skill when he operated and was impressed with the way he carried on in a calm unruffled fashion regardless of any commotion occurring around him. His recent promotion had come swiftly, after an evening where he continued to operate despite shells falling so close to the tent he was in. Everyone else not directly involved in the surgery that day was evacuated to a safer place. It was rumoured that he may be awarded the Military Cross for his actions that day, a fact his promotion to lieutenant colonel seemed to confirm.

Blackstone, who had always assumed she would continue nursing until she either retired to a small cottage somewhere or collapsed in the saddle, was beginning to question her future. The thought that she may have met a man who was interested in her as a woman was a little difficult to comprehend, after all nurses with good career prospects did not have time for men. Slowly she was beginning to think that a life away from caring for the sick may be an attractive proposition.

Blackstone, who had been immersed in these thoughts, while Chardingly discussed the merits of a cigar he wished to smoke with the café proprietor, gave a start. Coming from behind her she heard a familiar voice laughing. She did not need to look to know that shortly they would be spotted and that Lady Julia Hadleigh would be aware of their assignation.

***

Lady Julia Hadleigh glanced across the café as she walked in to where Major Max Standish was sitting and noticed Sister Blackstone was having dinner with Lieutenant Colonel Chardingly. For reasons of her own she did not wish to be spotted having dinner with an Australian officer, but thought it likely that nothing would be said as Blackstone was also breaking a few rules.

Hadleigh was very concerned. After months of fighting in the Belgian Sector, Major Standish had been posted to the French part of the Western Front. Rumour was rife that the Australians were regrouping around

Amiens where intelligence pointed to an imminent German attack, and that in order to repel the advance a second Battle of the Somme was being planned. Aware that they were not alone, Hadleigh did not give Major Standish the customary kiss on the cheek but sat down beside him rather abruptly.

'I'm sorry to be late. Briggs and I were made to scrub out some bed pans before being allowed to leave the ward for the evening off. We have a new Sister, Norma Morris, who is fresh out from England and is a little rigid in her approach. She keeps finding fault with everything I do, I'm not sure she likes VADs terribly much,' Hadleigh said as she sat down.

'That's all right, darling. Now listen to me for a minute! I have to leave on the midnight train. It looks like the battalion is being transferred back to France; I'm sure the Casualty Clearing Station will eventually follow, so we may meet again soon, but some things need to be sorted out before I leave.' Standish spoke hurriedly. 'I have something for you which I've carried throughout the war, waiting for this moment.'

Standish reached into his breast pocket and took out a small leather box, which he handed across the table to Lady Julia. Nestled on top of a silk lining was the most exquisite opal Lady Julia had ever seen attached to a gold chain. In the dimmed light of the Café Bleu it was possible to see the deep blues and greens glinting as the candle on the table flickered.

'This belonged to my grandmother and was found on land they owned to the north of Sydney; it's more practical than a ring, because no one will know you are wearing it. Julia will you marry me?' Standish asked.

Without needing time to think Hadleigh agreed immediately. Maxwell Standish removed the opal from its box and leaning forward hung the chain around her neck, making sure the clasp was secure.

'I will buy you a proper ring once this war is over,' he murmured.

May 1918 – London

Viscountess Hammond tried to sit still at her dressing table and allow Emily to finish combing her hair. She had spent an hour getting ready for a charitable gala, to be hosted by the Worshipful Company of Clothworkers in aid of the war effort; time which she felt could have been better spent doing something more practical. After a month as a member of the aristocracy, Viscountess Hammond felt a lot of things expected of her were an unnecessary waste of time. On her return to England she had initially been fully caught up caring for her husband who made steady progress getting stronger each day. More recently, with Hammond needing less help, she had time on her hands and began to wonder if she would not be of more use nursing somewhere.

The trip from Flanders had been difficult. An ambulance had transported Lieutenant Colonel Hammond from the Casualty Clearing Station to the railhead. He had been loaded into a lower berth on the train which had then spent nearly two days travelling, before reaching the port. The journey was punctuated by long stops, spent waiting for the line up ahead to be repaired, as German aircraft had been more accurate at bombing the track than usual.

Lady Hadleigh and Viscountess Hammond both travelled on the same train. For Viscountess Hammond this was to be her last nursing act as part of the QAIMNS. She had been asked to accompany her husband on the train, taking care of him and the other occupants of the carriage; with a degree of regret she knew that once the train arrived in London her nursing career would be over.

Lady Hadleigh had travelled in a carriage behind the engine, which was usually reserved for senior officers travelling to London. She had spent the journey worried that every jolt of the train may cause Gerald pain and was relieved to finally reach the port. Waiting at the quayside HMS *Stapleton* had finished loading and was ready to leave when the train arrived. With extra space on board the ship's captain made the decision to delay sailing and load the wounded.

After taking on the wounded, the ship was ready to sail within the hour; giving Lady Hadleigh only a short period of time to spend with her daughter at the café. The sea crossing had been rough with delays entering Dover harbour, which was full of ships unwilling to put to sea until the weather improved. Eventually, several days after starting out, the train carrying Lieutenant Colonel Hammond pulled into Charing Cross Station and he was moved to a convalescent hospital.

Hammond had been released from hospital a week previously. After an intense period of physiotherapy, he was able to walk with the aid of a single walking stick, although the muscles in his thigh remained weak giving him a pronounced limp. He was hoping that with time he would be able to give up using the walking stick, even though his doctors warned he may never be able to do without the support.

Walking into their dressing room, Hammond crossed the room and spoke to his wife. He was wearing Mess dress, which had not seen the light of day since the start of the war and Buxton had spent the day cleaning and polishing to look immaculate.

'Darling, you look stunning! I do so love those earrings you have on.' Hammond opened a box he was carrying, which contained a matching diamond necklace; leaning forward he bent to fasten the necklace around his wife's neck. 'Now that looks better!' he commented. 'Will you be ready to leave in half an hour?' he asked.

'I'll talk to Buxton and arrange a carriage. Will you join me in the drawing room for a glass of sherry before we leave?'

Viscountess Hammond entered the drawing room, where Gerald and Lord and Lady Hadleigh were already present. Buxton was pouring sherry.

'You look splendid, my dear,' Lord Hadleigh commented. 'Can I get you a glass of sherry before we leave?'

'Thank you, William, that would be lovely!' she replied. 'I am very much looking forward to this evening. It is such a relief that we are getting back to a more normal life now that Gerald is out of hospital.'

'Yes, we are very relieved Gerald is on the road to recovery. It has been such a difficult time for you both. How long do you think it will be before you are hounded to report for a medical examination?' Lord Hadleigh asked, looking in the direction of his son.

'I have been asked to make an appointment to see the CO at the end of the month, Papa,' Hammond responded. 'It will be a while before I'm passed fit for the trenches though.'

'I do hope that neither of us is asked for an opinion on the war tonight!' Margaret interjected. 'It feels as if everywhere I go I have been invited only to give an opinion on the situation on the Western Front, because I have been there. I'm not sure anything I have to say is of much value. After many years of watching men die needlessly my opinions are a little jaundiced.'

'People are interested, my dear. You have done what so many of them wish they had the courage to do. Some of them may even be a little jealous. You should give an honest opinion. If nothing else it will provoke thought,' Lord Hadleigh observed.

***

The evening which followed was typical of most arranged to assist the war effort. Arriving at Clothworkers Hall, Lieutenant Colonel Hammond, his wife and Lord and Lady Hadleigh climbed the sweeping staircase. At the top of the stairs an elderly man dressed in Clothworkers livery was announcing guests as they arrived. The Livery Hall had been decked out with Union flags adorning the walls. In a show of patriotism red white and blue was used throughout the hall as a colour theme; circular tables each able to accommodate ten people were set for dinner, with alternating red and blue table cloths. A centrepiece of white roses and white napkins completed the theme. An area had been cleared for dancing later in the evening; next to this was a grand piano, above which hung a banner announcing the Worshipful Company of Clothworkers supported the war effort.

People turned as Lieutenant Colonel Hammond and his wife entered. Hammond was one of only a few young people present in uniform. Most of the people attending were elderly and had sons away fighting; a few were there because their sons had died for the cause and supporting the war effort was the only hope they had left. The War Office had responded to this charitable event by sending some staff officers as representatives.

Finding people who were enthusiastic for fundraising activities was becoming more difficult as the war progressed, and the population of London became weary. Too many families had been affected by the war and were in mourning for sons and in rarer cases daughters, killed fighting the enemy.

Lieutenant Colonel Hammond and his wife found themselves seated with a mixture of family friends and two couples they did not know. Lord and Lady Arbuthnot had been family friends for years; the Moncrieff's were also present. Both families were anxious to know how Gerald was recovering now that he was out of hospital. Throughout dinner the conversation was light with some discussion on German gains since March when they had started their first spring offensive of the year, managing to push the Allies back at Picardy.

Sitting opposite the Hammonds were two people they had never seen before. The man was dressed in civilian clothing, which looked newly acquired from an expensive tailor; on his hands were several large gold rings, which Hammond thought slightly ostentatious, believing firmly that a gentleman should only be seen wearing a signet ring. His wife was also wearing an expensive new evening gown and was adorned with jewellery with the trademark look of Paget's of Bond Street. Introduced as Jeremiah and Fanny Pritchard of Pritchard's Fine Foods, the couple did not enter into conversation until they had eaten every last morsel of food on offer. Wiping his mouth with a linen napkin, Pritchard looked across at Gerald Hammond.

'I was hoping to catch you here tonight, Colonel.' Pritchard opened the conversation. 'You will have heard of me, of course. Pritchard of Pritchard's Fine Foods.'

'You make the blackberry jam we get supplied with in the trenches?' Hammond asked.

'Yes, yes! "The berry to make you merry!"' Pritchard replied, quoting the slogan present on every tin. 'I don't mind telling you this war has been good to me. My business has expanded rapidly over the last few years and looks like growing still further. Wars and rationing are always good for the humble grocer.'

'The company has grown rapidly from almost nothing four years ago.' Gesturing to the other couple seated at the table Pritchard continued. 'Let me introduce the Lampards; Jonathon and Nancy have been with me from the start, Jonathon is a joint shareholder in my company. We are looking for someone such as you to join the board. I find a lot of people at government level will only do business if there is a member of the upper classes on the board.'

'Do you not already have almost exclusive rights to supply jam on the Western Front?' Hammond asked. 'I've wondered for years what kind of man is able to go to bed and sleep at night, being responsible for sending such poor-quality produce to men fighting to keep this country free of the Kaisers type of tyranny?'

Abruptly Hammond stood up. 'Now if you will excuse me, my wife and I have people to speak to, who are here tonight with a genuine desire to assist the soldiers fighting with their backs to the wall. I would not wish to be associated with a company wishing to profit from supplying poor-quality food to the people who need it most.'

'Now hang on a minute!' Pritchard replied. 'We only use the freshest of ingredients. I may have been a victim of my own rapid expansion at times, having to contract some of the work out to smaller operators. As a soldier who has been there I would be interested in hearing from you about supply issues and what's wrong with our current product. I have no one to talk to with such first-hand knowledge.'

Hammond paused, 'If you are genuine, then I would be happy to help. Too often I have opened a tin of jam only to find the contents are covered in mould, or worse still the tin is full of maggots. I would be happy to meet tomorrow afternoon to discuss what you have in mind.'

Chapter Twenty-Three

They ask me where I've been,
And what I've done and seen.
But what can I reply
Who know it was not I,
But someone just like me,
Who went across the sea
And with my head and hands
Killed men in foreign lands...
Though I must bear the blame,
Because he bore my name.

Wilfrid Wilson Gibson

August 1918 – France

Major Maxwell Standish had attended a briefing and was confident it was getting closer to the end of the war. In March he had returned with his battalion to France; Allied Command having agreed that the AIF, who up until now been spread all over the Western Front, should unite to form an Australian division. Standish and his battalion had played a pivotal role during the German attack on Amiens earlier in the year, holding the line and halting the German advance. Once the allied line held, plans were immediately made for a counter attack; aimed at pushing the Germans as far back as they could.

In April the AIF had received a much-needed boost when the Australian Prime Minister paid a visit and addressed the troops. As a result of the visit, Standish and his men felt as though they were not forgotten and went into battle even more determined to fight for what was right as the cause was just.

Standish had recently been promoted to Major and was serving as adjutant. Based at headquarters he was no longer in charge of a company fighting on the front-line; he was missing the action and the camaraderie. For the forthcoming attack he had managed to leave the safety of headquarters behind, attaching himself to a tank, after he was promised a ride by Captain Montague Swift, a friend from home.

The attack was planned for the early hours of the morning, when it was thought the Germans could be caught unprepared. To assist with a surprise attack, no preliminary artillery barrage was planned. The barrage, when it did happen, would be a creeping barrage; the artillery firing off shells which would land just in front of the advancing soldiers. Major Standish had hitched a lift to where the Tank Corps was located, arriving at the Front just after midnight. The tanks were parked on the outskirts of a small wooded area taking advantage of the natural camouflage the trees provided. The area was full of activity; men were scurrying around carrying out last-minute checks to the huge metal tanks, so that all would go well when the order was given to move. Standish spoke to the first person he could find, who was standing ticking off completed checks on a clipboard.

'Corporal, can you tell me where I will find Captain Swift?' he asked.

'Further down the track, sir. I think he was dealing with an engine problem tank number three has developed,' was the response.

Walking further down the track Standish counted a dozen tanks parked close to the wood's edge. An attempt had been made at rudimentary disguise; tree branches had been used to cover the tanks to make them difficult to detect from the air. At the end of the track a machine gun emplacement had been constructed to take pot shots at any passing German aircraft.

Standing beside tank number three, Swift was deep in conversation with a staff sergeant wearing the insignia of the Royal Engineers. Standish arrived just as the staff sergeant took a step backwards, saluted and then marched rapidly off in the direction of a small supply area.

'Montague, it's good of you to allow me to travel with you.' Standish spoke.

'Happy to have you along, Max; I have a feeling we may be about to witness one of the more decisive events of the war. If we can get these tanks to cover the ground without being bogged down, we may manage to push the Hun back,' Swift replied. 'Once we have taken down the disguise and done a few checks we should be on our way. You will find this a very different way to travel,' he added.

The attack started just after four o'clock. A thick fog had descended making it difficult to see very far ahead. The tanks fired their engines. Fortunately, the sound was muffled by the barrage which started as they began to move. Slowly the large metal hulks left the safety of the woods and began to move across no man's land. Resistance was sporadic with the occasional ping as bullets hit the tanks' metal sides but failed to penetrate.

As tank number three arrived at the German front line Standish could see scores of German soldiers surrendering en masse. The Allies were well prepared to take prisoners; just behind the lines several large cages had been erected to accommodate them. Military policemen were ready and waiting to guard the men as they surrendered. The huge volume of Germans laying down their arms came as a big surprise though, as did the number of weapons that fell into Allied hands that day.

From his position perched on the top of a tank, Standish was privileged to see the end of a stalemate that had lasted on the Western Front for nearly four years, claiming countless lives. The Allied attack continued without respite until they reached the

Hindenburg Line, where resistance was stronger. Intelligence gleaned before the attack suggested it would be prudent to regroup and attack again after the troops were rested. The Allies dug in, aware that the tide had at last begun to turn in their favour and that there may be an end in sight after all.

September 1918 – London

Lieutenant Colonel Gerald Hammond eased himself up and grabbed hold of his walking stick. After several months his limp was slowly improving, but he still found it difficult to walk on unfamiliar ground so carried a stick more for security than of necessity.

As Hammond prepared to leave the meeting he looked up to see Teddy Moncrieff approaching him from the other side of the room.

'Ah, Moncrieff, very glad to see you could make this meeting,' Hammond said. 'I'm told that we are starting to make a difference to the quality of food supplies being sent out to the Front. It's taken a while to convince suppliers that poor-quality food is simply not acceptable as well as being damned unpatriotic.' Gesturing to Pritchard, who was standing beside him Hammond continued. 'I met Pritchard at some charity bash my wife was involved with. Have you two met?'

'Yes, we have been dealing with Pritchard Fine Foods since 1914. I'm very happy to see you are involved in this campaign, Pritchard. It simply doesn't do to have malnourished fighting men; especially now, when we are making such phenomenal ground on a daily basis. The War Office is happy to help with the supply of food in any way it can. Quality is the issue though,' Moncrieff replied. 'We must crack down hard on the people I am hearing about, who seem to be driven by profit at the expense of the fighting man.'

'I agree, we have spent the last month or so touring some of the factories which supply the Western Front. In some the quality was appalling. We have closed two factories down and have given notice to three others that unless they improve significantly, they will go the same way,' Hammond responded.

'My profit margin has decreased considerably since I met Viscount Hammond at Clothworkers Hall. He is a very persuasive man,' Pritchard commented. 'I have made a great deal of money from this war but have always tried to do it honestly. Until Viscount Hammond came along with a few months of time on his hands, I was too busy to spend much time with the group of businessmen working for me. Now I've made that time and I think you will all agree quality has improved.'

'Well I must take my leave, gentlemen,' Hammond said. 'Margaret is expecting me for a late luncheon at the Ritz. It is not often these days that we are able to find the time for this kind of indulgence. Margaret has become very involved with all sorts of war committees, attending meetings almost every day.'

***

The Long Gallery at the Ritz was crowded; officers in the uniforms of every possible Service and Dominion seemed to be represented, with very few men in civilian clothing. Most present were obviously on leave and were either waiting to meet loved ones, or were seated taking refreshment.

Lieutenant Colonel Hammond walked as quickly as his leg would allow through the Long Gallery to the restaurant which had views looking out over Green Park. His wife was already seated at a small table next to a window. Leaning forward he kissed her on the cheek before easing himself into his seat.

'Darling, that meeting was interminably dull. It would seem that Teddy Moncrieff is the only person at the War Office worth talking to. Some of the generals present were asleep before I had finished the first sentence of our report.' Hammond coughed, before picking up the menu which had been placed in front of him. Although improving he still coughed on colder days after being exposed to mustard gas the previous year.

'Never mind all of that, Gerald; I have some news. This morning while you have been at the War Office, I went to see Dr Fortescue, in his rooms on Harley Street. I didn't want to tell you before he confirmed it, but I am pregnant. The baby will be due in March,' Margaret said.

Hammond dropped his menu back on the table and looked up, his face drained of all colour.

'I never expected this to happen,' he stated. 'Not so soon anyway. I am so pleased; we must have some champagne,' he continued before beckoning to a waiter. 'Bring me a bottle of Bollinger. We have something to celebrate.'

October 1918 – Belgium

Victoria Standish walked down the ward glancing at the patients on either side as she did so. She was looking for Violet Briggs who had appeared at breakfast that morning looking pale and unwell, with the early signs of a fever brewing.

For several months now, Spanish influenza had become part of the daily lives of the staff working at the Casualty Clearing Station. It seemed ironic that just as the Allies had the Germans on the run and casualty numbers were lessening, an influx of men suffering from influenza kept the staff working just as hard as during any push. The disease was a killer; striking even the fittest of men. Unfortunately, most soldiers who had been engaged in trench warfare for several years were not the fittest of men. By September they were dropping like flies and were bought to the hospital in their hundreds.

Standish had been in charge of a team who spent hours of each day sponging down men who were suffering extreme bodily temperatures. Most reported feeling exhausted, before suffering headache and fever. Within hours they had difficulty breathing and then started to cough and cough, until they were coughing up bloodstained froth.

At the end of the ward Standish could see two VADs preparing a trolley with bowls of tepid water, clean linen sheets and other items necessary to treat the febrile soldiers. Walking up to them she spoke.

'Have either of you seen Briggs?' Standish asked. 'I'm a little concerned that she was not well at breakfast, she insisted on working though and with this epidemic we need everyone we can.'

'Yes, Sister, she went to the linen store to collect more sheets, but has been gone for a while.'

'Thank you, I shall look for her there.'

Standish left the ward and walked hurriedly through the grounds to the small building where linen and other stores were kept. She was concerned that Briggs had been gone for some time, on what was a routine errand. Opening the door to the storeroom her concerns were vindicated, collapsed on the floor Briggs was clutching her head.

'Briggs, can you hear me?' Standish asked, before kneeling beside her.

'Yes, Sister, my head it hurts so much. I suddenly felt very faint and could not stand any longer,' Briggs replied.

'Lie still and I will go for help.'

Standish sighed as she watched Briggs being carefully lifted onto a stretcher and taken to a wing of the hospital where nursing staff were being cared for. Hundreds of soldiers were being brought from the battlefield each day with influenza; despite stringent precautions, for most nurses it was only a matter of time before they too caught the disease. The Casualty Clearing Station was currently combating the second wave of influenza. The first wave had been less virulent and milder with far fewer deaths; causing staff to be caught by surprise when young men died almost as soon as they arrived, during the far deadlier second wave.

Within hours of being found in the storeroom, Briggs was delirious with fever. Sister Blackstone, who was responsible for all of the medical staff with the disease, was worried that the fever did not appear to show any sign of breaking and that Briggs was getting sicker each minute. Walking from her office to the bedside she noticed curtains were drawn around the bed; immediately she became concerned that Briggs who had weaker lungs than most, after the sinking of the *Ariadne*, may have succumbed to the disease. Stepping behind the curtains she was relieved to see her fears were unfounded and Hadleigh was sponging Briggs in an attempt to keep her as cool as possible. Rolling up her sleeves she looked across to Hadleigh.

'Pass me that sponge and I'll give you a hand, Nurse,' Blackstone said. 'Has she shown any sign of waking yet?' Hadleigh shook her head. 'I thought not. When we have finished here I will talk to Colonel Chardingly. Hopefully he will have finished the day's surgery. There must be something else we can do,' she continued.

Cold-sponging Briggs took more than twenty minutes, with cold compresses applied to her groin and axillary areas. Sponges of cold water were then used to bring her temperature down. Throughout the treatment Briggs did not stir. After remaking Briggs bed with fresh linen, Blackstone addressed Hadleigh.

'I must try and find Colonel Chardingly. If you need anything while I am away Sister Morris should be called from the soldiers' Influenza Ward. I hope not to be too long.'

Blackstone walked quickly to the Doctor's Lounge, where she hoped Lieutenant Colonel Chardingly would be relaxing with a cup of tea and newspaper. Knocking on the door she entered the room and looked around. Chardingly was seated in an old leather arm chair, by a window which looked out onto the canal. As she entered he looked up from a medical journal he was studying.

'How lovely to see you, Sister; what brings you here?' Chardingly asked.

'Sir, we need you to come at once. Briggs is very ill with influenza. I think we may lose her. Cold sponges are not having any effect. She is drifting in and out of consciousness and has been quite delirious at times. I am not sure what else can be done,' Blackstone replied.

Chardingly closed the journal and stood up. 'You must return to her immediately, Sister! Please set up the equipment needed for an infusion and also to take a sample of her blood. I have just been reading in this very journal of a treatment the Americans have come up with, which we may be able to try. Apparently, an infusion of someone else's blood might be the key to this.' Pointing at the journal article he continued, 'I believe the American Hospital has a stock of blood collected from victims who survived the first wave of this dreadful disease. Injecting some of this blood into Briggs may be her only hope. I will take a motorcycle and see if I can persuade them to give me some blood.'

Blackstone and Hadleigh were both standing at the end of Brigg's bed when Lieutenant Colonel Chardingly strode back onto the ward carrying a glass bottle, which contained a small amount of blood. 'We will need to take some blood from Briggs and analyse it to make sure both samples are compatible, before giving her the contents of this bottle,' Chardingly stated. 'Sister can you pass me the hypodermic needle, please, and a tourniquet, so that I can remove a small amount of blood.'

Chardingly lifted Briggs left arm and applied the tourniquet he was given. Tightening the tourniquet, he started to feel for the vein from which he intended to take a sample of blood. Using an alcohol solution, he prepared her skin above where he thought he could feel a vein and then slowly inserted the needle. Pulling back on the plunger her blood started to flow freely into the syringe. Withdrawing the syringe and needle, Chardingly handed the blood to Hadleigh.

'Take this to the lab and ask them to test it against the blood in this bottle for compatibility, as soon as they can,' he ordered.

The results when compared were favourable and a couple of hours later the bottle of blood was transfused into Briggs. Blackstone and Hadleigh continued to work into the night, sponging her every hour, until at last her temperature started to subside.

In the early hours of the morning the danger seemed to pass, with Briggs waking and declaring she was thirsty.

October 1918 – Camden, New South Wales

Constance Standish climbed into the trap and turned towards the hospital. She was in a hurry after finally getting Hector to agree that he was sick enough to require the services of a doctor. The previous evening, having spent a day in the fields, Hector arrived back at Oakfield House feverish and with a headache which he admitted he had been suffering from since first light.

Spanish influenza had finally reached Australia, a little later than it had spread through Europe. Newspaper reports spoke of a number of people dying within hours of being struck down. A few days previously Hector had read an article which described the symptoms to look out for and gave advice on treatment. It appeared not much could be done other than keeping anyone affected cool. Hector had started to cough the day before and was now showing signs of being very unwell indeed. He had a headache which was so severe he had asked Constance to close the house shutters, so that he could lie very still in darkness. More recently his skin had taken on a bluish tinge, which Constance knew must be serious. On her way to the hospital she could not help wishing her daughter, who would have known what to do, wasn't half a world away.

Bringing the trap to a halt Constance was pleased to see Matron McNally standing on the veranda deep in conversation with some wounded soldiers.

'Matron, can you spare a moment?' she called, as she arrived at the front of the hospital.

'Of course, what can I do for you?' McNally replied.

'It's Hector, he is very sick. I think he may have influenza. He has been feverish since yesterday and has an appalling headache. I cannot seem to keep his temperature down; I need advice and don't want to disturb the doctor unless I have to,' Constance replied.

'Go home immediately and I will follow. I shall need to arrange a replacement here, but Sister Collins is always keen to take charge on the odd occasion I am called away. I am sure she will be available.'

Matron McNally was as good as her word and within the hour arrived at Oakfield House. Both women worked tirelessly nursing Hector, but were unable to prevent the disease from taking its course; Hector Standish died in the early hours of the following morning.

Chapter Twenty-Four

*I do not like to 'let the audience down,' but I have no
news for you. I may perhaps have it tomorrow, but the
issues are already settled. In the spring we were being
sorely pressed. Our Channel ports were threatened,
and the enemy's steel was pointed at our heart. It is
now autumn. Constantinople is almost within gunfire;
Austria is shattered and broken; the Kaiser and the
Crown Prince have abdicated, and a successor has not
been found — a regency has been proclaimed. This is
the greatest judgment in history. Germany has a
choice to-day; she will have none tomorrow. She is
ruined inside and outside. There is one only way to
avoid destruction — immediate surrender.*

David Lloyd George. British Prime Minister,
November 1918

November 1918 – Belgium

Victoria Standish walked quickly towards Matron
Gillespie's office. She had been sitting at her desk with
yet another equipment inventory wondering how on
earth she would explain the loss of three thermometers,
half a dozen sheets and two blankets, when Hadleigh

delivered the message that Matron had summoned all of the AANS and QAIMNS sisters to her office immediately. Hadleigh was unable to elaborate on the reason for the order, but did say in her opinion it couldn't be bad news as Matron had been smiling.

Only a couple of weeks previously it had been left to Matron Gillespie to break the news to Standish that her father had passed away after a very short illness. Devastated, she had thrown herself into her work, thankful that there was plenty to keep her fully occupied. She had spent fruitless hours, of what little spare time she had, trying to get in contact with her brother who was known to be somewhere in France, where the Germans continued to be pushed backwards at an astounding rate.

After being summoned Standish rolled down her sleeves and attached the white starched cuffs she wore when not directly caring for the wounded. Pausing at the end of the ward she quickly looked at her reflection in a small mirror attached to the wall, making sure her hair was still in place.

As Standish entered the corridor where Matron had her office, she noticed it was not just nursing staff that were present. Lieutenant Colonel Chardingly and the chaplain were both standing in a corner talking to Sister Blackstone; the commanding officer was also there talking to the quartermaster sergeant.

Matron Gillespie stepped out of her office and walked over to the commanding officer, where she had a short, muted conversation before turning to address the people gathered in the corridor.

'I have some news which could not wait,' she announced. 'After more than four years I am able to tell you that the German Kaiser has fled and that the German Government has requested an end to this war. It is intended that the guns will at last fall silent tomorrow morning at eleven o'clock. As I speak, this message is being relayed to Allied Commanders throughout Flanders and in every other theatre of war.

'Some of you left Australia with me in 1914, full of hope and with the expectation that after a short skirmish the war would be over by Christmas; you have served your country with courage and distinction. You have suffered the depravation of war and have endured appalling conditions, to bring what skills you have to men in the direst of need. I count myself privileged to have served with you.'

Gillespie's speech was greeted with a collective sigh. Most present could not believe that it was almost over. This disbelief was heightened only moments later, as a convoy of badly wounded men arrived, putting an end to the subdued speculation from some of the Australians present about when they would be allowed to return home.

Several hours later Victoria Standish went for a walk. Wishing to be alone she followed a well-worn path across some fields nearby, which led to a river. She arrived at the riverbank pausing to sit and think for a while; a fallen tree providing a seat which was quite comfortable. Sitting down Standish's thoughts turned to her mother and the enormous grief she must be feeling. It sounded as if her father must have been a victim of the Spanish influenza that was having such a devastating effect everywhere. He appeared to have been all right one day, sick the next and dead the day after. Spanish influenza was a disease that could kill quickly and was not fussy about its victims.

Standish shivered with cold and thought of home. In Camden the Jacaranda trees would be starting to bloom and the weather would be improving. Soon the extreme heat of summer would have people wishing they could live somewhere cooler. Standish wondered how her mother would manage the farm without her father. It was difficult not knowing where her brother was and what his future plans were. Weeks had passed since he had last written. Once the war ended Standish was not sure she intended to return to Australia straight away, but with her father's death felt one of them should.

The sound of footsteps on the path behind her caused Standish to look around. Coming towards her carrying a letter Lady Julia Hadleigh looked excited.

'Victoria, I've had a letter from Max!' Hadleigh exclaimed. 'There's also one for you. He's all right but has been very busy chasing the Germans who are retreating as fast as they can. He has attached himself to an old school friend, who is in charge of a tank, so he can be at the forefront of any action.'

'Thank heavens he is safe,' Standish replied. 'It worries me that he is so keen to avenge Stanley's death that he may do something reckless. Let's hope he takes it easy until tomorrow morning.'

'Yes, let's hope he does.' Hadleigh sat down on the log beside Standish, idly picking up a stone, she threw it towards the water skimming it along the top. 'Can you believe that this will all be over soon?' she asked. 'I feel as though I have never known any other life. It will be odd not to have my life ruled by when the next convoy of ambulances is due. What will you do when it's over? Will you continue nursing?'

'I'm not at all sure,' Standish replied. 'It will depend very much on my brother. One of us will have to go home, to help with the house and look after Mother. I have already been asked by Matron Gillespie if I would consider remaining in London for a while; it's an appealing thought. The AANS will need someone to look at how well we were prepared for this war and if we can do anything to prepare better for next time. If I return to Camden, I will see Stanley in every tree and building. We grew up so closely it would be hard not to.

I do not know when, if ever, I will be strong enough to cope with that.'

In response Hadleigh removed the stud securing the starched white collar to the top of her dress. Hooking her finger through the chain hanging around her neck she showed Standish the opal she was wearing.

'Your brother gave me this, instead of an engagement ring,' she explained. 'We plan to get married, once the war is over. Probably in London, after which I think he would like to show me Australia; he talks so much of the house and where you grew up that I almost feel as though I've been there. Maybe telling you this will help with your decisions. I would have told you before, but neither of us could bear the thought of tempting fate by planning ahead.'

Standish responded to the news with a small excited gasp. Leaning across she hugged Hadleigh and kissed her on the cheek. 'Congratulations, I really cannot think of a nicer piece of news to celebrate the end of the war with. Tomorrow we will not only celebrate the Armistice, but will also toast you and my brother. I think the Wild Poppy Café may well have some champagne that needs drinking!'

November 11th 1918 – London

Lord and Lady Hadleigh were at home when church bells rang out signifying the end of the war. Lord

Hadleigh had spent the previous day at his club, where news that the war was almost over and the Terms of Peace were the only topics of discussion. Teddy Moncrieff had joined him in the early afternoon, confirming the time peace would be declared. He asked that Lord and Lady Hadleigh be present for luncheon in the House of Lords, where he hoped the celebrations would last well into the evening.

Buxton uncorked the first bottle of champagne in the morning room of the house in Bedford Square at exactly eleven o'clock. As he popped the champagne cork, cheering could be heard coming from the direction of Tottenham Court Road. Viscount Hammond and his wife were present and accepted glasses proffered by Buxton. Lord Hadleigh picked up two glasses, one he handed to his wife; he then walked across to Briggs who was sitting quietly on a sofa.

'You must join us in a toast, my dear,' he said offering her a glass. 'The war has ended at last. This is an historic day which has been a long time in coming. We have suffered as much as some families, but less than others. To those who have borne a loss with courage and for whom this day will not be seen as one of triumphant victory I would like to raise a glass, in the hope they may find some peace with the wars end.' After drinking a toast Lord Hadleigh continued.

'Buxton, you must make sure the servants all share in a glass of champagne this morning and then after you have driven us to the House, you may all take the rest of the day off. I'm sure some of you will want to go along to Trafalgar Square to join in celebrations there; my wife and I have been invited to a function at the House of Lords, so will not require any of you to be here. What are your plans, Gerald?'

'I am off to the Officers Mess shortly, Papa,' Hammond replied. 'This afternoon I shall return here to accompany my wife and Briggs to a function for nurses being held at the Guildhall. For most of us it is difficult to believe it is all over and at last we may be able to get on with a normal life.'

Lord and Lady Hadleigh left the house shortly before midday. The family motor car had been rescued from its garage and cranked into life. A small supply of petrol, saved in case of an emergency, was poured into the empty tank; oil was also added. Progress to the House of Lords was slow with crowds of people spilling into the roadway; Buxton drove the motor car sounding the horn continuously to clear the way.

The crowds were a sea of uniforms. Amongst the thousands there were several hundred nurses and girls from munitions, whose job had been providing the ammunition during such a dark time. Women in Naval uniform jostled with the First Aid Nursing Yeomanry. Clutching on, halfway up a lamp post, waving a Union flag one nurse was shouting across the street to a group of colleagues, who had been allowed the day off from University College Hospital, which was nearby.

Reaching for the voice pipe connecting the front of the motor car to the back, Buxton spoke.

'I think it may be well to avoid Trafalgar Square, my Lord; although other routes may also be difficult.' As he was speaking a total stranger dressed in the uniform of a VAD nurse jumped onto the running board of the motor car, kissed Buxton firmly on the cheek, before jumping back down and disappearing into the crowd.

'Do whatever you think is best, we are not in a hurry,' Lord Hadleigh replied, smothering a smile. 'This is after all quite entertaining.'

After a considerable period of time Buxton stopped the motorcar outside of the House of Lords. Helping Lady Hadleigh from the motorcar Lord Hadleigh looked back to see a mixture of motorcars and carriages drawing up behind them. It looked as though every peer of the realm, that could, would be attending the House that day. Linking his arm through his wife's, Lord Hadleigh began to walk toward the entrance of the House of Lords.

Throughout England, celebrations began that morning to celebrate the end of hostilities; in some places the party continued for several days. The news, that men who had been away fighting for years were on their way home, was to have a profound effect on the women who had been left behind; with some exhilarated by the news and others, having gained a degree of independence, not quite so happy.

November 1918 – Camden, New South Wales

Constance Standish trotted up past the hospital and turned into the road where Agatha Marshall lived. Arriving at her cottage she was pleased to see Mrs Marshall ready and waiting, sitting on the veranda. As the trap approached, she stood up and walked down the short path to the gate. Carrying a basket containing a bunch of freshly cut flowers she climbed up into the carriage and sat down before speaking.

'It's good to see you, Constance,' Mrs Marshall said. 'I have cut some flowers this morning, which we should have time to place on the graves before the thanksgiving service.'

'That's very kind, Catherine. It is such a shame Hector did not live to see such a joyous day.'

St John's Church was starting to fill with people arriving from all over the district. Dismounting from the trap, Constance Standish tethered the horse to the fence. She and Mrs Marshall then walked around the church and down the hillside to the area of graveyard that both of their husbands were buried in. After a few moments of silent contemplation where both women considered their losses, they laid fresh flowers before climbing back up the hill to attend the service of celebration the Reverend Sharpe had planned.

Standing in front of his congregation the Reverend Sharpe looked around the church. In his opinion the end of the war had come not a moment too soon. Every second family sitting in front of him had lost a close relative; fighting for a remote cause, on behalf of a country most would never see. It was hard for him to understand why the young men of the district had been so keen to fight and die far away in Europe and on the shores of Gallipoli. Sharpe was relieved that his role as the deliverer of bad news would come to an end soon.

With the service over Constance Standish and Catherine Marshall took the trap down into the centre of Camden. Argyll Street had been festooned with banners. Flags hung from every building and tables had been set out to put food on for a giant street party, which had been organised in something of a hurry. The Plough and Harrow had supplied several barrels of beer for the occasion. Cuthbert's bakery had donated bread and some large pies, while the grocer at the other end of town had supplied several fruit platters.

People were everywhere, milling around in small groups; every now and then a spontaneous cheer would erupt as people expressed their excitement. The biggest cheer of the day was reserved for Matron McNally who appeared at the intersection of John and Argyll Street driving a large hay wagon; in the back were half a dozen wounded soldiers immaculately turned out in uniforms of the AIF, ready to tell stories of their war.

The party continued long into the evening people scarcely able to believe the end had come.

November 11th 1918 – France

Major Max Standish was cold. It was just before dawn on the eleventh of November and he was several miles away from headquarters, holed up in a tank with his good friend Captain Swift. Progress had been rapid with the German Army in full retreat.

Standish had been wakened by his batman advising a courier had travelled through the night from headquarters with an urgent dispatch for him to read to everyone in the vicinity, at exactly seven o'clock. Walking outside of the ruined farmhouse they had camped in, Standish was pleased to see a group of men huddled around a fire, over which a makeshift arrangement to boil water had been constructed. The chill morning air made the cup of tea he was given very welcome.

'Sergeant Wilson, I need to assemble all of the men for a briefing at seven o'clock,' Standish ordered.

'I will make sure they are all up and ready to listen, sir,' Wilson responded. Removing the kettle from the fire he filled a mess tin with water, which he handed to

Major Standish before continuing, 'You may want some hot water to shave, sir.'

'Yes, thank you, Sergeant, I shall use it now.'

At seven o'clock Standish arrived back in the clearing to find about fifty men waiting for him. Standing in front of them he waved the dispatch he had received earlier that morning.

'Gentlemen, I'm pleased to announce there will be a general ceasefire at eleven o'clock this morning. The Kaiser has fled and Germany has asked for peace. With only a few hours left of the war I would suggest you do nothing to antagonise any Germans remaining in this area. If we do not fire on them we may see this out, without any more bloodshed. I for one am looking forward to returning home unscathed.'

'Our orders from headquarters are to continue to show a presence, moving slowly forwards this morning. At eleven o'clock when all fighting stops, I think we can expect to see some Germans surrender. Sergeant Wilson will coordinate the surrender accepting guns and other ammunition. The rest of you will be detailed to perform various tasks after the ceasefire. Keep alert and calm, the war is not quite over yet.'

For Standish and his men, the war seemed to fizzle out rather than end with a bang. The morning crept on slowly with sporadic fire being aimed at their tanks as they edged slowly forward. At eleven o'clock, suddenly there was complete silence so that the battlefield took on an eerie quality. Bringing his tank to a halt, Captain Swift waited for a few minutes before opening the hatch. Beckoning to Standish to join him he climbed out onto the roof of his machine and sat watching the far end of the field where Germans began to emerge from a wooded area, in complete surrender.

After this, the day took on a surreal quality with tank troops engaged in marshalling the enemy and retrieving their weapons. The only thing to have changed after the ceasefire was a lack of gunfire. It would be several days before Standish and his men truly believed it was over.

Beneath the folds of the grand old Union Jack, the emblem of the British Empire, we are the freest people on God's earth, and to those whose names appear on the panels of the monument we owe a debt of gratitude that can never be paid.

Camden News (NSW), 16th February 1922.

"I unveil this plaque to perpetuate the memory of the brave men whose names appear thereon. They set higher store on glory than on life, and valued great deeds above the length of day. Let us with bowed heads salute the sacred dead."

Elizabeth Macarthur Onslow

Camden News (NSW), 21 September 1922.

Despite the February heat the crowds of people were dressed in their Sunday best, with collar studs in place, ties knotted and shoes gleaming in the morning sun. Those in uniform and some who were not, wore a full set of campaign medals; bestowed on them, with thanks, from a country keen to forge its own identity and never be placed in the same position again, by a country half way around the world.

The stone memorial to the dead had been in the planning almost since the last of the guns in Europe fell silent. Debate had raged in the *Camden News* about the type of memorial, where it should be erected and most importantly who should be included as amongst the dead. A number of men from the District remained 'missing,' with no known grave, their families living life wondering if every knock on the door contained news.

Matron McNally had taken the trap from the hospital, the short distance along the road to Macarthur Park. Loaded into the back of the trap were three of the long-term wounded; not well enough to live independent lives, the three had taken up residence in a small cottage in the hospital grounds, paying for their keep by working as general handymen. Arriving at the smart white wooden gate, which had been given a lick of paint in honour of the occasion she jumped down from the trap and strode into the crowd which had gathered; quickly finding Constance Standish, her son, and daughter-in-law, who was heavily pregnant with their second child.

The ceremony eventually started. The Reverend Sharpe delivered a moving eulogy for those who had gone and not returned. After a moment's silence he nodded to Mrs Marshall who had been seated with the Standish family. Rising slowly, prematurely aged from the loss of her son, she made her way to the large sandstone memorial, where a small cloth curtain hid the names beneath. Not wishing to delay the moment she quickly pulled the curtain to one side, revealing the names inscribed beneath; a generation of men who had made the ultimate sacrifice in a senseless war.

Decked out in the uniform of a matron in the Australian Army Nursing Service with captain's pips on her shoulders and chocolate brown stripes on her sleeves, the nurse stood motionless and unnoticed in the shade of a large Jacaranda tree. She had caught the early train from town determined to arrive on time. Walking through the township nothing much seemed to have changed. As she had walked through the near-deserted main street the shops looked the same as last time she was there; the Plough and Harrow's doors were open as if ready to serve a drink to anyone passing. Vaguely she wondered how this could be – when the world had changed beyond any recognition. Continuing up John Street towards, and then past, the church, she was reminded of the last time she had made this journey, when her only pressing concern was what to do next, after newly qualifying as a nurse.

Listening to the eulogy and watching as the names were unveiled on the country's newest memorial, Victoria Standish at last allowed herself to think of what might have been; tears streaming down her cheeks, she started to walk towards her family.